ULTIMA

ULTIMA

L.S. HILTON

ZAFFRE

First published in Great Britain in 2018 by
ZAFFRE PUBLISHING
80–81 Wimpole St, London W1G 9RE
www.zaffrebooks.co.uk

A CIP catalogue record for this book is
available from the British Library.

Hardback ISBN: 978-1-78576-089-1
TPB ISBN: 978-1-78576-091-4

also available as an ebook

1 3 5 7 9 10 8 6 4 2

Typeset by IDSUK (Data Connection) Ltd
Printed and bound by Clays Ltd, St Ives Plc

Zaffre Publishing is an imprint of Bonnier Zaffre,
a Bonnier Publishing company
www.bonnierzaffre.co.uk
www.bonnierpublishing.co.uk

For Michael Platt,
with thanks

Prologue

The night before the sale, we had walked across the city hand in hand. London seemed remade. A rare, soft night, the lights strung out along the Embankment a stream of phosphorescence in the river's tail, the still pools of shadow in St James's Park amethyst beneath the summer-heavy trees.

Later, in our bedroom, there was still the ghost of my scent on his mouth when he kissed me. I didn't switch on the light, just opened the window. I wanted to feel the watershed of the sweet, dirty London air as it met the heat of my skin. I straddled his face, feeling the spread of the lips of my cunt around his tongue. Slowly, I leaned back, arching towards the tip of his cock, his hand gripping the tense column of my neck, my bent body a comma of anticipation, suspending us, holding us there, before he flipped me onto the side of my hips so that my legs lay along his chest. He kissed the inside of my ankle as he slid inside me, moving lazily, his fingers splayed across my belly.

'*Ti amo*, Judith.' I love you.

'Show me.'

'Where do you want it?'

I wanted it everywhere.

'I want it in my cunt. I want it in my hair, in my throat, on my skin, in my arse. I want every drop of it. I want to drink you, I want to drink your cum.'

He turned me again, setting me on all fours with my palms against the bedhead. He grabbed my wrist and twisted it behind my back, pitching me forward into the pillows, slammed into me with all his weight, just one heavy, dull stroke. I spread my legs wider, offering him the wet slash between them.

'Again?'

Another.

'Again?'

He knelt back to slide a finger into me, then two, then three.

'I want to hear you beg for it. Go on. Beg for my cock.'

'Please. Don't stop. You have to fuck me. Please.'

'Good girl.'

I was so soaked I felt him slip when his cock pushed up me again, I reached round under my thigh to cradle his taut balls as he went faster, faster, shoving into the red core of me until I came in one acute, twisting gasp.

'Now. Turn over and open your mouth.'

Later, I felt for his face in the dark, kissed his eyelids, the sides of his mouth, the sweet hollow under his ear.

'Can I ask you something?' My face was in his neck, my lips on the steady, familiar throb of his pulse.

'Anything, my love.'

'Just when exactly were you planning to kill me?'

His heart remained quiet. No tension, no reaction. He turned on his elbow above me and set his mouth on mine, a kiss with the warm promise of a bruise.

'Tomorrow, sweetheart. Or maybe the day after.'

PART ONE
PRIMING

1

Six Months Earlier

I'd never been to the south of Italy before, and the way things were looking my visit was going to be both short and final. Mainly because Inspector Romero da Silva of the *Guardia di Finanza* was aiming his gun at my heart. We were standing on a beach somewhere in Calabria; more precisely on a concrete platform built into the churning, sulphurous sea. A boxy, rusted container ship was moored about a hundred metres out, connected by a thick rubber pipe to the low cube of the water purification plant next to us. I'd thought about swimming for it but da Silva had already informed me that the currents would have me if he didn't. And although I'd worked out in the past few hours that da Silva's ability to lead a double life made me look like an amateur, I believed him. On the other hand, I get a kick out of risk. And I could see something da Silva couldn't. Over his shoulder, the man who was moving slowly and purposefully towards us along the beach. I doubted he was a random passer-by, since he was holding an assault rifle.

'Either we stop here or you come back with me and we see if we can work together for a while.'

Da Silva's voice was as steady as his hand on the gun.

'"Work together"?' I hissed.

I could have thought, then, of all that I'd done, of all that had happened to bring me here, of all that I'd been and all that I'd become. But I didn't.

'Go on, then,' I answered. 'Do it. Go ahead.'

When the shot came, da Silva looked more surprised than I did, but then this was the second time in a week that someone had tried to kill me. The bullet was not from da Silva's Caracal, which was still aimed firmly at my chest, but from behind, on the beach. Slowly, maintaining his position, da Silva swivelled his head until he saw the figure at the foot of the cliff. The man had fired in the air, a warning. I was tempted to point out that at least someone round here meant business, but it wasn't the moment. Faintly, I could smell the powder as it rose to the dull steel of the hard December sky.

'The girl. Leave the girl!' the man shouted.

I hissed to da Silva, 'Can you swim?'

'The currents,' da Silva answered slowly. 'I wasn't joking about the currents.'

'Grab me,' I told him. 'Move me in front of you. Then use the pipe.'

'What if he shoots you?'

'You were just about to shoot me.'

'The girl!' The rifle was pointing towards us now. Da Silva lunged forward, seized my shoulder, flipped me against him as he spun as though we were dancing so that we changed places, his back to the pulsing waves. The rifle was now definitely aimed at me. At least that was a change.

'I told you. Leave her!' The gun and the man behind it were now advancing down the litter-strewn shingle. Shielding his body with mine, his arm crooked under my chin, da Silva took a step back, then another. One more, and I felt his grip ease, then he released me and a second shot cracked over my head as I hit the concrete flat, palms under my shoulders. A splash, and a long moment of silence. I twisted my head. Da Silva had told me just moments ago that if I tried to escape the currents would finish me off in minutes, but he'd made it to the pipe. I could just see his locked arms, crunching his body along its length beneath the scurf of the waves. The man on the beach had started running. I had maybe twenty seconds before he reached me, which didn't make for a considered decision. The pipe was to the left, I could reach it in a few strokes. Rolling sideways, I held my breath and let my body drop into the water.

Da Silva hadn't lied. The undertow was so strong I could hear it, a thick, insistent gulping in the swell beneath the thud of the pressurised pipe. The cold would have knocked the breath out of me, but the current had already done that. My heavy down jacket, already a sodden shroud, was tangled over my head. I flailed and clawed, blind with salt and the fatal tremors of panic, broke the surface in time for another bullet, straining desperately for the pipe's ridged curve. I got my leg half over, slimy rubber digging into my face, swaying on the pulse of the contained water, used my teeth to tug the jacket from my shoulder and get my right arm loose. Reaching it back under the pipe for purchase I let my left arm flop free just as a wave hit me full in the face and the musty water sucked the bastard thing off me. I was smaller than da Silva and the pipe was too wide for me to move underneath it for protection and still breathe; I had to hump along half on top, pulling my weight forward with my arms. At least that meant I could see, though when I looked up and saw the man from the beach straddling the pipe where it joined the platform, lining up another shot, I rather wished I couldn't. He fired again, but he wasn't aiming at me. If he needed to get lower, da Silva must be somewhere along the water ahead. The man moved forward tentatively, gripping the thick column Comanche-style between his thighs. There was no sign of life from the bobbing ship. Were the three of us going to duke it out on the deck, if we made it? I hadn't got anything to defend myself with except the hairclip in the back pocket of the jeans I'd pulled on last night in Venice, when I was convinced da Silva was arresting me for murder. Back when life was relaxing. If I'd had the time, I could have felt quite wistful.

It was a Concorde clip, about four inches long, curved to fasten hair into a chignon. I flexed my icy fingers and tugged it out. *Think, Judith.* The clip was no kind of weapon, even if the gunman allowed me to get close enough to use it. He'd done his bit for chivalry; I doubted he had any profound qualms over collateral damage. I shoved it between my teeth and strained forward, a few further, desperate metres, then slid sideways towards the sea, my legs gripping the pipe, reaching out the clip as I took in a lungful of air. Eyes scrunched tight against the salt, I felt between the stiff ridges with my left hand behind my thigh, then stabbed the clip into the thick rubber of the pipe. It went in clean. Squeezing with all my strength, I pulled it loose.

The pipe cracked violently to the right like the tail of a giant rattlesnake as the compressed water shot free. It bucked me momentarily to the surface before another wave twisted me back under. I tried to reach my arms around it, but it was too thick and I had no grip; it thrashed again and spun me off altogether. A few heaving upward strokes brought me back to the air, though I could feel the insistent tug beneath me, dragging me in the direction of the roiling pipe. There was no sign of the gunman. Gasping, I trod water, hacking burning brine from my throat. The container was still about fifty metres away, but the currents were already pulling me in the opposite direction at alarming speed. I bobbed helplessly. Any attempt at swimming was futile; already exhausted, encumbered by my clothes, there was nothing to do but drift. Float for a while. As I let my head fall back into the deep, indifferent water, I remember thinking how strange it was that I no longer felt cold.

'Here! Over here!'

I wondered why I hadn't heard the engine of the dinghy, but da Silva's voice was almost swallowed by the swishing shellsong in my head. His cries cut through the odd, soft calm. *Why couldn't he just give up, just leave me?* At least I could deprive him of the satisfaction. I stopped moving my legs then, and slipped down, into the cradle of the sea.

It was dark when I opened my eyes. That is, it seemed to be night – the clouds were charcoal against brief glimpses of a crescent moon. The cold had woken me. Inside my soaked, sea-stiff clothes, my whole body was trembling, my teeth clattering together like one of those wind-up children's toys. I seemed to be lying on the board bottom of the dinghy, which bumped painfully against the small of my back each time it bounced over a swell. The hum of the engine drilled icicles into my throbbing ears. A row of LED lights in the stern showed da Silva sitting placidly at the rudder. For a moment, I considered the idea that this might be Hell – maybe I was condemned to cruise the Styx for eternity with da Silva for company? – but the ache in my thighs and the cloying thirst in my throat suggested, disappointingly on the whole, that I was still in the land of the living. I tried to sit and banged my head on the boat's rear seat. Da Silva turned at the sound.

'You're OK, then.'

My bare right arm was stretched uncomfortably above my head; when I tried to move it I felt metal encircling my wrist, chafing the wet skin. Da Silva had cuffed me to the underside of the bench.

'There's some water next to you.'

My left hand groped, found a plastic bottle. The Evian tasted better than a '73 Lafitte.

'You fucker,' I remarked conversationally.

'Why?'

'I saved your life back there! He could have shot you. He could have shot me instead of you!'

'I saved you, didn't I?'

I had to admit there was a certain logic there.

'Where are we going?'

'Shut up.'

'I'm cold.'

'Shut up.'

I stretched my sore legs as far as they'd go, but there was still a decent gap between da Silva and my feet. Even if I succeeded in kicking him overboard, there was no way I could reach the tiller with the cuff attached. And then? Then I had no money, no phone, no ID. If I reached land, wherever land was, I supposed I could hitch the 700-odd miles back to my flat in Venice. Which currently housed a corpse. Not the most appealing of prospects. Plus I felt appalling – nauseated from swallowing seawater, limbs bruised and aching, freezing in my sodden jeans and T-shirt in the December dark. So here I was, marooned in the middle of nowhere with a crooked Italian cop who'd planned on shooting me hours ago, a man who was himself, it seemed, being pursued at the wrong end of a rifle. Quite the little mini-break.

'What's with the boat?'

'I borrowed it, OK? From the container ship. There wasn't time to ask permission, I just untied it.'

'Did you see what happened to our friend?'

'I told you about the currents. He's no longer a problem. I thought I asked you to shut up, by the way?'

'I need to pee,' I whinged.

'You can piss in your clothes. I'm not untying you.'

'Charming.'

'I told you to shut the fuck up.'

There didn't seem to be much else to do apart from watch the scudding skeins of cloud cobwebbing over the blackness. When I got tired of that, I watched da Silva. When I got tired of that, I somehow went back to sleep.

The second time I awoke, it was to the crunch of the boat being pulled up the beach, hard ground beneath the hard boards. Da Silva stooped over me, kindly setting his kneeling weight on my stomach, as he unsnapped the cuff. Footsteps on the shingle told me we were not alone, though my vision was blocked by da Silva's chest.

'You can ditch the boat.' He sounded calm, but I could smell the salt on his skin, the sweat beneath it. He was afraid.

'On your feet.'

I stood, gingerly. The back of the dinghy, where da Silva had been steering, was still lurching in the waves. Hands reached under my arms and lifted me clear as I peered into the darkness, trying to make out a face, but as soon as my feet touched the shingle a cloth was tied around my eyes, so swiftly and professionally that I knew there was absolutely no point in screaming.

'You two walk her. I'll follow.' Da Silva wasn't speaking Italian but a thick southern dialect that I could scarcely follow.

A grip under each elbow.

'Come this way, *signorina*.' Fish and onions on the speaker's breath. My frozen legs protested as I stumbled up a steeply inclined beach.

'Just a minute. Here we are now.' Fish-Breath's voice was flat and practical, as though he'd done this many times. 'You're going to get into the car, now. That's right. *Attenzione alla testa*.'

Soft leather pillowed under my bruised backside. Fish-Breath leaned over and snapped a seat belt over me as the car shifted with the weight of the other men. Warm – blissfully, deeply, luxuriously warm. *If they'd just get on with it now, I could die happy.*

At first, as we drove, I tried to count the seconds, so as to know how far we were from the sea, but soon gave it up. Anti-kidnap strategies weren't exactly relevant: it wasn't like there was anyone to send my sliced-off ear to who cared. They were presumably taking me somewhere quiet, out in the country, where they'd shoot me and roll my body into a ditch.

'Time to get out.' Da Silva's voice, as the engine stilled. We repeated the awkward perp-crouch, Fish-Breath's hand on the top of my head.

'Over here.'

Fear thrashed inside my chest. Forcing what was left of my strength into my limbs to quiet the wild urge to run, I heard a door being unlocked as he pushed me forward a few steps. Sharp click. I started despite myself, but they had only turned on a light, a slight shift in the blackness beneath the cloth binding my eyes.

'Stand there,' ordered da Silva. 'When you hear the door close, you can unfasten the blindfold. Not before. OK?'

I managed a nod. Footsteps again, the creak of a hinge, slam, flare of a naked bulb.

The room looked like a garage or outhouse – breeze-block walls, dusty concrete floor, no windows. There was a grubby blue sleeping bag in one corner, a plastic garden chair with a bucket next to it, a towel folded with curious neatness over the chair on top of a man's shirt. Next to the chair a flowered china plate with a sandwich and an orange. A two-litre bottle of water. Absolutely nothing else. For several minutes I shivered against the wall, straining for the sound of their return. When I was finally convinced I was alone I dropped into a feral crouch over the sandwich, gobbling it down in huge bites, gulping water to swill the dry lumps of bread and ham down my salt-strafed throat. I couldn't remember when I had last eaten – two days ago? When it was gone, I used a palmful of the water to wash the sea-sting from my face, then peeled away the wet pipes of my jeans and pulled the shirt over me. I would save the orange for later. Nice to have a treat to look forward to.

A few laps of the concrete floor, stretching the weariness from my bones, and that seemed about it for this evening's entertainment. Listening again at the locked door, I heard nothing, not the spark of a lighter or a muffled conversation, not the impatient shift of waiting feet. There was no handle on the inside; I pushed my palms against the door and listened for the drawn bolts. Wherever I was, they had abandoned me for the moment. Peeling the orange slowly, I broke it into segments and sat down on the floor. *Would they bother feeding me if they planned to kill me? Who were 'they,' anyway?* Da Silva's colleagues, I supposed, but not the kind who wore the same uniform of the *Guardia di Finanza*. I didn't fancy the sleeping bag much, but I wriggled into its musty warmth and rolled myself up in a corner like a larva. The bare bulb burned away the dusty shadows in the corners of the room.

Toppling between exhaustion and alertness, my brain careered in and out of sleep. When I dozed, my subconscious treated me to a montage of the past days – Alvin Spencer's skeleton crackling to the floor of my flat in Venice, da Silva's questions at the police station, the long, silent car ride down the spine of Italy. Waking, I tried to arrange my thoughts lucidly, but when Cameron Fitzpatrick walked through the door with a bunch of bloodied linen in his hand, I realised I was still deep in a feverish dream. Fitzpatrick was dead. I knew that because I'd killed him, years ago, in Rome. And da Silva had been there then too. I saw him in the dinghy, steering under a black dream-sky whose waves became the lapping water of a bathtub, cold water that smelled of almonds, gently, so gently, pulling me down . . .

My own hoarse gasping pulled me round, stiff on the concrete floor in the monotonous glare of the bulb. At first, I had no idea if minutes or days had passed. There was the faintest line of light beneath the door. I humped myself over to it caterpillar style in the sleeping bag, clutching the water, and heaved myself into a sitting position.

I had believed that I was playing one game, to rules of my own making. Yet that game was woven into another, knitted long before, whose strands were as invisible as they were binding.

I unpeeled myself from the sleeping bag, shook out my body, tried to force my swamy mind to concentrate. A faint skittering noise made me start – *a rat? Fuck, a scorpion?* – but it was only a beetle, fat oily carapace the size of my thumb, beating its wings senselessly against the concrete walls. I watched it for what might have been hours, until it fell to the floor, waved its legs in feeble comedy and seemed to die. I flicked the crisp carcase gingerly. Nothing. Somehow that revived me. Using a scrap of the paper that had been wrapped round the sandwich, I scooped up the bug and set it in the middle of the floor. Then I tore the leftover orange peel into lumps. My hair was a sea-damp mat; I yanked on a knot until it came free and tied it round one of the sections of peel. Judith. I placed it next to the beetle. He would be da Silva. Romero da Silva. *Who had been there all along.* Da Silva was a cop. Da Silva was a crook. He'd brought me down here to Calabria. Why? More pieces, arranged around the beetle like the numbers on a clock. On the skin side of each I etched an initial with my fingernail. Here was Rupert, my old boss, head of British Pictures at the House, the auctioneers where I had once been a junior in London. And here – I scraped another rune – was Cameron Fitzpatrick, the art dealer. Rupert and Fitzpatrick had been planning to scam the House by selling a fake painting, which I had stolen after Rupert fired me, after I had killed Fitzpatrick. I removed the 'F' section from the circle. Fitzpatrick had been working with a man I had known as Moncada, flipping fakes through an Italian bank. I bustled another piece of peel next to the 'M'. Cleret. Renaud Cleret. Da Silva's colleague in the police. I had killed Cleret. I shot him out of the circle with a snap of my fingers.

What then? I felt alert now, purposeful. I had moved to Venice, established a new identity. Judith Rashleigh vanished. I became Elisabeth Teerlinc, curator and owner of the Gentileschi Gallery. Carefully, I pulled a thread from my rotting T-shirt and tied it over the Judith peel. Then another, 'K' for Kazbich. Moncada had been dealing with Kazbich and his co-conspirator, Balensky. Another section. The pair of them had been laundering money obtained from arms sales through the art market. I flicked Moncada and Balensky out of the circle. Both now dead. What a shame. Who was left?

A feather from the sleeping bag made a little banner for a new entry: Yermolov. Pavel Yermolov, a wealthy Russian art collector. Kazbich had been trying to sell him a Caravaggio. At least, he was claiming it to be a Caravaggio. Yermolov and I had worked it out together, the connection between Kazbich, Moncada and Balensky. I left Yermolov in the ring. What I hadn't understood, had been blind to, was the presence of da Silva, creeping along in the darkness. All the time, he had been watching me. I muttered over my little rubbish tip like a voodoo priestess. 'A' for Alvin Spencer. Alvin had been . . . in the way. An art world drifter with connections to the House. A bit too curious about me. So he had to go, except that somehow I hadn't quite disposed of the evidence. I picked up the peel, set it down near the corpse of the beetle. Da Silva had found out about Alvin and made out that he was going to arrest me. Except he hadn't arrested me. I lay down and contemplated my mosaic of fetishes.

Da Silva wanted me to work for him. He had said so, on the beach. And if I didn't? Presumably it would be easier to dispose of me here than in Venice. Obviously da Silva had friends, connections he could call upon – the men who had brought me here, wherever here turned out to be. Mafia. Rolling over seemed more efficient than standing, as my legs weren't feeling quite themselves, so I scrabbled over to the peelings, rearranged them once more around the beetle. Moncada had been Mafia; Kazbich and Balensky were connected to the Mafia too. Da Silva had been the missing link. Crazily, I waddled my peel-people closer to the beetle, like a child playing with Lego figures.

I'd learned quite a lot about the Mafia, one way or another. Though there were still many powerful people in Italy who denied its existence. As little as twenty-odd years ago, the Archbishop of Palermo had been questioned in an anti-Mafia trial. Asked what the Mafia was, he had replied that as far as he knew it was a brand of detergent. The Sicilian Church was later found to have close ties with Cosa Nostra bosses. Such official denial of the very concept of organised crime indicated the extent to which, in Italy, it had penetrated the state itself. If a bishop could be bent, why not a policeman? That would explain the ease and discretion with which da Silva had got me here, but if he was so powerfully connected, who was the man on the beach, the assassin whose body was now spiralling gently towards the coast of Puglia? My waterlogged mind gave out at that moment, and I slept again, deeply this time. When I woke, the light beneath the door was gone.

Lying on my side, my head pillowed on the sleeping bag. I must have passed out again. It was even colder than before. Night. A sense of thicker, softer stillness in the unseen world beyond my prison. My eyes travelled over the clutter of my makeshift model, its contours meaningful only to me. A pellet of bread lay outside the circle. I pinched it, rolling it between my fingers until it was malleable, made a head, the suggestion of a tiny round body. Katherine. My sister, Katherine.

At the police station in Venice I'd confessed to killing Alvin Spencer – what else could I do, since his corpse was sitting in an armchair in my home? I hadn't been able to get rid of it, to tidy things up. And when da Silva had asked me why, all I could think of was my baby sister Katherine, who had died. In a bath that smelled of almonds.

I never thought about Katherine. I couldn't allow myself to. Because when I did, my memories swirled and muddied, opaque as the oil when it met the water. You know what you did. But it wasn't your fault. It wasn't, was it? It was your mother's fault.

Urgently then, I scrabbled all the little pieces together, staggered across the room and dumped them in the piss bucket, where they belonged. The beetle bobbed foully in the mess.

There was no real way to tell how much time passed while I was in that room, but I think it was three days. The second time I awoke, it was to the sensation of thumping on the door at my back. A voice I recognised as Fish-Breath's heavily accented Italian instructed me loudly to stand in the corner with my face to the wall and replace the blindfold. I scurried to obey him. Three bolts creaked before he came inside. He didn't speak. I heard him cross the room and set something down, then the slight slosh as he picked up the bucket. I was glad he had to do that, it would humiliate him. The door opened and closed again; in that brief moment I tried to smell the air-traffic fumes or olive leaves – fertiliser perhaps, or even the smell of bread – anything to indicate where I might be. All I could scent was dust. Locks clicking again, then his voice, telling me I could remove the blindfold. I rushed to the door and listened, made out his receding footsteps, then, faintly, the sound of a car starting.

My provisions consisted of another bottle of water, a packet of wet wipes, another ham sandwich, a packet of chocolate biscuits, a small frayed towel, a banana and a strawberry yoghurt. No spoon. I did my best to wash and pulled on my damp jeans, which were beginning to give off a mouldy smell. Still wrapped in the sleeping bag, I ate the food slowly, mindfully savouring each bite of nourishment. A fag would have been nice, but it wouldn't do me any harm to have a bit of a detox. I cleaned my teeth with a wet wipe and the grainy inside of the banana skin.

The same procedure was repeated the next day. I'd passed some of the time in walking laps of the room and doing press-ups and burpees to keep warm, and the rest of it elaborately plotting my escape. The plastic of the yoghurt pot was too flimsy to fashion into a shiv, but I reckoned I could wait behind the door, swing the bucket at Fish-Breath and be out while he was still wiping the piss from his eyes. His footsteps sounded as though they were going downhill, to the left, towards the car, so I could run right – to where exactly? Even if Fish-Breath wasn't carrying a gun, there was no certainty that he was alone. I didn't even have any shoes, since the sneakers I had dragged on in Venice had been lost in the sea. If the shed, or whatever it was, was somewhere remote, which would seem to be the case from the silence which surrounded it, how far would I get over rough ground with one or more men chasing me, one of them nicely riled up from a shit bath? Could I strangle Fish-Breath with the blindfold? It wouldn't be my first attempt at that trick, but I would have neither strength nor surprise on my side. And compared with Alvin Spencer, who had become dead in my bathtub in Venice, Fish-Breath was definitely a professional.

The other option was to greet Fish-Breath naked and offer him a fuck in return for my freedom. Even without a mirror in my quarters, I had a sense that I wasn't looking particularly ready for love, but even a rancid fuck is still a fuck, and Fish-Breath himself didn't seem overly troubled by personal hygiene. Yet even if I really went to town, I doubted I could render him sufficiently cunt-struck to defy da Silva and release me. Diverting as it might be, it was a crap plan. If da Silva wanted me dead, it would have happened by now. Hadn't he mentioned my working for him? So I had something he still wanted, something I could do, even if its value was only measured in sandwiches and bananas.

Since I've always believed that if one makes up one's mind not to be happy there's no reason not to have a perfectly good time, I objected to those days of captivity much less than might have been expected. Since there was nothing to be afraid of, fear was of no benefit to me. I just decided not to feel it. The hours were long, but since there were no contingencies to react to, they possessed an almost hypnotic quality that increased as the hours passed – a pleasant torpor, if not peace. I slept, and did my exercises, and declaimed verbs in Russian, and when I wasn't doing that, I thought about pictures. I'd heard of prisoners reciting poems, or passages from the Bible to keep themselves sane. I took imaginary walks around the National Gallery in London, the place where I had first seen real pictures. I went back to one, in memory, most often: Cézanne's *Avenue at Chantilly*. I'd looked at it many times, the composition all in greens, just a path in a wood bisected by the wooden rail of a ride, dusty earth underfoot and, in the background, low white buildings and the pure orange ball of a rising or a setting sun. At first, it seems a tranquil, even rather stolid canvas, but then you see that the vagaries of the light are captured so mischievously that the leaves seem to flutter with your breath. So still, yet so vividly alive.

2

Either da Silva's Caracal had survived its swim or he was aiming its replacement at me when he eventually opened the door. Waiting obediently in the corner for Fish-Breath and today's exciting culinary surprise, I started at the sound of his familiar voice.

'You can come out now.'

After the endless electric glare, the colours of the winter landscape swirled like a Kandinsky as I groped my way outside, into an impossibly vivid medley of green and gold, blue and grey which resolved under the winter sun into a rocky hollow fringed with thin oak trees and low shrubs. Sharp scents of myrtle, leaf mould, pine. Da Silva was back in uniform, smelling brightly of shower gel and cologne. I was painfully aware of my own reeking mouth and matted, greasy hair. There was no sign of Fish-Breath. Da Silva handed me a plastic carrier.

'Happy Christmas. Go and get ready.'

The clean air emphasised the staleness of what I now saw was a breeze-block hut, a storage space with a tangle of farm machinery rusting in a corner of a dirt yard. I had a feeling we were high up. Da Silva kept the gun trained on my back as I fumbled in the bag. More water and wet wipes, a toothbrush and toothpaste, soap, deodorant, a comb. I peeled off my filthy jeans and T and began to clean up, not caring whether Da Silva was watching me or not. There wasn't much I could do about my hair, but the mint and the soap, even in cold mineral water, felt wonderful.

'They're not what you're used to.'

He had provided navy sweatpants, a white cotton shirt and a shiny down jacket, supermarket underwear and a truly horrible pair of mock-leather loafers in burgundy.

'I had to guess your size. And most places were shut, for the holidays.' He sounded faintly apologetic.

'They're fine. And you can put that away, you won't need it.'

'I don't think so. Are you done? Come on. Put the blindfold back on.'

He took my arm to guide me outside. A loaded gun against my heart, and yet my heart stayed quiet. Strange what one can get used to. As my feet negotiated the downward slope, I felt an odd pang of loss for the peace of my little room. A pause, and da Silva turned me to unfasten the blindfold.

'Wow.'

We were standing on a roughly concreted track at the crest of a cliff. In front, the view stretched out for miles: first steep wooded hills, then a wide plain dropping to the bright sea, ribboned with silvery beaches.

'It's beautiful.' So far, Calabria had struck me as a bit of a dump, but from up here the motorways and half-built concrete horrors were invisible to my starved eyes. Da Silva pointed to the left.

'I was born just over there. Siderno.'

'Is that where we're going?'

'Maybe. We have a visit to pay first. Get in the car.' The secret kiss of the pistol's nub still jammed against my ribs. *Don't let him see you're scared.*

'Oooh. Will you put your siren on, Inspector?'

'Shut up.'

'A little conversation might be nice. You know, I've been a bit lonely, what with you locking me up for days.'

'Save your breath. You can have a look at these on the way.'

He handed me a phone, but not before he had cuffed my wrists and fastened the seatbelt. I waited until we had twisted our way down the steep track and joined a road before gesturing at the device where it rested on my lap. He reached one hand off the wheel and pressed a button, lighting the screen on a close-up shot of a grey-haired man with a hole in the back of his head and quite a lot of brain on his collar. That made an ID rather difficult, but the next shot, of the man's prone body lying across a desk with a view of swagged red velvet curtain to one side confirmed what I had suspected: this was the body of Ivan Kazbich.

I had met Kazbich early in the summer when he had called at Gentileschi, my gallery in Venice, with a request to value the paintings of his employer, the Russian collector Pavel Yermolov. The connection between da Silva and Kazbich was what I had been so fruitlessly seeking over the past months. The valuation had been a ruse; Kazbich had been cheating Yermolov and here were the consequences – the dealer shot from the back like the traitor he was in his art gallery in Belgrade. Yermolov had told me he would take care of it.

I scrolled through the next few shots of the body, letting Da Silva register the lack of interest on my face.

'Well?' he asked.

'So Kazbich is dead. Do you expect me to care?'

I thought for a moment, then continued.

'You think you're next. Is that what that scene on the beach was about?'

'Go on,' said da Silva. He looked amused.

'You and Kazbich are – were – running arms with art as a cover. Kazbich was trying to take Yermolov for a whole lot of money, but now Kazbich is dead. The question is . . .' I paused, recalling the trash I had assembled on the floor of the shed. 'Why did Kazbich need Yermolov's money? Because he owed it to someone. Someone who wants it back. And now there's only you to pay it.'

'Very good.'

I felt absurdly pleased, like a diligent pupil who has just recited a lesson. Why did I give a shit about da Silva praising me? Had I developed Stockholm syndrome in the shed?

'But to whom do I owe this money?' he asked. 'Assuming you're right? Who do you suppose sent me these pictures?'

'Why would I have any interest in knowing that?'

'Dejan Raznatovic.'

'Ah. I see.'

Raznatovic was the supplier of the weapons, the last piece of the scam.

I'd tracked him down in Belgrade, and I'd thought our encounter in his study had gone pretty fantastically, but if the chap with the gun on the beach was anything to go by, the post-coital glow had apparently worn off.

'So Raznatovic sent our friend Rifle-Man to off you? No Kazbich, no money?'

Da Silva shrugged. 'Yes and no. As for Mr Raznatovic, a few crossed wires. Let's just say I needed to see you urgently in Venice.'

'Not that urgently, since you've had me on the *panino* detox for three days.'

'I am sorry about that. I needed to keep you safe.'

'Safe?'

'From Raznatovic. You'll see. Things have been straightened out. Would you shut up now, please?' he added, as he opened the window and lit a cigarette.

This time, he didn't say it harshly. He offered me one, but though I could have murdered a gasper, I didn't accept. The stale smell of tobacco in cars reminds me of my mother.

We were driving along the coast road now, with the sun over the sea to our right and a tatty strip of empty tourist apartments and shuttered outlet stores to our left. The light bounced off the water, giving a silvery taste to the air. I gulped it in, relishing the coolness on my clean face. Altogether, I felt quite gay. Just days ago I had believed I was looking at a considerably longer period of incarceration than a few days, and no one had even tried to shoot me for over seventy-two hours. Admittedly, I was unemployed, homeless and handcuffed, but that meant things could only get better. Positive thinking is so important.

After we had passed Siderno, the journey lasted about forty minutes. Every few hundred metres, we passed women, alone or in groups of two or three, waiting in the sight of the sparse incoming traffic. They were all African, mostly young, all dressed in bright-coloured, skintight minidresses, or hot pants with crop tops, despite the December temperature. Some sat on plastic chairs, smoking, chatting, playing with their phones, others swayed and posed as the cars passed, their eyes far behind over the highway. One girl was wearing a red satin micro-skirt trimmed with white faux fur and a Santa hat.

'What's with the girls?'

Flyover hookers are a familiar sight on the fringes of most Italian cities, but I'd never seen so many.

'There's a camp down the road. Capo Rizzuto.'

They were refugees, then, these women. Asylum seekers.

Da Silva slowed down and pulled into the emergency lane. 'Get out.'

'I really don't think I'm dressed for doing business.'

'In the back. I'm bringing you in, OK? No need to say anything.'

He holstered his gun and helped me into the rear seat.

We joined the road and continued a little way before da Silva pulled over at a gate manned by two *Guardia di Finanza* uniforms. They saluted as we drove through a compound of brown concrete office buildings to an open field with a landing strip and a sagging windsock. A dark-blue official helicopter waited on the tarmac, its blades beginning to whirl as the car drew up. Another officer jogged over to open da Silva's door, then the two of them walked me to the steps and shoved me up beside the waiting pilot, who did not acknowledge me even with his eyes. The officer reached in and set the harness over my head, fastened it, and released the cuffs before da Silva climbed in beside me. We were given headphones and the officer handed the pilot and da Silva various papers to sign before we took off.

I knew better than to ask da Silva where we were going, even if my headphones had been wired in. He and the pilot were conducting a conversation over my head, but all I could hear was the muffled drone of the engine. We banked over the low hills beyond the coastline, then the 'copter wheeled and set out across the sea. I twisted my mind from its tangle of questions and tried to think of something cheerful. My friend Carlotta, for instance, the party girl made good who had finally snared her old-fashioned billionaire. Carlotta had passed on several useful tips, one of which was that you should always fly private.

Without a watch, I estimated that we were in the air for about three hours. We made one landing on what appeared to be a military base, where I was unloaded and led, cuffed, to a bathroom by a self-conscious young officer. He waited outside the cubicle and then handed me a bottle of water which I drank as I watched the helicopter being refuelled. Taking off, we moved further up the coast before swinging out over the open sea. In a while, we dropped over another stretch of coastline and the pilot began speaking on the radio again, preparing to land. We flew low over jagged high-rises stuck with tumbling balconies and TV aerials like crazy, elaborate hats and came in on a roof marked with a huge white 'H'. Several uniformed men ran towards the chopper, doing that irrational head-duck that the whirling blades inspire. Da Silva helped me out and cuffed me again as soon as my feet were on the tarmac. I kept my head down as we passed through a door, descended a flight of stairs and took a shabby aluminium-lined lift to an underground garage, where a plain black BMW waited with a driver. Da Silva didn't speak until the two of us were settled in the back, and when he did, it was in English.

'Are you OK? Not feeling sick?'

'I'm fine. Why have you brought me to Albania?'

'How do you know we're in Albania?'

'Well, let's see. We left Italy, heading east. The Breda Nardi NH500 has a maximum range of 263 kilometres, so we had to refuel before getting here. Anywhere else would be too far. Plus you're speaking English – many Albanians speak Italian so English is more discreet.'

Da Silva looked slightly alarmed, but I wasn't going to give him the satisfaction of an explanation. In truth, the only reason I knew about what kind of helicopters the *Guardia* used was that when I had researched a Caracal pistol I had stolen, the same pistol Da Silva carried, I'd poked about a bit in the *Guardia*'s set-up. I'd thought it would be handy to be able to recognise an Italian policeman, even in plain clothes, by standard-issue equipment, and facts have a tendency to hang around in my brain. I'd be a demon in a pub quiz. What the fuck we were doing in Albania I supposed I'd find out in good time, but I had a fair idea that it wasn't official police business, for all that da Silva's little outing was on company time.

'So you might as well tell me where we are!' I added brightly.

'A place called Durres,' answered da Silva. He seemed a bit deflated by my Inspector Montalbano routine.

'Here,' he added, reaching over to unsnap the cuffs. 'We won't be needing these now.' I might have imagined it, but his thumb remained a moment too long, massaging the inside of my wrist where the metal had rubbed a slight welt into the skin. I looked out of the window. Durres off season made Calabria look like Mustique. The car bumped wildly along gnarled and pitted streets crowded with women in grubby nylon burnouses hauling pushchairs and shopping trolleys between dingy food stalls and open drains. There seemed to be an extraordinary number of stray dogs, who ricocheted fearlessly between the churning traffic. Despite the clear fastness of the winter sky the light was murky, strained through the teetering heights of apartment blocks whose top storeys were clouded with a miasma of smog. Da Silva's face was incurious – he had obviously been here before – unmoved even when a beggar, stark naked except for a flowered tablecloth draped over his shoulders, banged on the rear window as we stopped for a light. The driver stuck his head out and shouted something that may have involved the moral continence of the gentleman's mother, and he shambled away.

Eventually we left the town and headed out on a spanking new motorway. There was less traffic, but what drivers there were seemed to regard all six lanes as their own private race track. I shut my eyes as a huge truck loomed before us, swerving away only at the last second. Da Silva patted my shoulder.

'Crazy, right? And they say Italians are aggressive drivers. You should see the road to Tirana – always covered with bodies.'

'Thanks for that.'

Our destination was a huge peach-coloured villa whose driveway led directly off the road. As we pulled through high electric gates topped with barbed wire, a reedy man with a watermelon paunch under an open-collared purple shirt and a beige cashmere blazer shambled busily up to the car. He greeted da Silva effusively in Italian, with plenty of handshakes and backslapping, but I sensed a wariness in his pouchy, pebble-coloured eyes. He opened the car door for me and bobbed briefly and formally over my hand, watching da Silva over my shoulder. Did he think I was his girlfriend or something?

'This is Miss Teerlinc.' Da Silva used my alias, the cover for what I had fondly imagined was the life I had always wanted.

'*Buongiorno, signorina*,' said the man formally.

I was glad we hadn't had to shake hands. His would surely have been as slimy as the nervous sheen on his forehead.

'Is everything ready?' da Silva asked brusquely.

'*Certo, certo, tutto a posto!*'

There was white spittle drying at the corners of the man's mouth. He was really hopped up.

Da Silva spoke to the driver, who pulled the car ahead and disappeared behind the house. The three of us followed on foot along a dainty crazy paving path, into a large concrete-walled yard with a children's swing set in one corner and a fountain featuring a plastic swan in the middle. The rest of the décor consisted of various old Mercedes, a plastic table and chairs and a kneeling man with his hands held behind his back by two shaven-haired bouncer types in jeans and tattoos. When the man saw da Silva he started shouting, or pleading, attempting to explain in Italian that there had been a mistake, that it wasn't his fault, that he had never . . . As though his voice could stretch out the seconds. I didn't get to find out what he had never done, as da Silva moved past me swiftly, pulling out his gun as he walked, and shot the man three times in the chest.

Our host crossed himself ostentatiously and nodded at da Silva. The body was slumped between its grim-faced minders, pumping vivid gouts of blood onto the tarmac, the heart a few hideous seconds behind the brain. I could smell the sickly, ferrous tang of the blood and the powder lingering on da Silva's hand as he guided me towards the house. From the expression on his face he might just have flicked a spot of ash from his uniform trousers.

A tiny, invisible gravity between us. *You're like me.* Both of us knowing it, for a moment, without a word.

Looking over my shoulder, I saw the two heavies loading the corpse into the wide boot of one of the cars. The reedy man came up on my other side. His sallow face was pale and damp as though he was about to vomit, but he attempted a smile.

'Please, *signorina*,' he rasped, 'come this way. Lunch is ready.'

3

'I don't want any lunch.'

Actually, I was starving – I hadn't eaten since yesterday's dry *panino* – but our little jaunt was really beginning to give me the pip. Paradoxically, despite what I had just seen, any revived vestiges of fear I felt towards da Silva had evaporated along with the scent of the powder off the 9mm slug. And it wasn't as though I'd never seen a dead body before – if da Silva really knew as much about me as he implied, he'd have to put in a bit more effort on the shock and awe front. I was bored of being hauled about like a parcel, and whatever it was da Silva wanted from me I was quite prepared to get it over with and get him the fuck out of what was left of my life. I shook myself free of them and turned on da Silva.

'What do you want, Inspector?' I demanded in English. 'Just explain to me what exactly it is that you want. Because I'm really not interested in your friend's hospitality, any more than I'm interested in that little pantomime you just staged. OK? Just tell me.'

Da Silva shrugged. 'Fine. I just thought you might be hungry. Come with me, then.'

'No. Was that shit supposed to frighten me?'

The other man was fiddling nervously with three place settings at a large, ornate mahogany table with a glass top, pretending he wasn't paying attention. I took a breath and lowered my voice.

'You didn't bring me all the way here as a witness. So what was that?'

Da Silva looked wearily amused, which provoked an intense desire in me to break his handsome nose.

'It's not always all about you. That was a message. None of your business. Now, will you come along? Mr Raznatovic can't wait all day.'

'He's here?'

'As you said, I didn't bring you here to watch me shoot someone. Please.'

The long rooms of the villa were furnished with hideous faux antiques, though the style didn't extend to the floors, which were bare concrete, like the stained yard outside. Da Silva led the way past the table into a sitting room with a huge flat-screen TV, then upstairs into what could have been a bedroom if it had contained anything apart from three folding chairs, one of which was occupied by the huge bulk of Dejan Raznatovic.

I was acutely conscious of three things – that the room was extremely cold, that my hair was a disaster, and that Raznatovic could wear my spine for a necklace if he only bothered to stretch out a hand.

'I believe you've met,' offered da Silva, obviously thinking himself very witty.

I gave him a blank look as I sat down on one of the chairs facing Raznatovic. My last encounter with the Serbian had been too brief to properly refer to him as a lover, but when I saw his heavily carved features and the heft of those impossible shoulders I did feel a little twitch of remembered desire. He was a talented man. Not that he looked particularly happy to see me. On the other hand, I thought, if he was really unhappy, he wouldn't have risked arrest under various European extradition treaties to meet me in person. He'd have just had me killed exactly like the man in the yard.

'Miss Teerlinc,' he began.

'Hello again, Dejan. I believe I told you that you could call me Judith.'

'Judith, then. Shall we come straight to the point? You lied to me, in Belgrade. I passed on your message to Ivan Kazbich on the condition that you would return the – item – as you claimed you intended. You told me you would hand it over in Switzerland. Yet it appears that Mr Kazbich is no longer with us, and the item is nowhere to be found. Where is it?'

The 'item' was an ingenious cartoon on linen, a supposed Caravaggio. Kazbich had been attempting to sell it to Pavel Yermolov, but I had got in the way. I seemed to have a talent for that.

'You could say I abandoned it. What was left of it, anyway. It was worthless, as no doubt you are perfectly well aware.'

'Indeed. Nonetheless, it was very useful. You have caused me a good deal of trouble. In fact, had it not been for the inspector there' – Raznatovic's eyes moved to da Silva, who had taken a seat next to me – 'you might have gone the same way as Mr Kazbich. But the inspector proposed a better solution.'

'What do you want?' I was really getting tired of asking that.

'When the . . . item disappeared, I spoke to Mr da Silva. He knew certain things about you which I did not, but collectively – I think that's the word? Yes, we decided collectively that you might be able to help us both to resolve our mutual obligation.'

'Yeah, yeah, and if I refuse you kill me. Old news.'

I didn't actually want to die. I didn't particularly want to redeem my life of evil by spending the rest of it helping lepers either, but I really didn't want to die. However, since I wasn't dead already, I knew they were doing nothing. At least, not yet. Just trying to bully me. I don't react well to that.

'Naturally,' said Dejan, 'but not straight away. First we'll kill your mother. Show her the photographs, please.'

Da Silva was pulling out his phone. He scrolled though and handed it to me. It was, indeed, my mother. My mother going into the pub on our old estate. I supposed I could be grateful that they hadn't photographed her coming out of it. My mother pushing a trolley in the supermarket. She was wearing a jacket I had posted to her from Italy for her last birthday, a navy waxed canvas MaxMara pea coat that I'd known she would think dreary but hoped might smarten her up a bit. I was surprised to see she'd actually worn it. The last shot had been taken through the window of a café, where my mother appeared to be enjoying a cappuccino with her friend Mandy. I could never quite get over the fact that cappuccino had made it to Liverpool. The pea coat had been replaced by a heavy fake fur jacket for colder weather, but in case I was in any doubt of the timing, Dejan's spy had placed a copy of the *Mirror* with yesterday's date on it in the foreground. Gently, I reached out and touched the screen, then looked up into Raznatovic's heavy dark eyes. I'd stared down a fair few gun barrels recently, but those eyes were far more frightening. I would have told myself not to show I was scared, but I found that I wasn't scared. Dejan wasn't really with the programme on this one. Apart from my life, everything I'd ever had to lose was long gone.

'So, I know you can get to her. Am I supposed to be impressed that you can fly a goon to England? Like I said, old news. I don't care if you kill my mother, I really don't.'

Da Silva made a small grunt of surprise. Italians have that sacred thing with *la mamma*. Even Raznatovic looked momentarily shocked.

'So then, two things,' I continued. 'I'm assuming that the guy with the gun on the beach a few days ago was one of yours, Dejan? Because you wanted the money from the "item" that our friend here had mislaid? That's why da Silva hid me away, out of your reach, until you could work things out?'

Raznatovic nodded slowly. I turned to da Silva.

'And the guy in the yard? That would be the other dead one? He's the one who organised the hit against you on the beach? So now you get to off him to prove to everyone in your gang that you two are best friends again? A "message", you said? A gesture of faith in your renewed collective bargain?'

Both men were staring at me. Dejan made to speak but I waved it away dismissively, a gesture I had to say I enjoyed.

'It's beyond me why you lot feel the need for that kind of crap. All that *omertà* shit is really ageing, you know. Haven't you got anything better to do? And the Big Brother routine with my mother? Whatever. Anyway, bad luck to the bloke in the boot. I think you both want a replacement for your "item", yes? And you think I can sort it out for you?'

'*Ho detto che e brava*,' muttered da Silva. 'I said she was good.'

'That's correct,' put in Raznatovic. His tone had warmed up a bit.

'So, yes. As I say, I don't give a toss about my mother, but the answer is still yes. I'll do what I can. But first, can we please stop all the nonsense? Let's be more businesslike. Can we agree on that?'

I was hoping they were buying the bravado. If I could convince them I didn't take them seriously I could play for time, discover what they needed. And then there might be a chance I could walk out of here on legs that still functioned. Acting the part was also quite useful in preventing the powerful

urge to vomit currently fomenting under my revolting jacket.
I knew just what both these men could do to me. So it was a
relief to see that Dejan was smiling.

'What did I tell you when you visited my home in Belgrade,
Judith?'

'That I was very brave. And also stupid.'

'Quite. But I agree. We can dispense with the nonsense, as
you call it.'

'So, your solution? What is it?'

'When you came to Belgrade, you offered to sell me an
artwork? I suspect that it wasn't genuine, that you had . . .
manufactured it, yes?'

'Well, I was just desperate to be introduced to you, you see.'

'Do you think you can make another?'

The 'artwork' I had shown Dejan was no more than a few
photos, a mash-up of a Venetian icon and some fairly foul
contemporary pieces. It had never been real – serving as a
ruse, no more. I hesitated.

'I know about pictures. Quite a lot. But I can't make them.
I can't paint.'

'My colleague has people who can see to the execution.'

'I gathered.'

'Please do not be flippant. You have already wasted a good
deal of my time. Your job will be to invent the piece – the
artist, the provenances. It will need to be impeccable. Impec-
cably valuable. Do you understand?'

'Yeees.'

'So, do you think you can do this?'

'Why me? Surely you two big shots have a whole team of
bent dealers on the payroll?'

There was a pause. Then da Silva said quietly, 'Actually, we
don't.'

Kazbich, Moncada, Fitzpatrick. All gone. I didn't need him to explain. Basically, all the other candidates for the post were deceased.

'So, when Mr Raznatovic and I had our little . . . misunderstanding, I thought of you. You have a legitimate gallery. You have proved you can spot a fake, you're good at research. I've been watching you for a long time, remember? Without a . . . plausible dealer there is a gap that needs to be filled, quickly.'

I turned back to Raznatovic.

'I'll need time. Maybe quite a lot of time. I'll need to research it, to speak to the people who will make it. But yes, if you can provide me with the resources.'

I looked at those lazily calm eyes again. For the first time since Kazbich had approached me and asked me to view Yermolov's collection, I felt suddenly gleeful. After thinking I would never see a painting again, unless it was an illustration in the prison library, I was being asked to forge one all of my very own. A serious picture. Though why that should make me so excited I couldn't quite see, immediately. As far as art was concerned at least, I had always been on the side of integrity. Hadn't this whole business with da Silva started because back when I had worked as a junior at the House in London I had been on a righteous crusade to expose a fake? But the time I had spent trying to be Elisabeth Teerlinc had implanted a contempt in me for her world, for its posturing, its snobbery, its venality. I might love pictures, but I had no reason to love the people who sold them. And then – oh, and then . . . I might even have laughed out loud.

'Let me get this clear,' I continued, once I had suppressed my internal glee. 'You,' I jerked my head at da Silva, 'or at least you and your "family" – do you still call it that? You owe him a fuck of a lot of money. So this picture needs to fetch – how much?'

'One hundred,' put in Dejan. He didn't need to add the million.

'So the person who should really be worried here isn't me?'

'You could say that.'

'OK. So this is how it's going to work. Yes,' I repeated, 'if you give me the resources, I can definitely do it. But not a private sale. That's my condition. A public auction. And anything in excess of his debt, we split, fifty-fifty.'

'You're very confident.'

'Indeed, gentlemen.' I'd always wanted to say that. 'And no more nonsense. We're partners now. A collective, if you like. Done?'

Dejan paused. 'Very well. Do you agree, Inspector?'

Da Silva nodded.

'And if I fail, well, you can off us both together, can't he, Romero?'

'Smart choice. I'm sorry I can't join you for lunch, but as I'm sure you understand, I have to get back to Belgrade. Since you agree, the inspector can introduce you to your assistant. We will provide everything you need.'

'There's one more thing. Something in my old flat, in Venice. It needs to be tidied up. Da Silva here can take care of it, I'm sure, but I want it done.'

'Inspector?'

Da Silva shrugged. 'Not a problem.'

Dejan was getting to his feet. His head almost reached the ceiling.

'Wait. What's your budget?'

'Budget?' I appreciated his aristocratic air of surprise. 'Whatever you require, of course. I'll be most interested to see what you produce.'

The conversation was clearly over. Da Silva ushered me briskly from the room, the track pants flapping over my dreadful loafers. Perhaps we could also swiftly dispense with my outfit, now that we were going into business together? I was distracted from that thought by the slam of the bedroom door. I may have felt a teeny pang that Dejan hadn't bothered to say goodbye.

Da Silva escorted me back to the dining room. The anxious man had laid out salad, bread and a plate of wizened, spiteful-looking sausages. I constructed yet another sandwich and munched it down.

'I hope there's pudding? The catering in that hole you had me in wasn't up to much, you know.'

Da Silva was eating more delicately, peeling a slice of cucumber.

'You meant that about your mother?'

'Why do you ask? Because if you know I'm an emotionless psycho you look less of a tit?'

Da Silva massaged the bridge of his nose. It was a nice nose.

'Do you always talk so much? Look, how can I explain? This thing. Our thing. It's not just about money. There are ways of doing things – codes. Mr Raznatovic is a very rich man, you know that. But if it looks as though he isn't getting paid, if it looks as though we don't make examples of people who step out of line, it makes us seem weak. Which is very bad for business.'

'A show of strength, then, all the dramatics?'

'Not a word most people would have chosen. Mr Raznatovic's men work frequently between Albania and Italy. One of them got a little enthusiastic when he heard of our recent misunderstanding. We agreed it was important that he should be made an example of somewhere his colleagues would be . . . clear about it. Also, Albania was convenient for Mr Raznatovic to see you, in person. He was quite clear about that.'

'Fair enough.' I speared a pallid tomato.

'So . . . your mother?'

'Did you study Dante at school? You must have done, you're Italian.'

'I'm not really into poetry.'

'In the *Inferno*, Dante reserves the ninth circle of hell for treachery. There's a kind of VIP area for people who betray love and trust.'

Da Silva was giving me the same look as when I had started banging on about helicopters.

'Your mother betrayed you?' he asked slowly.

How could I even begin to tell anyone about my mother? Least of all da Silva? 'Never mind. My mother's a drunk. She never cared about me, never looked after me. What do I owe her?'

'I'm . . . sorry.'

'No, you're not. Anyway, don't we have work to do? And I'm far more interested in you telling me what the actual fuck has been going on than in talking about my mother.'

'You'll know what you need to know.'

'Uh-uh. We're a team now, remember? Your mate Dejan says so, and he's the boss, it seems.'

The idea I'd had – I might even have gone so far as to call it an inspiration – was fizzing inside me so brightly that this latest surreality hardly registered.

'I think I'd like a cigarette now.'

Like all sophisticated pleasures, the first taste made me sick, but after that every drag was ecstatic.

'So, Romero, what's next? When do I start?'

'You said you wanted to see the person who can make it?'

'Ready and waiting.'

'So – we're going back to Calabria.'

'Joy.'

I'd thought I didn't believe in fate, but da Silva and I obviously had some karmic number going on. So many bodies, so many ghosts. We were beginning to seem like the last men standing, so perhaps we might as well be friends.

4

My new quarters were a considerable improvement on the shed. The honeymoon suite at the Grand Hotel President di Siderno, no less. By the time we arrived late that evening, da Silva's elves had already been busy. As well as the small bag I had packed in Venice when I had thought I was going to be doing time, there was a collection of my things from the apartment in Campo Santa Margherita, including my laptop and phones, jewellery, clothes, underwear, toiletries, running gear, all my art books. I was pleased to note that they had resisted the temptation to include any pieces of Alvin.

'You'll be comfortable in here? I'll be just next door while you're working.'

'I wasn't planning to start tonight. I'm a bit tired, what with the death threats and everything.'

'I mean, I'll be staying here while you prepare.'

'The whole time?' I asked disbelievingly. 'But what about Christmas? Won't Franci and the kids miss you? Giovanni and Giulia will be devastated if Papa isn't home. And work – what about the day job?'

Da Silva was flicking idly through the illustrations of a biography of Soutine.

'What? Oh no. Sick leave. I was unfortunately shot in the leg last week. Injured in the line of duty.'

'Seriously? You can get away with that rubbish?'

He looked at me pityingly. 'You really don't know anything, do you?'

'And your wife?'

'She understands. Better still, she's not always asking questions, unlike some people. I'll leave you to settle in. But I'll be taking these.'

He held up a brown envelope. My passports – the original in the name of Judith Lauren Rashleigh and the two fakes I had bought a year apart from a 'cobbler' – a fixer in Amsterdam who faked documents. Elisabeth Teerlinc and Katherine Olivia Gable. My sister's names – our mother adored classic Hollywood films.

'That's really not necessary. Where do you imagine I'm going to go?'

'Why do you imagine I'd trust you?'

'Trust is what you do when you don't have a better alternative.'

'*L'ultima spiaggia*?'

'We say the last resort.'

'I'm taking them. If you want anything, food – order whatever you want.'

'Have you got any fags?'

He handed me his own half-finished pack.

'Thanks. I suppose. I'm dying for a bath.'

Da Silva gave me a funny look as he closed the door.

Locking it behind him, I turned on the taps in the marble tub, pouring every bottle of complimentary foam and shampoo into the steaming water. While I waited for it to fill, I started checking my computer. My bank accounts in Panama and Switzerland were all in order, I was still relatively rich, and aside from a (disappointingly few) queries from bewildered clients asking about the abrupt closure of Gentileschi, I had four messages. Steve, Carlotta and Dave, the three people who were the nearest thing I had to friends. Another from Pavel Yermolov. I tapped Yermolov's first.

Judith. Please contact me. Just to let me know all is well. Everything fine here, as arranged.

Yermolov was a bit late with that announcement. *Fine* didn't quite cover it. When he'd assured me he would take care of Kazbich it had never occurred to me that I might have to take his place. Sort of touching, though, that Yermolov should sound so concerned. We had shared a few days of decent sex and world-class-spectacular pictures, but I hadn't fooled myself that it meant anything, though I admit I have low standards in that department. On the whole, the less I know about my lovers the better. Their names, for instance.

Carlotta's message was typically brief: two baby emojis and a thumbs-up sign. I smiled. After hooking her elderly but extremely high net worth husband, Carlotta's next scheme had been to get pregnant, ideally with twins. Carlotta was an impressive example of getting what you wanted, if what you wanted was to cash the cheque after the wedding. I couldn't envy her, but I was glad for her.

Dave's message was also brief.

Hope all OK. Great news about my book! Can't wait to tell you – drop me a line. Love, D. xxx

I felt bad about that one. Dave had worked as a porter at the House in London, back when I had been a junior in British Pictures, but his earlier experiences in the army had proved pretty useful. That and his capacity for not interfering, just like da Silva's wife. He'd helped me in all sorts of ways he didn't know and would certainly never wish to know. When I had last seen him, he had explained that he had written a book on his experiences of art as trauma therapy for soldiers.

I'd finished most of it, but being arrested and kidnapped had distracted me from the final chapters. His shy enthusiasm and his genuine, passionate love for pictures deserved better. With a pang I remembered our conversations over snatched cigarettes in the yard beneath the House where the works were brought in. I doubted he'd think much of what I was involved in now.

Steve, or rather Steve's latest assistant, informed me that his boat, the *Mandarin*, would be in the Caribbean for New Year, and would I care to join? I replied regretfully in the negative.

Unsurprisingly, there was nothing from my mother. Still, tomorrow was Christmas Eve. She'd probably be in touch.

The hot bath and two orders of tagliatelle with prawns and vodka followed by fruit salad and tiramisu should have soothed me, but I was too excited to think of sleeping. Wrapped in a robe, I combed out the tangles in my blissfully clean hair and went onto the balcony for a smoke. My terrace even featured a hot tub. Below me, the old centre of the city stretched towards the sea, the glittering illuminations along the promenade wavering like the tentacles of a jellyfish. Siderno. I was dying to get started with my work for Raznatovic, but there was quite a lot I needed to know first. Such as what Mrs da Silva was doing. I fetched the hotel-issue notebook and pencil from the desk, opened Facebook and began snooping.

Running next morning felt wonderful after the days of confinement. Looping down from the hotel I made for the front, pushing myself into a sprint every hundred metres, feeling the stretch and twang as my muscles opened. I wasn't surprised to meet da Silva on my return, bundled up in a heavy hooded sweatshirt, though it really wasn't that cold. He was doing push-ups off a low wall, swapping his hands alternately behind his back.

'Bravo! Fancy a coffee?'

Da Silva peered up at me from under his shoulder. My own workout gear was a considerable improvement on the sweat-pants and I daresay the sea air had brought a becoming flush to my cheeks.

'Sure,' he answered, straightening up. We walked into the lobby together, the clerk at the desk giving da Silva a respect-ful nod. Apart from an elderly couple in wheelchairs who had been parked at the breakfast table by a dreamy-eyed Filipino nurse, we appeared to be the only residents over the festive season.

On the terrace, Da Silva pulled a packet of Marlboro Gold from his sweatshirt pocket and offered me one as our *cappuccini* arrived. It seemed we shared an approach to exercise, amongst other things. He lit me up with a heavy gold Dupont.

'So,' I began, once the waiter was out of hearing, 'maybe we should speak English again? It might be more discreet.'

'OK. What have you been thinking?'

'About how this works. About what you do.'

'I said yesterday, you'll know what you need to know.'

'Yes, I will, in the end. But it would be much less painful if you just told me. I'll start with what I think.'

Da Silva sat back, quizzical, taking a long drag on his cigarette.

'I friended your wife on Facebook. Quite some time ago.'

'Yes. And? I don't like you mentioning my wife.'

'Her family name is Casachiara. Francesca Casachiara.' Ital-ian women do not customarily take their husbands' name. 'And she's from Casilino in Rome,' I went on, 'where you grew up.

But you told me you were born here, in the south, in Siderno.'
Casilino was a fairly grim sixties suburb not far from the city
centre. 'The Casachiaras are quite a big deal in Rome, aren't
they? When Francesca's grandfather died his funeral shut down
part of the city. The police helicopters couldn't even get near – it
was a scandal. Even the British press picked up on it, you know.
They love a good Mafia story.'

Da Silva winced at that word. I knew that only amateurs
used it, really, but I enjoyed his discomfort.

'So – Romero from Siderno and Francesca from Casilino.
What could the connection be? This is what I think. Round
here' – I gestured over the parapet of the terrace – 'they reckon
one per cent of the men are involved in – that thing. Many of
you come from Siderno, or Bovalino.'

'So?'

'Do you remember where we first met, Romero? Lake Como,
wasn't it? So beautiful up there. You'd come to ask me about
Cameron Fitzpatrick's death.'

'Yes, we've already been through all this.'

'Keep your hair on. Bovalino. Cameron Fitzpatrick's mother
was from Bovalino. Chambermaid in a Roman hotel, wasn't it?'

Da Silva's lighter clicked again. I continued.

'Fitzpatrick was born here, like you.'

'How do you know that?'

'There was a memorial service for Fitzpatrick in London
last year. Such a tragedy, the murder. His mother flew over for
it – her name was in the obituary. And then – electoral register, declarations of residence at the *commune*. You lot do love
a document. The thing is, though, anyone who wants to play
in your gang has to be born down here. Your blood family are
also your clan family, if you like. This is where it all begins.

This place. You're all connected, though I admit it took me a while to work it out.'

Da Silva appeared to have eaten his fag.

'Shall I go on? I like the next bit.'

He nodded.

'There was a bit of a recruitment problem, wasn't there? Too much muscle, not enough brains.'

'*Brava.*'

Researching official documentation on the Italian Mafia was not such a thrilling activity as its subject suggested. *Generational Hindrances to Internalisation of Competencies in Illegal Markets* was one of the catchier titles. Basically, in a town where there was nothing much to do in winter except use sheep for target practice or fuck your sister, the quality of locally born clansmen was deteriorating. One too many thumbs. The strict rules about membership through birth were getting in the way of profits, particularly when it came to infiltrating legitimate businesses. So the families, the clans, devised a solution. College scholarships, business school, English lessons. All the training for a twenty-first-century operation.

'There are ten big Calabrian ... groups, do you prefer? – operating in the north of Italy. Connections with the Roman ... groups are crucial. And you're one of the new boys, aren't you, Romero? With your dynastic marriage, your connections. You're all over the place, with your university degrees and your nice suits and your taste for sushi. Law firms, planning offices, civil service? Even the Senate, if the press have it half right. All legit. Except you're bent as fuck.'

I took another fag without asking and watched him. He looked back impassively, lizard-eyed.

'Go on.'

So you and Fitzpatrick and Moncada were in on this arms thing together. Kazbich was your adviser, Raznatovic your supplier. That's how Kazbich found me, over the Caravaggio. That's how you knew what was in my apartment.'

'That would be Alvin Spencer. The man you confessed to murdering?' His voice was flat.

'You didn't arrest me then and you're hardly likely to now. I think . . .' I put my head to one side. 'I think you would have killed me, the other day.'

'I'm only sorry I was interrupted.'

'Yet here we are.'

Da Silva stretched his arms above his head, flexing his triceps diagonally one after the other.

'So, back in Paris,' I went on. 'What was it, four years ago? A cop calling himself Renaud Cleret found me. He believed you were working together. I was all set to skip town, and you were waiting for me, at the airport. I assume you have to catch the odd criminal now and then, to maintain the cover? But you lost me. If it hadn't been for that text . . .'

The text I had sent from Cleret's phone: *Does the name Gentileschi mean anything to you?* Eight words that had pursued me ever since.

'What happened to him? To Cleret?' The question showed he had dropped all attempt at ignorance, that the bones of the story it had taken me most of the night to piece together were correct.

'Your old colleague? You don't want to know. Really.'

Some memories have a synaesthetic quality, the prompt of one sense discovering the recollection of another. The thick gulp of Renaud's carotid artery as the knife entered his neck conjured the wine-coloured spiral of his blood sluicing down the drain, its foetid sweetness ever present, that night in Paris. I'd wrapped his head in clingfilm, then a plastic bag, then into a cheap sports-carrier and dumped it in the Seine. As far as I knew, it had never been found.

I stubbed out my fag in the floral border. 'Well?'

'I'm going to take a shower. And then I suggest you stop interfering and get on with what you're here to do.'

'No. I want to know. I've said I'll do the work. It's not as though I have much choice, is it? But I want to know what it's going to pay for.'

'Why do you care?'

'I'm an artist now. I need inspiration. And you need me, so you'll tell me. Raznatovic isn't going to wait for his money forever.'

'You're not indispensable, whatever line you gave in Albania.'

'No. But Fitzpatrick is gone, Moncada is gone, Kazbich is gone. They were the ones who designed the fakes for you. Who moved them. You've already admitted it. Whilst I'm already so deep in crap with you, you know I can't escape. You won't find anyone who knows piss about pictures who's got such good reasons to keep their mouth shut before Raznatovic runs out of patience.'

5

An hour later we were in da Silva's car, the same black one that had brought me from Venice, heading back up to Capo Rizzuto. There were more women than yesterday working the lay-bys, taking advantage of the family holiday. Da Silva drove in silence. He had changed into jeans and a navy V-neck sweater over a white shirt, the preppy clothes and his short hair making him seem younger than in uniform. I had to admit he was in pretty good shape. Navy had been my choice too, a button-through suede Chloé dress, gathered at the small of the back, under a softly tailored tweed three-quarter jacket, with flat Ferragamo boots. The elves had forgotten my scent, without which I didn't feel quite dressed, but with a whisper of make-up I felt quite like my old self. More like my old self than I had in a long time. It was an absurd outfit for a visit to a police station, but the pleasure of having my own things again made me want to dress up a bit. At least, that was my story and I was sticking to it.

'The port's along here,' said da Silva finally, as we pulled off onto a freshly tarmacked track.

'This is where the boats go out, to pick people up. The camp's about a kilometre up the coast.'

He flashed his ID at the sentry on the barrier and we found a space in the crowded car park.

'How come it's so busy?' I asked.

'Christmas. They'll be getting the boats ready for the search – they'll expect plenty of refs tonight.'

As he spoke we were walking down to a pier, where three large motorboats striped with the *Guardia*'s insignia were moored. A group of uniforms loaded orange lifejackets and crates of water bottles, radios crackled, a bale of blankets was tossed up into waiting hands.

'The traffickers charge extra at Christmas. More chance of a sympathetic reception,' explained da Silva matter-of-factly. He stooped to give a hand to a young woman struggling with a heavy red first aid box. She glanced curiously at me as she thanked him and he wished her a happy Christmas. I marvelled at his assurance amongst his colleagues, the cool fit of his mask. Did none of them have any idea? Or did they just not believe in asking questions? Some of these people would be setting out later, leaving their own families to rescue others. How could they be unaware of what was going on under their noses? I remembered something I had read yesterday evening, a miraculously lucky victim to a botched Mafia hit who had refused to testify. 'It's true they put sixty-three shots in my back,' the man had said, 'but I'm sure it was by mistake.' Maybe it's easier to keep silent about something whose very existence is never acknowledged.

We passed to the end of the pier, where the waves chopped through the sound of our conversation.

'You said you wanted to know,' da Silva murmured. 'Here it is. The equipment goes on the boats. When they connect with the right agent, we exchange it for the refs.'

'You mean the weapons?'

'What else would I mean?'

'And then?'

'Libya, Syria, Iraq – even further. Wherever the customer wants to take them, that's not our business.'

I had to admire the simplicity of it. And the audacity. Humanitarian rescue as a cover for shifting AK47s.

'What happens to the people?'

'Most of them end up there, to start with.' He indicated a headland across the bay to our left. Shielding my eyes against the sun, I could make out heavy twists of barbed wire, blocking access to the cliffs, and what looked like a holiday camp, rows of small wooden chalets. A group of men were playing football between the low buildings. One of them wore a red and blue striped shirt with 'MESSI' stencilled on the back.

'But how?' I still couldn't get my head round it.

'The crates are unloaded into the dinghies. The guys who take them off don't know anything more than that. Or they know better than to ask.'

'But how does the gear get here in the first place?'

'God. Don't you ever shut up?'

I turned to face him, the wind blowing my hair back from my face. 'I saved your life, you saved mine. You said you'd explain.'

He pointed up the coast as though he was showing me the view.

'Military trucks.'

In the decades following the collapse of the Soviet Union, Raznatovic had made his fortune as an arms dealer. A huge swathe of eastern Europe had basically become a car boot sale for state-issued weapons – at one time you could pick up an AK47 for a hundred dollars.

'No bother with the borders,' I observed.

Serbia was perfect for moving military contraband into the Schengen area of Europe – once inside, army vehicles could move freely.

'Exactly. Once the stuff's out of Serbia, it's stored in bar-racks and moved in trucks. Some of it official, most of it not. We get the refs to unload it, further down the coast. Takes a few minutes per truck. We pay them,' he added, when he saw the expression on my face. 'Two euros an hour. Same as they'd get for tomatoes. Then it's divided up; some of it comes here, the rest distributed along the coast. Got it?'

One of the distant football players had saved a goal, throwing himself theatrically to the ground as he dived for the ball. I thought of those hands, how they would rest tiredly in his lap after a night moving heavy boxes, shifting the very tools that had shattered his life. It was grotesque, when you thought about it. But then no one ever really thinks about it. They look at the shot of the dead kid on the beach and scroll down their feed to the amusing kittens, the inspirational yoga poses.

'Impressive,' I murmured.

'Shall we go back now? It's bloody freezing.'

Da Silva disappeared after we returned to the hotel. He said he was joining some of his family for the Christmas Eve din-ner and then going to Mass. I spent the afternoon reading, then took myself for a walk. The last of the shops were clos-ing, people were busy buying emergency gifts and supplies, everyone wishing each other happy Christmas. Walking alone through the cheery crowds felt like the worst kind of cliché. For a while I sat on a bench overlooking the sea while it got dark, and smoked until I felt dizzy. Then I called my mother, but she didn't answer. Pissed, of course, sleeping off Christmas Eve afternoon in the pub. I left a message apolo-gising for the late arrival of her gift, blaming the Italian post, and said I was planning 'a quiet one'. She wouldn't have been expecting me to come back. I wished her all the best and hung up.

One of the more useful lessons of my childhood is that junkies always know where to score. They'll find the place on the outskirts of town with the twisted dropped wraps hiding in the paving stones, the bent spoons in dustbins. When I saw the Santa girl from the roadside strolling along the front, I reconfigured my plans for the evening. I hadn't been all that keen on dining *à trois* with the wheelchairs anyway. I stubbed out my umpteenth fag and followed her. Dressed in skinny jeans and a purple satin Puffa jacket, she wasn't working, but she remained conspicuous – not only for the colour of her skin, still a rarity in Italy, but for the way she carried herself, erect and graceful, moving through the remains of the festive shoppers according to some invisible choreography. She glided a little further along the marina and then turned up one of the ugly modern streets which divided the *centro storico* from the sea. Trailing about twenty metres behind her, I crossed a wide boulevard into a polished marble square with a small baroque church at one end, its cream stucco gleaming in the winter dark. Behind the church, I dropped back as we entered narrower streets; I didn't want the sound of my boots on the smooth stone to alarm her. She stopped to check her phone and I hung back in a doorway, elated by the sensation of pursuit.

The ancient streets rose as they twisted until we came out on a perpendicular alley, running against the grounds of the white mass of the Siderno castle, the highest point of the old city, where she ducked under an arched stone gateway. Tea lights in brown paper bags of sand lit up bare walls which had been laid by the kings of Aragon. There was music playing faintly, something wailing and jazzy as I descended a narrow flight of curving steps into a cellar. It looked like my girl already had a date – she was enveloped in the sturdy arms of a shaven-headed woman, old-school man's shirt and braces over a thick, squat body, the cluster of piercings in her ear twinkling through Santa girl's hair in the candlelight. A high bench and a shelf of bottles made a bar. I ordered a tumbler of filthy red and looked around for a plan B. There were maybe about twenty people in the small space, a mix of hipster Italian kids proudly escaping Christmas Eve and several groups of Africans and Arabs, maybe some of them from the camp. Two men, a short bearded Italian boy and a tall black guy in a patterned shirt, slow-danced rapturously near the speaker, eyes locked as they swayed. A line of crates topped with mismatched cushions along the back wall made for the seating, I took one and lit a cigarette, waiting and watching the dancers.

'*Ciao.*' A guy two crates along, not bad, long legged, narrow, a wide clever forehead. I smiled and he bumped his seat over. The room grew busier as we chatted over the music, he bought me another drink and rested his arm over my shoulder, testing. I let it stay there. When we'd ascertained I spoke French we switched from his jerky Italian. He said his name was Serafim, that he was from Egypt originally, he had a job as a mechanic, studied English in the evenings. He told me he dreamed of going to London one day. 'Carnaby Street,' he smiled. I didn't have the heart to tell him it was all Zara and noodle bars. A wave of cold air from the door preceded another gust of drinkers, four Italians. Serafim waved one of them over, introduced him as his friend, Raffaele.

'Seriously? Serafim and Raffaele? Are you making that up?'

'No. Maybe, if you like.'

OK, then. Raffaele was blondish, shorter than his mate, tight, gym-stoked body. He had the look on him, I thought, and when Serafim went up to the bar he pulled me in for a kiss. I opened under his mouth, letting my hands find the tight muscle of his torso under his sweatshirt, and when Serafim came back I turned my head and smiled again and gave my mouth to his. So familiar, so easy.

'Do you want to go somewhere else?' Serafim asked.

'With both of you?'

Raffaele nodded slowly.

'Sure. I'll grab a bottle.'

We left arm-in-arm, me in between their shoulders. 'This way,' said Serafim. So they'd done this before. All the better. They guided me up the steps to the alley, crossed it and moved a little way along the castle wall until we came to a wooden door with a half-hearted padlock.

'Shhhh!' one of them giggled as we slipped through the gap. The door led to another flight of steps, between the castle walls, much darker and colder. A part of my brain asked if I should be frightened, but it was the part of my brain that doesn't work properly, so I ignored it. We came out into a wide, scruffy courtyard, tufts of grass sprouting between huge, ancient paving stones. Serafim led the way, crossing to an open loggia that I guessed would give a view of the sea on the other side. Cats skittered in the corners, the occasional pair of green eyes flaring spookily. At the end of the loggia, an enclosed space, barely even a room, just a curved wall with a row of candles in tomato cans tracing its shape. Serafim lit them one by one. We passed a bottle of more filthy red, each of us taking a single, solemn drink. It was freezing, but my skin felt hot, plump with blood. For a moment, we all paused, looking at one another, then I took off my coat and laid it on the ground, followed by my dress.

'Come and keep me warm.'

They lay down on either side of me. Raffaele, bolder, slid his hand into my pussy at the same time as his tongue found mine, Serafim buried his lips in my neck, grasping at my breasts. One of them told me I was beautiful. Raffaele began to move his mouth down my body; I gasped as he found the inside of my thighs, slowly circling his tongue, taking his time. I pulled Serafim against me harder, reaching for his cock, released it, fumbling in the darkness, then guided him onto his knees, straddling me, to take it in my mouth. Little nuzzles and whispers, then the fat bulb of smooth flesh pushing my throat wider as I stretched my jaw to swirl my tongue over the tip, supporting my neck with one hand as finally the other man's tongue found the soaked lips of my cunt, lapping upwards in long strokes. I sucked harder, pushing my mouth down Serafim's cock to its shaved mount, reaching my other hand to cup his balls with my thumb firm on the base.

'*Si, bella, si, cosi.*'

'Wait. *Attendez*. I want to see you.' Pulling back, I sat up against the damp plaster, the yellow flames glowing on a single skein of juice between my pussy and Raffaele's lips. He wiped the back of a hand against his mouth, grinning.

'Show me. Stand up, go on. One of you to fuck me and the other one over me.' They obeyed, both of them stroking their cocks outside their jeans. I took a good hungry look. Serafim was definitely the best of the bargain.

'I'll have you. Lie down.' As we changed places I kissed Raffaele again, tasting the clear musk of my cum on him, lemony tonight.

'Touch it,' I instructed him. With my back to Serafim, I lowered myself onto him, bringing my knees forward as I lay back against his chest, until I had his cock fully inside me, pinioned. As Raffaele began to wank himself off with a tight, urgent fist, I ground my weight against the thickness inside me, circling my arse against Serafim's belly, squeezing the muscles of my cunt upwards with every stroke until he began to moan, then slowly sitting up, bringing his hand to my hips so he could push deeper at me, feeling the pulse of his closeness as I spread my legs just a little, wide enough for my fingers to find my clit, wanting him to flood me, wanting a lake of sperm up me as I began to come, his cock a dull weight now, swelling, stretching me, until he came as Raffaele cried out and thumped his load over my face, sending it dripping down my jaw to pool in my clavicles as I scooped a palmful of Serafim's cum and gulped it and let it fall over my chin, glistening silver against the freezing burn of my skin, and that got me there, drenched, worshipped.

Serafim sank his teeth into my shoulder as I fell softly back against him, reaching my arms to Raffaele, who pillowed his head on the cooling slip between my breasts. A time when I could hear all three of our hearts. Then the shock of another pair of eyes a little behind us, and another at the edge of the wall, somewhere a half-stifled gasp.

'I think we have company,' I said, very slowly.

'Don't worry, they won't bother us,' murmured Raffaele. 'They were just watching.'

Both my boys were still dressed; we rested there, my nakedness between the weight of their two bodies, until silent, shuffling footsteps told me our silent audience had melted away, and the ice in the wind off the sea began to bite.

* * *

It was about one in the morning when I began the walk back to the hotel, clutching my coat around me. My dress was a ruin, the thin suede stained and scuffed, but I didn't mind. The churches were letting out the worshippers from midnight Mass, stretching in their smart jackets, ferrying drooping children hurriedly to their cars. *Oh come all ye faithful.* Somewhere far out on the black water, the boats were searching. I'd bought a carton of fags earlier. I wrapped a sheet of hotel notepaper round a pack, scrawled 'Happy Christmas' across it, and left it outside da Silva's door. I planned to spend Our Lord's birthday asleep.

6

Boxing Day morning. The industrial estate was as ugly and nondescript as all such places are. We passed anonymous warehouses and loading bays, a few Chinese workers snatching a cigarette break outside. Two rows of flat-pack garden sheds, similar to the chalets of the refugee camp, with washing strung between them, a heap of bunk beds glimpsed through an open door. Many of the buildings would be crammed with sewing machines, men and women bent over the seams of delicate, expensive clothes like the ones I was wearing, the big designers paying sweatshop rates to achieve the crucial 'Made in Italy' label. One low block had huge security doors and two guards with patrolling Alsatians. There was a sharp smell of chemicals in the air, and when I looked up, two sinister chimneys leaking white smoke. Perhaps they were cooking smack in there. Perhaps I gave a shit.

We stopped a little further along, at a smaller red-brick building where another Chinese man waited outside. He was middle aged, paunchy, dressed in a blue overall like the other factory workers.

'This is Li,' offered da Silva. 'Li, this is Miss Rashleigh.'

'Judith, please.'

'I'll leave you to it, then,' said da Silva. He returned to the car, opened the window and lit up.

'Don't you want to see?' I called.

'Old news,' he smiled back.

Li held the door courteously and asked me in perfectly accented Italian if I would like something to drink. I declined, and followed him eagerly into the workshop. The space was larger than it looked, replete with natural light from several wide skylights and an enticing smell of oil paint and varnish. We walked along a partitioned corridor to a heavy door in a brick surround. Li punched in a security code, waited for the door to click.

'This is the storeroom. What would you like to see?'

'Anything that's ready to go perhaps, please?'

Li paused a moment, then grinned and reached for the handle of what looked like a giant fridge. Inside was a revolving rack, which he turned with a small remote control. I saw the edges of canvases clicking by, until Li paused it and pulled out a Kandinsky.

At least, it wasn't a Kandinsky. I knew, rationally, that it wasn't. And yet, weirdly, marvellously, it had exactly the same effect on me as the real ones I'd seen. Had it been real, the picture would have belonged to the artist's earlier period, around 1911. A landscape with houses, a meadow in the foreground, a river curving round a hill. The simplest of colours – green, red, yellow, blue – the childish precision of the buildings contrasting with the daubs that gestured at earth and water. The kind of picture about which people still say 'My three-year-old could do that!' as if the point was a mere clumsy rendering of what the painter saw. Until you look again and see the glazed depth of the water within the apparently flat layers of the paint, the dance of shadow as the invisible sun plays on the roofs, watch the colours bloom out and out so that the damp of the plaster walls and the dust on the shore grass haze your eyes, until you feel, rather than see, even though what he has drawn is the front of your own iris.

It's estimated that about ten per cent of the works that hang in major museums are fakes. Looking at Li's work, I could easily believe it. Perhaps this picture wouldn't have withstood complex technological analysis, but I suspected it might. And if it did, then where did the reality of a Kandinsky lie?

I didn't need to tell Li it was good; that would have been an insult.

'Something else, please.'

Again he clicked the rack and selected a larger canvas, a classic seventeenth-century-style Dutch still life. Deep coffee-blue background, a lawn-covered table, a silver dish of pome-granates and black grapes, the light from a trio of candles in an ornate holder burnishing the must on the skins of the fruit. On the rim of the platter, a tiny, vivid green caterpillar crept out towards the viewer, so realistic it seemed at first to be glued to the canvas. A standard trick, inserting a miniature, playful detail as a flourish of virtuosity.

'Got a loupe?'

Li handed me the magnifier from the pocket of his overall and laid the picture down on the workbench. I moved it care-fully over the surface. The 'craquelure' is the pattern of tiny fractures made on the top level of a painting as the oils and varnishes dry. The right effect can be faked – often by baking the finished work in an oven, but a poorly executed craquelure can catch a forger out, identifying them in the same way as human fingerprints. I was no expert on still life of any period, but I'd seen enough similar compositions back at the House to be pretty sure that this one would pass.

'The pigments?'

'All correct. We grind them ourselves.' He crossed the room to a bookshelf and took down a large square volume in a plain red dust cover, the *Dictionary of Historical Pigments*. He proffered another, reading the title carefully in English, *Optical Microscopy of Historical Pigments*.

'I've heard of them.'

'And here's our checklist.'

He pointed to a handwritten notice in Chinese characters pinned to the wall.

'Canvas, stretcher, panel, layer, ground, priming . . .' – he hesitated, found the word – 'binding, patina. Each piece is checked before it leaves, but this is only a reminder, of course. Not necessary.'

'I shouldn't think so. Thank you. May I see the workshop?'

'Of course.'

When people think of artists now, they mostly imagine a lone genius, toiling in solitary confinement in a garret. But that's a fairly recent invention. Until the nineteenth century at least, artists ran their studios as production lines, with canvases passed between the newest apprentices, who would block in the ground, up through the specialists in landscape or drapery, and finally to the artist himself, who would execute the final strokes to a face or the shadow of a cherub's wing. Not altogether different from the processes going on around the industrial estate. Many pictures that pass as Old Masters have precious little of the old master in the paint – a picture by Rubens, say, might actually be no more than a portrait of a hand. Li's atelier seemed to be based on the same principle. Several men, middle-aged like himself, were working quietly at long tables to the gentle sound of classical music from a radio. One was laying in ground in dark oils, another – meticulously

– the thick white underpaint of what was probably an Impressionist with a small wooden tool that resembled the stick of an ice lolly. They moved unhurriedly between their tasks in their dark overalls, intensely concentrated, like monks in a medieval scriptorium. I thought of the fake Stubbs, the painting my old boss Rupert had tried to move through the House. Had it been altered here to appear genuine? Watching the men work, I couldn't summon any outrage on behalf of the clients they were defrauding. What they were doing required such patient, rare skill, such precision, such love. They were only doing what generations of apprentices had done before them, after all, and the results to my eyes were far better than the wank coming out of the average art school.

'What's your usual time for a piece?' I asked. I found myself whispering.

'Usually three months maximum. For something more modern . . .' Li grinned mischievously.

'A Pollock, say?'

'Oh that. We can do that in an afternoon.'

'You can work on wood?'

'Wood, paper, anything. Once we did something on a . . . lady's dress?'

The Caravaggio. I knew all about that one.

'I'm going to try to bring you some wood. You'll need oils, late nineteenth century, nothing earlier than 1860, nothing later than 1905.'

'Varnish?'

'Maybe. Applied and then removed, I think.'

'Easy, then?'

'I think anything would be easy for you.'

* * *

My first question had been: who? Which artist should I choose? An Old Master – Rembrandt or Velazquez, say – would obviously be the most reliable in terms of the price it would fetch, yet even if the identical period paint was used, if the canvas, sizing, pigment density and brushwork were impeccable, just as on Li's checklist, there remained the problem of history. To forge an artwork, there has to be the possibility that it really existed, a fissure in the chronology into which the forger can insert the fake. The Rembrandt Research Project had spent forty years in microscopic examination of every single attributed canvas, erecting a barrier of scholarship around van Rijn that only an idiot would nowadays attempt to scale. Occasionally, it's true, a lost work by a master is discovered – a Leonardo had been sold in Paris quite recently – but such miraculous discoveries make international news, and their rightful ownership can be a matter of disputes between governments. Way too complex, too public, too slow.

That left more modern works, late nineteenth to midtwentieth century. Impressionists or Abstract Expressionists are much easier to fake, especially the latter, as it's not actually necessary to know how to paint. If Li was going to make a piece that would fetch over a hundred, that would be the most promising area. Willem de Kooning's *Interchange* had fetched three hundred million, Cezanne's *Card Players* two hundred and fifty, Pollock's *17A* two hundred, placing all of them ahead of poor old Rembrandt, whose double portrait *Soolmans and Coppit* had gone for a measly one-eighty. The biggest challenge was the gap in the catalogue. I knew that Modigliani, whose works also sold at well over one hundred, had often been faked for that reason – the painter had spent much of his life near destitute and had often exchanged canvases for food, making the extent of his output notoriously difficult to track. Yet for that very reason, Modigliani might be too obvious, too risky.

Then I had thought of Gauguin. Often, when I had worked at the House in London, I had been sent to the archive at the Courtauld Institute on the Strand. There was a Gauguin in the collection that I always took time to visit – *Nevermore*, painted in Tahiti in 1897. At first, it had seemed ugly to me, a heavy-flanked nude on a brightly coloured counterpane, her head supported by an acid-yellow pillow. The pose was ungainly, the patterned decorations of the room clumsily gay. And yet I had found myself drawn back to it, rushing up from St James's past Charing Cross, weighed down with heavy files, to steal a few minutes in front of the picture. The gallery notes told me that what I was seeing was an exploited teenage girl, the artist's *vahine*, his Tahitian 'wife'; that the composition, with its two watchful figures placed at the right and the vicious-beaked bird, a raven, to the left, was sinister and troubling. But that wasn't what I saw. To me, the girl just looked sulky and bored, impatient with her older lover's demands that she sit for him. I had liked that defiance, and I liked the artist for showing it, for laughing at himself. But I also remembered that *Nevermore* had been painted over another composition, a tropical farmyard of energetic palms, with a horse and a chicken, revealed by the infrared examinations of the museum. From what I knew of Gauguin's life, it had been restless, peripatetic – he had painted in Paris, Brittany, Arles, in Copenhagen and Martinique, Tahiti and the Marquesas Islands. Gauguin did not only work on canvas, but in ceramic, woods, fresco. And that had given me another idea.

Yet as I left the workshop, I realised that my job was going to be far, far more difficult than Li's. Li could make the pictures, but he couldn't sell them. Inventing the backstory, the provenances, was also technical, and Christ knew, I'd faked enough versions of my own life. A laborious detective story run backwards. But Raznatovic wanted me because I might be able, had to be able, to convince the buyer. Li could make something that looked exactly like a Kandinsky, but what made it a Kandinsky was the conviction of its owner that it *was* a Kandinsky. In any encounter involving desire, the person whose need is greatest is the submissive. It was as true of commerce as it was of sex. I was going to have to elicit that complicity, to make our buyer believe, to make them feverish with want, possessed by the urge for possession.

There were three fag butts outside da Silva's car window. Leaning against the wall I lit one of my own. A compact of faith sealed with money. A hundred million. I blew a zero of smoke, watched it quiver and dissipate. Eight of them. I'm a good actress, but was I that good? Though the alternative wasn't looking too appealing. I shook myself, pulled out my phone and typed my reply to Pavel Yermolov.

Happy Christmas. All well. Though I may need two favours. Can you call me?

I hesitated, then added a kiss.

Next I called Dave.

'Judith! It's great to hear you, love! Happy Christmas!'

'Happy Christmas to you too! I'm not disturbing you, am I?'

He sighed. 'Got the mother-in-law here. She and the missus have gone to the John Lewis sale.'

'That's . . . er . . . nice. So tell me about the book!'

I'd finished it on Christmas Night, in bed with a bottle of Ciro and a club sandwich. It began as a memoir, describing Dave's time in the army, the loss of his leg and the solace he had found in beginning to learn about art. The second part discussed his work with injured servicemen, research on art and therapy for PTSD, ending with a passionate plea for the continued teaching of art history in schools. I could see that readers would find many of the stories moving, and Dave wrote well, simply and unpretentiously, his enthusiasm springing off the page.

'It's really good, Dave. I was proud to read it.'

'But guess what?'

Dave's wife had suggested he self-publish the book online, and it had been downloaded so many times and received such positive comments that a literary agent had picked it up. He had an advance from a publisher and everything, he explained. 'And the BBC have been in touch. They wanted some ideas for a documentary, about the work we've been doing.'

'Don't be modest. They want to make a film about you!'

'Yeah, well. It's ace, anyway, isn't it?'

'More than. I'm really so happy for you. Your wife must be just thrilled. Good for her, too, putting it out there. You'd never have done it on your own.'

'Thanks. And you – everything's all right, is it?'

I knew what he meant, was grateful that he didn't ask more.

'Just fine. One thing, though – maybe you can help me – what do you know about recent sales of Gauguin?'

'Well . . . there was that big one – funny name? Fetched over two hundred?'

'*Nafea Faa Ipoipo*. Yeah, I know about that. Anything else, further back?' Decent online research is only good for about a decade; after that, it's easy to miss things from the good old days before everything was online. Here in Siderno, Dave was as close as I could get to a proper archive.

'Nasty bugger he was, that Gauguin. Couldn't half paint though. Hang on – let me just have a look . . .'

I heard Dave's stick tapping away from where he'd laid his phone.

'Here you go. I cut it out of the paper. So, there were two versions of the same picture. Up in 2000. *Vase des Fleurs (Lilas)*, they were called. Our place had one in their spring catalogue. But they both came from the same dealer, some crook in New York. Our lot was withdrawn, the Other Place sold what they said was the original.'

'Two versions? OK, thanks a lot. Just a bit of research.'

'Anytime, love. You take care now.'

'You too.'

I tapped on the door of the workshop and Li reappeared. 'Sorry, I forgot something. Prussian blue. You'll need lots of Prussian blue.'

Back at the car da Silva was having a snooze. I prodded him in the shoulder.

'Yo Cha-Cha. We have to get ready. Bit of winter sun.'

'What?'

'You might need to take me to Tangier.'

At the President, I set a grumbling da Silva to research flights while I packed a bag and paced up and down my terrace, smoking and waiting impatiently for Yermolov to call. I started as da Silva stuck his head over the adjoining parapet.

'What do you want to go to Morocco for, anyway?'

'Don't you want to go?'

'Why would I? *Perchè è pieno di marocchini!*'

'Well, who else would it be full of, you racist twat? Anyway, we're in a hurry.' I made a gun with my fingers and pointed it at him. 'Tick-tock goes the clock. Raznatovic isn't going to wait forever. If you take me to Tangier, we can maybe have your piece ready for sale in six months.'

'Six months? *Cazzo.*'

'Which reminds me.' I pointed over the front wall of the terrace to the hotel gardens below, where the wheelchairs were enjoying a morose airing. 'I'll be needing a new house. This place is way too depressing. And I've made a to-do list for you. Stuff I'll need. Do you speak French?'

'No,' said da Silva wearily. I was really enjoying the Mafioso-is-my-bitch shtick, I had to say.

'Then you won't be any use to me there. You can stay in the hotel and get on with the prep.'

'No way. And if you think—'

My phone rang, stopping him mid-sentence. 'Sorry,' I whispered, 'got to take this.'

Da Silva slammed his terrace door.

'Здравствуйте, Pavel, как дела?'

'Your accent hasn't got any better, Judith. But you are well?' It was good to hear his voice.

'Fine – I'm in Italy. How are you? How is . . . Elena?' Elena was Yermolov's estranged wife. She had been the one to drag me into the Caravaggio business.

'Good. She is much calmer, on holiday now with the boys.'

'I'm glad. You're in France?'

'Yes. In my bedroom.'

There was a pause. I remembered that bedroom. Considering what we'd shared – nights of sex and pictures and wine, blackmail, Balensky's murder – I felt oddly shy.

'You said you needed a favour. Two favours? Perhaps you might elaborate? Though I don't exactly see why I should do you a favour.'

'Yes you do. What we had was so special, Pavel. Plus there's a tape somewhere in Serbia which shows you cracking Balensky over the head with an ashtray.'

'You said you'd destroy it!'

'Just teasing. Maybe. Anyway, the second favour depends on the first. You went to Balensky's house, right? The one in Tangier?'

'The Man from the Stan' had owned a place in the famously louche port town, where he had given famously louche parties.

'Several times, yes.'

'And you said something about the décor. Polynesian stuff? I know Balensky had crappy taste in art but you said the house itself was surprisingly OK?'

'There were some pretty things – why do you want to know?'

'Doesn't matter. I've looked online but there's tons of villas in Tangier and nothing to say which one belonged to Balensky.'

The existence of Balensky's home in Tangier was common knowledge, at least if one enjoyed a read of *OK!* in one's leisure time, but any details had remained discreetly vague.

'He bought the house from a Frenchman, I think. An architect.'

'Do you remember the architect's name?'

'I'm afraid not. But the house had a name, wait a minute.' He paused.

'апельсины. That was it.'

'Oranges?'

'I think so, yes. Something to do with oranges.'

'Дарлинг, где вы?' A woman's voice, cutting in – *where are you, darling*? Oh well.

'Umm, OK. Anyway, sounds like you're needed. Thank you. That was all I wanted to know.'

'And the second thing?'

'I'll be in touch. Thank you, Pavel. Really, thank you. Say hi to the paintings for me.'

I found I didn't much want to think about Yermolov's lady house guest, her presence in Yermolov's bedroom, or whether she had visited his private gallery, so I switched that part of my brain off and googled up houses in Tangier with oranges in the name. A few clicks took me to 'Les Orangers', formerly the property of one Xavier de St Clemente. A made-up name, for sure. And also a French architect. St Clemente had been a well-known member of what French *Vogue* quaintly referred to as '*les happy few*'. He had died of Aids in the eighties, and I found several gushing magazine pieces reviewing his career, with photographs of the Moroccan home – full title Chateau des Orangers – and its owner, plus antique celebrity guests. The construction of the house, which indeed included antique panelling and sculpture from French Polynesia, was illustrated in several shots. In others, Jackie O squinted balefully from the terrace. I ran a cross check through an article on dendrochronology, the dating of wood, on the site of the Philip Mould gallery in London and came up with what I needed. Then a search of estate agents in Tangier, until I found the house listed, only its name and one photo, with a note saying that price was on application. I took a few moments to open a Gmail account as 'kateogable' before sending an email with a brief enquiry.

'Romero!' I screeched over the terrace. 'We're on! Get your bucket and spade!'

'When?'

'Tomorrow!'

'*Cazzo*.'

'Don't be such a grumbleweed. You'll love it. You know, the Krays used to go on holiday in Tangier. Right up your alley.'

7

Da Silva had pushed for a modern hotel, with air con and satellite telly, but there was no way I was going to Morocco and staying in the Best Western. The discovery that we had to travel via Naples and Barcelona did nothing to improve his temper; after grudgingly handing over my old passport, he had spent most of the eight hours of flights bitching that we were bound to be harassed and robbed, timorous suspicions which only grew more wearying as an ancient mustard-coloured taxi deposited us at the top of the Kasbah, the old city, where a boy with a torch waited to guide us to the riad I had chosen. Dar Miranda turned out to be a tall cube of a house, with a huge light well dropping boiled-sweet patterns through its coloured glass into a central courtyard scattered with rose petals. We were shown up several chaotic flights of stairs to a narrow white room with two single beds covered in blue and white striped ticking and a view of the twilit ocean through the deep recess of its shuttered window. Above was a roof terrace of low, tiled tables with a few smartly dressed French couples dining on delicious-smelling tagines and salads of cinnamon-coated carrots. A tortoise wove ponderously between their feet.

'Look,' I gestured at the menu, 'they even serve wine! Cheer up – or are you missing Franci? Where does she think you are, by the way?'

'Business. Like I said, she doesn't ask questions.'

'But aren't you pleased to be here?'

'We usually go on holiday to Sardinia.'

'God, you're provincial.'

'Will you stop breaking my balls and let's just have dinner, OK? Whatever disgusting muck they serve here. I'm exhausted.'

Da Silva's misery was only adding to my pleasure. As he poked suspiciously at his perfectly lovely plate of chicken and preserved lemons, I sipped dark-red wine and looked out over the crazy jumble of Tangier's rooftops. Even now, after all the places I'd seen, there was still a part of me that couldn't quite believe that I was somewhere like this, somewhere that looked and smelled so . . . exotic. The sound of the call to prayer over the city seemed ancient and thrilling, even the faint tang of sewage wafting up from the mysterious streets below was somehow exhilarating.

Da Silva clattered down his fork bad-temperedly. '*Fa schifo*, serving meat with fruit.'

'What about *mostarda*? Can't you just relax a bit?'

'Maybe if you tell me why we're here.'

It hadn't seemed safe to discuss it on the journey, but now I listened to the conversations around us, which were mostly in French. I leaned forward, poured him some more wine. The waiter replaced our plates with little diamonds of cake soaked in orange flower syrup.

'We need some wood. There's a house here that I think has some, of the right age. If we can get it then Li can start work on the picture.'

'Why couldn't we just buy some?'

'Duh. Dendrochronology.'

I detailed the method of dating panels by analysing the growth rings visible in the end grain of the wood. By measuring the distance between the rings and comparing the sample with chronologies of known date and location, it's possible to determine the age of the youngest growth ring, giving the earliest possible date for the use of the wood in question, and hence of any painting on it.

'So if the thing we want to make is supposed to date from 1900, the wood has to be the right age.'

'It's not as though there isn't plenty of old wood in Italy.'

'Yes, but it's got to be the right kind of wood. That's why we're here. You can date oak, or beech, but they don't come from the right part of the world. You've heard of Gauguin, right?'

'Of course.'

'So you know that he worked in Polynesia? In Tahiti? The wood has to come from there.' I paused as the waiter set down wire-chased glasses of fresh mint tea.

'And so this place, this house, it has the right kind of wood,' I explained. 'Miro, it's called. Do you get it now?'

'Do you think they have espresso?'

'Jesus. You didn't have to come, you know. I can manage perfectly well on my own.'

'I told Raznatovic I'd stay with you. Besides,' he added, 'you might need . . . protecting.'

'As we both know, the most dangerous thing round here is you. Unless I'm abducted by a wildly passionate nomad sheikh? That would be nice, but we've got a schedule here, remember?'

Da Silva looked puzzled.

'*The Sheltering Sky*? Paul Bowles? The writer? He lived here, in Tangier.'

'I told you, I don't have much time for reading.'

'Whatever. Let's go down. We have to be up early for church!'

* * *

The heavy brass candlestick between our beds had been lighted and two starched linen bathrobes laid out. I changed in the small bathroom, navy silk pyjamas from Olivia von Halle, a monogram of a burning cigarette on the breast pocket. At least I could look the part. I slipped into bed and tried not to listen to the sounds of da Silva pissing and cleaning his teeth. As da Silva emerged in T-shirt and boxers and blew out the candles, his presence in the soft darkness was suddenly very loud. I found myself remembering that moment in Albania, when he had pulled the trigger on the kneeling man. The quietness of him. *You're like me.* Perhaps my hand strayed down under the sheet to the silk between my legs. Just for a second.

'Romero?'

'What now?'

'How do you do it?'

'What?'

'Your life. Being two things at once. I don't mean practically, I mean – how do you stand it?'

'*E cosi,*' he answered. That's how it is.

I heard him shift onto one shoulder, the crisp rustle of the bedclothes. There was a long pause, and I thought he had fallen asleep, but then he whispered.

'And you? How do you stand it?'

Staring up into the dark, I listed the names in my head.

'You know,' I whispered back after a while. 'That's how it is.'

He hadn't waited for my answer – all I got in reply was a snore.

White-towered and green-roofed, with an incongruous flag of St George on the turret, the Anglican church of St Andrew in Tangier looked more like a Moorish fortress conquered by the Crusaders than a dour outpost of empire. According to the InterNations website, the post-communion coffee morning was the hub of ex-pat life in the city, a bit of a comedown for a place which had once been considered a cosmopolitan hotbed of sin. Da Silva and I shuffled in at the back just as the vicar was launching the congregation into a rousing verse of 'Lo! He Comes with Clouds Descending'. Church hadn't been a big feature of my childhood and da Silva was a Catholic, but we knelt and muttered our way clumsily through the service. The building, with its cool colonnade and ornate marble screen might have belonged to another world, but the worshippers were straight from a costume-drama version of England circa 1953. Dark suits, stiff collars and red faces for the men, floral frocks and sensible sandals over tan tights for the women. Some of them even had hats. The only indication that we were technically in Africa was provided by a large woman in a brightly printed fuchsia ikat kaftan and severely bobbed grey hair, with a huge silver necklace and earrings that I had a suspicion she might describe as 'fun'.

The vicar and his wife shook the congregation by the hands as we filed through into the parish hall, a low wooden walled space to the side of the church, where the vicar's wife installed herself behind a large urn; da Silva looked disgusted as she handed him a brimming cup of watery Nescafé with a Rich Tea biscuit in the saucer. I made a beeline for the necklace lady who was loudly discussing her drains with a rather frightened-looking chap in a tweed waistcoat. 'So I said to Hassan, this is simply *impossible*. The fourth time this year! We'll be dead of bloody cholera before summer.' Her accent was ringingly RP, but as she got more excited about the iniquities of Moroccan plumbers a tiny bit of south London slipped in. I wondered if she'd retired on the proceeds of a cathouse in Putney. Tweedy Man and I waited for a pause in the flow, but when it showed no sign of coming, I just interrupted her.

'Morning! Lovely service, wasn't it?'

'Oooh!' beamed the woman, sensing fresh prey, 'A newbie! Who are you, dear?'

'Katherine Gable. I've just arrived.'

'I'm Poppet!' announced the woman, as though that explained something.

'Poppet's been here thirty years,' ventured Tweedy Man in confirmation.

'Well there's nothing I can't tell you about the place,' trilled Poppet. 'And what brings you here? Rellie at the consulate?'

'Not exactly. My colleague and I' – I pointed to da Silva – 'are here for work. We're property consultants.'

'Are you now?' Poppet was giving me a shrewd eye as Tweedy Man slipped gratefully away. I had chosen an A-line black skirt and a fine navy cashmere round-necked jumper which I hoped would give the impression of a string of pearls under the collar. 'From London?'

'Based in Montenegro, actually. I used to work at . . .' I gave the name of the House. It would impress Poppet, I knew.

'I *see*. So you must know Laura Belvoir?'

'Oh yes! Dear Laura!' I spluttered. Fuck. I'd been caught out by the name game. *Why hadn't I resisted that chippy little urge to show off?* Laura had once been my superior at British Pictures.

'She used to be out here all the time – staying with the Whitakers, you know.'

'Yes, of course, the Whitakers. Small world!' I pitied them, whoever they were.

'And you're looking for something here?'

'One place in particular. Les Orangers. I heard it was . . . for sale?'

Poppet obviously hadn't been this delighted since Princess Margaret's last visit.

'Les Orangers. Oh goodness, that dreadful business. Did you hear?' She leaned in, the claws of the necklace threatening to snag my sweater.

I assumed she was referring to the scandal surrounding Balensky's death in Switzerland a few weeks previously. Yermolov and I had taken care to make sure it was all over the internet. In the accepted version, the broke billionaire had been having a bit of a last hurrah with a piece of ski-station trade, complete with a saucy pair of PVC panties, when things had got slightly out of hand. A dead oligarch had made for spectacular headlines in the pre-Christmas lull.

'Not really. Just that the property was available. It's listed with Price and Henslop, but there are very few details and we weren't able to reach them.'

'Oh, you'll be wanting Jonny Strathdrummond. Are you at the Hotel Minzah? No? Well, you *must* come along to supper later. I have my little "at homes" on Sundays, everybody comes. Here, have a card. About seven.' She looked suddenly serious. 'We have *gin*, you know. Isn't it wonderful?' By the whiff off her, I guessed Poppet had had a go on the Tanqueray already, but I wasn't complaining.

'You're so kind,' I cooed, 'but you know – I should really be more discreet. Our client is a very private person.'

'Naturally.'

I thanked her again and retrieved da Silva. We were barely out of the door before I heard Poppet sensationally informing the company that someone had come to look at Les Orangers.

Da Silva had Google Maps up on his phone. 'The Kasbah's this way.'

'Yes. I can see it.'

We made our way up a steep street towards the main Tangier square, the Grand Socco. Taxis honked and crawled between crates of live chickens and Berber women in wide-brimmed straw hats with trays of eggs and herbs. First I took a look at the ex-pat estate agent's, Price and Henslop. Despite a number of fancy-looking modern villas advertised in the windows, the office had a flyblown air. There was no notice for Les Orangers. The cafés around the wide, irregular space of the Socco were full of men, smoking and drinking tea and Coca-Cola. The only female customers were tourists. We sat down outside the rather gorgeous art deco cinema and da Silva finally ordered his espresso. He lit two fags with the Dupont, glancing cautiously round for pouncing pickpockets.

'What now, then?' he asked glumly.

'Well, we're on the list! Worth the sermon, no?'

'How did you do that?'

'I used to work at the House. Magic password. The address of the place we need isn't listed online. Thought it was worth a try. Now you are going back to the hotel and I'm going for a walk. Without you. My passport's at the Miranda, I'm not going far.'

For a while after he had left, I wandered through the streets down to the port, revelling in simply, finally, being alone. I bought a paper cup of little grey snails in thin amber liquor from a huge steel cauldron and ate them with a pin. Then I retraced my way to the market, eyeing the goods tumbled out on cloths on the pavement. Ancient phones, single worn shoes, cassette tapes – it seemed incredible that anyone could have a use for most of the junk, but crowds of men were energetically picking it over. One cloth held nothing but rusted bolts and screws, another a variety of well-worn tools. Promising. I asked the stallholder in French if he had a hacksaw. He rummaged around in the heap and produced a new one with a red plastic handle. 'Only one dirham!' About ninety pence.

'*Shuk'haram*. Thank you. But I wanted something more like this, please.'

I held up a wooden-handled hammer. 'Something old.'

He pushed his gnarled wool beanie back on a bald head and sorted through the strata of iron to produce a little saw, the blade discoloured with age but the teeth still sharp-looking.

'Perfect!'

'Five dirhams for this.'

He looked almost disappointed when I immediately handed over a note, but it would have been indecent to haggle. I put the tool carefully in my bag and headed into the medina.

I was making for the Petit Socco, the smaller square which had once been the centre of literary Tangier. Pushing through swinging rails of djellabas, leather babouches stacked up for tourists, stacks of argan oil soap, I was lost in minutes, but getting up a map felt like cheating.

'You want something, mademoiselle?' A young guy, black – not Moroccan – in jeans, hoodie and box-fresh Nikes.

'*Non merci*.'

'You want the Kasbah, your hotel? You want . . . something to smoke?'

'Certainly not!' I sounded like an E.M. Forster governess.

'Why you here by yourself, then?'

'Please, I'm fine. You're very kind. Now I have to go.' I turned blindly down the nearest alley, which turned out to be the entrance to a hunched, shabby mosque.

'Lady. You is lost.'

I scrabbled in my purse for a few dirham notes. 'OK. You win. I want to get to the Petit Socco.'

'No charge, lady. This way.'

I followed him for an embarrassingly short period of time to a steep triangular space, lined like the larger square with cafés. He refused another offer of money, but didn't show any sign of fucking off as I took a seat at a yellow-enamelled table.

'You wanna buy me a Coke, lady?'

'No. Please go away.'

'OK.' He made to leave, rolling his shoulders emphatically. *Had he thought I was trying to pick him up? Of course he had. Christ.*

'Wait! Sorry, what's your name?'

'Abouboukar, lady. Abouboukar from Côte d'Ivoire!'

'Do you want that Coke?'

'Sure, lady.'

'Can you drive?'

'Drive? Sure I can. Well, I haven't got a licence, but—'

'Grand. Have a seat.'

We had a very satisfactory conversation over his Coke and my mint tea, exchanged numbers and agreed to speak the next day. He offered to escort me back to the Miranda – no charge – but I didn't see any reason for he and da Silva to meet just yet. Instead I asked Abouboukar to find me a taxi to the Café Hafa, just out of the old city on the cliffs above the sea, and ate grilled sardines and flatbread on my own, just the way I liked it.

* * *

Poppet's card took us to a street of fifties apartments between the old town and the new, three- or four-storey buildings with Spanish-style, glass-enclosed balconies. We took a wheezing lift to the top floor, where the door was opened by a servant in white shirt and trousers and a fez. As he was taking our jackets, a small woman in a headscarf bustled down the hall with a tray of empty glasses. She offered them to the man, who refused to take them, and the two began a vigorous argument in Arabic. Poppet barrelled out of a side door in a black and gold number with matching turban, snatched the tray, screeched at the woman in pidgin French and actually kicked the man's backside as he turned to stow the coats.

'Twenty years they've been at it!' Poppet crowed. The servant had resumed his post by the door, apparently unperturbed. 'The cook won't serve drinks because of alcohol. Hassan there won't take the tray because he maintains it's woman's work. Really. Well, here you are, dears. Come in, come in! Katherine and er . . .'

'Giovanni,' I supplied quickly. Da Silva took that and dipped over Poppet's outstretched hand, which seemed to rejoice her. He was wearing a pressed pale-blue linen shirt that flattered his dark hair, though he had balked at my suggestion of a tie. Evenings in Tangier were cool, so I had stuck with the Sunday-best look, an ivory-silk shirt worn under my old black Chanel suit. Poppet handed us an enormous gin and tonic each and conducted us to the drawing room, a mixture of Edwardian chintz and velvet with Moroccan tables and carved ottomans. The thick dark-red velvet curtains were drawn, though it was barely sunset outside, and the air was heavy with tobacco and the tinny, oily breath of people who have been drinking through a long afternoon.

'Now, where's Jonny?' asked Poppet busily. 'He's not here yet. Never mind, you can talk to—'

A girl with a curly cap of red hair sprang up from behind a sofa. 'I'm Muffie!' she announced. 'Sausage?' She was proffering a plate of chipolatas. 'Heaven, aren't they? We all bring them over from Marks and Sparks, when we go *home*.' From the way she sighed the word you would have thought London was beyond a distant ocean, involving a three-month voyage with a stopover in Port Said. 'And this is Juancho.'

Juancho looked like a miniature polo player, a wizened cheroot of a man in riding boots and jodhpurs with a sun-strafed forehead and artful grey curls hanging off his collar.

'They're after Les Orangers,' whispered Poppet conspiratorially.

'Are you now? And is that *all* that brings you to Tangier, dear boy?' This voice, which boomed and minced in equal measure, seemed to be attached to the stripe-shirted arm that was snaking its way around da Silva's shoulders.

'Leave him alone, Vivi,' slurred Juancho in a heavy South American accent. Apart from da Silva and me, all of Poppet's guests appeared to be well and truly pelted. The arm snaked down da Silva's chest as its owner turned towards us, a big fair Englishman in a paisley cravat. 'Vivian Forrest. You can call me Vivi, darling. But your girlfriend can't.'

'How do you do?' stammered da Silva.

'Fairly, fairly. Spotted you at church this morning, didn't we? Now tell me' – the arm was drawing da Silva away – 'you look jolly fit. Keen on the muscle exercises, are we?' They made for a corner where several more cravatted Europeans had corralled a couple of Moroccan boys.

'Darlings, look what I've brought you!' shrieked Vivi.

The camp sat weirdly with his rugby-player physique, but I reckoned da Silva was more than capable of handling a few old queens, so I turned back to Muffie. Juancho had subsided amongst the cushions, fumbling for a cigarette, though he already had a gold-tipped Sobranie between his withered lips.

'They say it's haunted, you know,' Muffie confided, 'Les Orangers. Jonny Strathdrummond says they can't get any of the locals to clean it.'

'I was hoping to meet him. But . . . er, what brought you to Tangier, Muffie?' I added quickly. I didn't fancy another round of working out who everyone knew in common.

'Oh, I make jewellery and bags and things. That's one of mine, over there.'

She pointed across the room to a woman in a dark trouser suit, burgundy lipstick bleeding onto her teeth. On the floor next to her brogues was a green silk pouch with two Moroccan bangles for a handle.

'Lovely,' I managed, which I suppose it was, if occupational therapy was your thing. 'You must give me a card. So tell me more about the ghosts!'

'Well, Jonny Strathdrummond says they've heard noises there. Groaning and moaning, like a banshee.'

'Really?' I had a feeling I knew what that might be. 'So it's pretty spooky?'

'Oh yah. Out on the cliffs, past the Hafa. You wouldn't catch me there on a dark night!'

We were interrupted by Hassan ringing a small handbell while the cook brought out a huge dish of what looked like shepherd's pie.

'Din-dins!' squeaked Muffie. Da Silva was practically sprinting for the hot buffet, out of Vivi's clutches. The food was actually delicious – peas with lettuce and crisp rosemary potatoes alongside the pie, though I doubted even they would soak up all the gin. We hung around, but the famous Jonny Strathdrummond didn't show, until Poppet kindly offered to ring him up.

'Migraine!' she announced. 'But he says he can meet you tomorrow evening, at the Club Maroc at six thirty.'

'You're a marvel, Poppet,' I thanked her.

'Well, we've got to stick together, haven't we? Are you and your colleague going to be here for the New Year?'

'I don't think so, sadly.'

'Such a pity! The dervish musicians are quite something – they go all over the town with their lovely drums. Now, do telephone if there's anything you need. And if you change your mind about New Year, the Whitakers always have the most wonderful party – they'd love to see any friend of Laura's!'

As I was manoeuvring us into the hallway, a hand clutched at me from behind a miniature orange tree on a brass stand. 'Want another drink?'

'No, thank you, I'm afraid we're leaving.'

'Oh. Well, if you don't want another gin and tonic, you can fuck off!'

I peered between the bright little fruits. It was the vicar's wife.

Da Silva glared at me all the way back to the Kasbah. '*Sono pazzi, gli inglese*. Are you all alcoholics?'

'Most of us. Burden of empire and all that.'

'And why did you feel the need for that shit? Montenegro?'

'Because the thing is . . .' I paused. How to explain the name game to an Italian? The slapping of mutual acquaintances down like cards, ascertaining precisely where someone stands in the hierarchy of status that everyone pretends doesn't exist any more?

'There's a certain sort of English person, who still thinks of themselves as part of a particular class. They care about stuff like how people speak, where they went to school – most of all, who they know in common. Knowing people is a password, like I said. And if people aren't in the club, they want to pretend. It's even more difficult because the club has invisible walls. So Poppet will think that because I said Montenegro, because I mentioned the House, that we are those sorts of people. Like her, or at least, who they're all pretending to be. So, when we do our thing tomorrow, all that information will confuse them. It will keep them explaining and gossiping for weeks, while we skip town. Besides, didn't you think it was a nice party?'

'I don't understand dick of what you're saying.'

'You don't need to. Just do as you're told.'

8

From the terrace at the top of the riad I had looked across the harbour to a long crescent of sand framed with tall modern hotels. Between the buildings and the Bay of Tangier was stretched a palm-flanked promenade, lumen-clogged with the lights of early evening traffic. From that perspective, Tangier was a city like any other, but up here, in the sinuous alleys of the Kasbah, it was almost impossible to believe it existed. As I walked uphill the next evening between the white walls and bright painted doorways, women in djellabas and sandals filled plastic containers at standpipes, precariously illuminated by the crazy web of improvised electric wiring that trailed like creeper between the houses. Grubby, half-dressed children streaked busily past me, a man pushing a handcart loaded with a luridly patterned velour sofa spat thickly as he laboured up a flight of shallow steps. The shadows were moth-soft with tumbling, skinny cats. The higher I climbed, the quieter it became, and the layered scents of the air – diesel, sewage, lemon, jasmine, cumin, sweat – peeled away until, as I came out into the square, I could smell only the clean ozone of the Atlantic.

The Club Maroc looked incongruously smart against the stillness of the crumbling, ancient citadel walls, its gleamingly restored colonial verandas shut in with spruce green blinds. A doorman in a white jacket waited outside; as I approached another chunky Mercedes taxi pulled up and he held the door open for a middle-aged tourist couple.

'*Bonsoir, madame.*'

Inside, it was the twenty-first century again, the standard version of Morocco peddled from Moscow to New York. Dark-red walls, low brass tables, intricate lanterns, embroidered cushions. I asked for the bar and was directed across a courtyard strewn with the inevitable rose petals to a roofed terrace furnished with stolid leather club chairs. I took a seat and a waiter appeared with a small brass bowl and a long-handled jug, from which he poured orange-flower water over my hands before handing me a monogrammed linen towel. I asked him in French for a *kir framboise* and sat back, watching the smooth dimming of the sky.

'Miss Gable? Miss Katherine Gable?'

The voice came from behind the high back of my armchair. It was the kind of voice I had become unaccustomed to hearing since I left my job at the House in London, a relic of a voice, marooned somewhere between D-Day and the Suez crisis, though its owner couldn't have been more than sixty.

'May I? Thank you. Jonathan Strathdrummond. Drink? Oh, very good, I'll take a gin and tonic, there's a good chap.'

'Thank you for meeting me, Mr Strathdrummond.'

'Oh, please call me Jonny. We don't stand on ceremony out here, you'll find. You must have seen that at Poppet's place, eh?'

Jonny wore a crisp pale suit, gleaming Church's brogues and what I strongly suspected was not an Old Harrovian tie. If he'd taken down the accent and removed the signet ring he might have passed, but then presumably the reason he lived in Tangier was so he didn't have to.

'Found the place easily enough?' He took a long swallow of his drink.

'Yes, thank you. I had a wonderful walk.'

'Game girl. Have to have your wits about you in the old Kasbah.' I was tempted to add that I'd forgotten my parasol and would he send his bearer for it, chop-chop, but I didn't think he'd laugh.

'As I explained in my email' – Jonny winced a bit at that, perhaps it was knocking a bit at the old colonial dream to mention technology – 'I'm interested in Mikhail Balensky's house.'

'Quite. Rum business, what?' *Christ, was the man ever going to let up on the dear old Raj shtick?*

'I understand it's for sale.'

'That's about it. Sorry I didn't get back to you. Christmas holidays and so on. Do you know Tangier well?'

I could see that estate agent hadn't perhaps been Jonny's optimal career choice but I was going to have to move things along a bit. Abouboukar had messaged me to say they were waiting at the property with the truck, but he and the boys wouldn't stand around all night.

'Would you care to see a menu, *madame*?'

Jonny looked at me hopefully. Close up, I could see the foxing on his shirt cuff, the grease in the carefully pressed seam of his trousers. Momentarily, I was rather sorry for him.

'Thank you, I don't think we have time.' I turned back to Jonny. 'The thing is, my client is very keen to acquire the house, and so I need to see it as soon as possible.'

'Really?' Any wistful longing for a pigeon tagine forgotten, Jonny was all business. He reached into his jacket for a diary. 'Well, how about the day after tomorrow? Got a few things pencilled in but I daresay I could bung them back—'

'I want to see the house tonight, please. Perhaps you could ask them to call us a cab?'

'Now? But, well, it's dark.'

'That's not a problem.' I leaned forward and laid a confidential hand on his arm. 'You see, the thing is, my client is a very busy man. He has a very significant portfolio and he tends to get . . . distracted. If we both want our – um – commissions, Jonny, we need to move on this.'

'Understood.' He rose to his feet, signalling eagerly to the waiter. 'I'll have to stop at my office for the keys.'

'Of course. And naturally I'll take care of the cab. Please allow me to offer you the drink too. I'm so grateful for your understanding.'

I had bought a beautiful soft leather bag in the medina earlier that afternoon. As I reached inside to extract my purse, I caught a brief glimpse of the handcuffs and the hacksaw, gleaming dully in the soft light of the tiny lanterns.

Da Silva was positioned in the café opposite the Price and Henslop office at Grand Socco. Like me, he was dressed in plain dark clothes, and I'd brought a scarf to cover my head for the walk home. As Jonny unlocked the door and I bent forward to the cab driver to ask him to wait, da Silva passed behind me and I handed him the bag like a relay baton. He disappeared into the office behind Jonny and I returned to the back seat. After what felt like only a few moments, da Silva slid in beside me.

'*Route de la plage Mercala, s'il vous plaît.*' I switched to Italian as the car headed uphill towards the Marshan Ridge.

'That was quick. You didn't hurt him too much, did you?'

'I just hit him once and cuffed him to the chair.'

'Gag?'

'Used his tie. There'll be someone along in the morning, he'll be fine. Here.' He waved a bunch of keys. We were driving through a quarter of elegant thirties villas, some of them smartly lit up, others romantically neglected. After the hustle of the medina, it felt very quiet. Then out past the terraces of the Hafa, along the coast road, with the wide beaches below us.

'It's beautiful,' remarked da Silva, as though he'd only just noticed.

The homes were sparser now. We passed a camel stable and a bus stop, then a long wall of smooth grey concrete began to the right. I'd already checked the place out on my morning jog – the wall ran for about five hundred metres, encircling the grounds, and ending in a modern steel double gate.

'This is it. They said they were waiting. Look, there they are.'

I asked the cabbie to stop and we got out. I pulled my scarf around my face to keep off the dust skimming in on the ocean breeze. We waited until the taxi left, then walked to where Abouboukar had parked the van, a battered Ford Transit. We nodded at his two mates, both African like him. I'd offered him forty thousand dirhams – just over three grand – for the job, plus whatever he and his boys took from the place. It was more than I guessed he'd see in a year, but there was no need to be stingy with Raznatovic's money. I had the notes, withdrawn from four banks on my morning's shopping trip, wadded in a hair elastic in my bag with the antique saw. Abouboukar had been instructed to bring blankets, a chisel, rope and torches. Our visit would look like a break-in – no one we had met at Poppet's knew our real names or where we were staying, and by the time old Jonny was found we'd have left on the 6 a.m. flight to Naples. It would have been more straightforward in a sense just to break in, but there were two reasons why I'd figured this way was better. Firstly because we needed a clear point of egress to get the wooden panel out. The views of the house online had shown the façade of Les Orangers was thick-walled, plastered in white, with tiny irregular windows like arrow slits and worn Moorish rinceaux carved on the cornices. Hence the keys, which would let us through the main doors. Secondly because the hoo-ha Jonny's capture would stir up might distract everyone from what was actually missing. The police might get round to showing our photos at the Miranda, but probably not any time soon.

'*Alors.* You can take whatever you can carry, while we're removing what we need. Then this gentleman will go with you in the van, and Abouboukar and I will go separately back to town.' I repeated this in English, then tried the first of the bunch of keys at the porter's door set into the gate.

From the photos of the garden I'd seen in the magazine, I recognised the long driveway lined with palm trees, their leaves flapping at every gust of wind. Another key let us through into the courtyard where the house proper began. It was pretty spectacular – originally a Roman villa extended with a series of white marble and glass Modernist boxes descending towards the sea. The pebble mosaics in the courtyard were supposedly original. I shone my torch over a goggle-faced Jupiter holding an eagle-tipped staff and into the swimming pool, empty now apart from a rank, greasy puddle in which bobbed the tattered remains of a gull. The smell of oranges was everywhere, from the espaliered walk that encircled the courtyard, thick with soft dungheaps of ungathered, rotting fruit. That and the sightless eyes of the gods beneath our feet did make the place seem sinister, malicious in its tropical fetor.

Da Silva and Abouboukar's boys followed me in silence as I made for the main door, one of three pairs in miro wood, which gave onto a stone atrium backed in glass.

'No lights!' I warned. The boys spread out, searching for loot, though I doubted they'd find much as the house had obviously been cleared soon after Balensky's death. The only signs of the original décor were several Asian statues, perhaps too heavy to move. A large Javanese statue of a god in soapstone reminded me of one of Gauguin's paintings, *Mahana No Atua*, which felt like a good sign. The torchlight illuminated the walls, washed in eau-de-Nil, and another set of doors, beautiful Moroccan intarsia work. Not those. A marble staircase led down to a low-ceilinged room with stone couches built into the walls. I had an image of the orgies Balensky had held here, leering old men fondling their boys while they watched the floorshow.

'Let's try the other way.'

Back along the courtyard wing, where a row of bedrooms opened onto the orange walk. In one of them, a bottle of Chanel Bleu stood abandoned on the edge of a seventies Jacuzzi tub, its grubby plastic adorned with a pale mollusc of used condom. Those moaning ghosts. A sound of breaking glass from deep in the house. *Fucking amateurs*. The corner bedroom had a wide terrace giving onto the gardens to our left, wooden pillars set in the smudged glass, two high narrow reddish doors between them. They were fastened with what looked like the mother-of-pearl mount of an antique musket. It was a shame to ruin them, but I told da Silva to get going. He took the hilt of the hacksaw to the hinges and had them smashed in a few blows, then we laid one of the doors upright on its side so I could steady it while he cut out a slice. Miro is a very dense wood and the old saw was small, but the panel would betray us if there was the tiniest trace of modern metal in the grooves of the wood. Da Silva sweated and swore as I tried to keep the door steady, pausing after a few minutes to throw off his sweater. The torch-light played on the muscles of his back as he worked. Every few minutes I glanced anxiously at my watch, but it took a full half-hour of wrestling to cut the panel free. It measured 150 centimetres by 75 – I'd bought a hideous silver-framed mirror exactly that size in the medina that was waiting for us in our room at the Miranda. Finally we carried it flat between us back round the house into the courtyard.

'*Cazzo*, that's heavy.'

'The remains of it need to go over the cliff. Out at the back.' At the Café Hafa the day before I had gazed down on huge ple-siosaurs of driftwood, thrown up on the beach by the violent Atlantic waves. At this time of year, the beaches were empty; the door would be unrecognisable by the time the warm weather came.

'Why?' asked da Silva.

'We can't leave it there with a hole cut out of it. It would look weird.'

'Good point.'

'OK – hurry though. Round up the boys, get them to drag it down and chuck it over.'

He jogged off in search of Abouboukar.

Once the door was disposed of properly, another fifteen minutes, the lads wrapped the panel in a blanket and loaded it into the van. Whatever swag they had recovered – cutlery, by the sound of it – they slung in afterwards, then da Silva got in behind and they drove slowly away.

I sat down on the edge of the pool and lit a fag. My watch read just after nine; we could hear the last call to prayer, between sunset and midnight, ululating over the city. Abou-boukar lowered himself down next to me.

'So?'

'So now we wait a bit. Give them time to get back to town.'

'You got my money, lady?' He was smiling, his teeth brilliant where they caught the orange glow of my cigarette, but I didn't like his tone.

'Sure. But like I said, we should wait a bit. If anyone does come, they'll be too busy with us to bother with the van.'

'I want it now, please.'

'Suit yourself.' I passed him the bundle of notes, watched as he shoved them inside his black hoodie.

'That all you've got, lady?' He wasn't smiling any more. Part of my brain gave a little sigh. Really? He was going to threaten me? All alone, here, in the dark? *You have no idea, mate. No idea.*

'None of your business. In fact, I've changed my mind. You can leave now, Abouboukar. Thank you. I'll wait on my own.'

He didn't move. I smoked in silence for a while.

'You still here?'

'I'm waiting, lady.'

'I've paid you. You can fuck off now.'

He was on me in one move, the whole of his weight forcing me onto my back against the lumpy pebbles. I was still holding the burning fag butt, so I stuck it in his neck. He screamed and struck my arm away, coming back with an open-palmed cuff across my face. A couple of dazed seconds before the red pain flared.

'You're a fucking bitch. You think you're a big shot, fucking bitch.' He spat where he'd hit me. I could smell the nicotine in his saliva, the cooked meat of his burnt flesh. Under that, unwashed clothes, sweat, the adrenalin high. I tried to wriggle back, but my legs swung into space over the pool, I couldn't get a purchase, and he was big, for all that he was thin, maybe eighty kilos of desperate sinew.

'You know,' I hissed viciously, 'the thing is, I just can't be scared of you. You smell too fucking poor.'

'Bitch!' He hit me again, a hook to the side of the head. His hipbone dug into me as he turned to fumble with his fly.

'Really?' I slurred. 'You're going to *rape* me? And what if I liked it? Could you get it up then?'

He pinned his left elbow across my face as he released his dick, wrenched my trousers with his right hand. I heard them tear and bit his arm, but it was pretty useless through the thick sweatshirt. My mouth was full of blood now. I tried to wrench my head to the side to spit it out, but I couldn't move, it was choking me, I couldn't breathe, I couldn't fucking *breathe*. Incredulity that this was actually happening, strangely distant irritation at my own stupidity, mostly no air, no air. And then the weight of him rose off me, I twisted over, coughing blood. Through my one good eye, da Silva in the starlight. He had Abouboukar in a headlock from behind; as I watched he twisted the boy's right arm back between their two bodies. I thought the crack was something falling in the house before I realised it was the bone. Abouboukar's mouth opened in a monstrous silent scream, silent because da Silva had smashed his right temple with the hilt of the saw. He must have been dead before he hit the ground.

'Give me a hand up?'

He set me on my feet as gently as if I was made of porcelain.

'You came back.'

'They're waiting up the road. They'll want their money.'

'They can have it. In his pocket. What will we do with that?'

Da Silva was running his hands over the body, passing the notes to me and checking the pockets.

'No wallet, no ID. He probably didn't have any papers.'

A refugee, perhaps. *Poor stupid sod.*

'But you're lucky he only hit you.' Da Silva was opening a wide-bladed clasp knife.

'OK – burglary, the thieves quarrel, they fight – step back – he's stabbed, here, I think.' Da Silva plunged the knife into Abouboukar's left side, in under the heart, gave it a twist, kicked the body over and held it with his foot while he stooped to withdraw it, keeping the first spurt of blood under the corpse.

'He falls on his right, blow to the head. They chuck him in the pool, broken arm *post mortem*, done.'

'Anyone would think you were a policeman.'

'We need to let him bleed out a bit. Can you manage the feet?'

'How bad's my face?'

'Pretty bad. But you can cover it with the scarf. If we pay off the guys in the van it'll be a while before they come looking for this one.'

I took a few deep breaths. My windpipe ached, but not more than my cheekbone or my jaw.

'I'm ready.'

'OK. Get him up. Over here. We're going to swing him. One, two, three.'

Abouboukar thudded down to join the seagull.

'We need to wipe down the knife.'

Da Silva produced a packet of antiseptic wet wipes from his back pocket. I suppressed my urge to laugh. The clean knife followed its owner.

'You good to walk?'

'A bit dizzy.'

'Here.' He wrapped his arm under my shoulder to support me. Not a tall man, our mouths were almost level as he wrapped the scarf over the mess. As we left Balensky's house, my head rested against his heart. It was beating steadily, just like mine.

'Ready? Keep the scarf over you, stay back. I'll give them the money and take the panel. Don't let them see you up close. OK?'

We set off at a jog down the road towards the van, where the first piece of my Gauguin was waiting.

At the riad, I made da Silva tape the panel in behind the heavy mirror before he tended to my face. It would look like a souvenir at the airport – faux-antique tourist tat. I looked away while he did it, not too keen on seeing what Abouboukar had done. Then I showered and wrapped up in a bathrobe, still without looking at myself. Da Silva fetched the cone-spouted jug of rosewater from the dresser and bathed the cuts gently, then used a hot flannel and another antiseptic wipe.

'This needs a stitch.'

'Will it scar?'

'Maybe.' *Great.*

'We can't go to a doctor. Shit.'

'Got any dental floss? There's one of those little sewing kits in the bathroom.'

Right next to the shoeshine mitt and the shower cap. Brilliant.

'It'll scar for sure if I don't.' I couldn't work out whether there was tenderness or spite in his voice.

'Is there a minibar? I need a stiff one.'

He found me a brandy, scorched a needle in the candle flame and had it done in a minute. Four quick stabs. I didn't cry out, though I made a mental note not to buy mint floss next time.

'Judith? That guy – he didn't—'

'No, he didn't. You arrived in time. How come?'

'Call it professional instinct.'

For a second I was grateful, but then I remembered Razna-tovic, and another dead man squirting blood. It hadn't been chivalry. Da Silva wasn't going to let me die, at least not until I'd paid his debt for him.

The alarm was set for 4 a.m. Before we slept, da Silva reached across the space between our beds and took my hand, rubbing his thumb against the palm.

'In Rome?'

'What about it?'

'How did you do it? I mean, Fitzpatrick was a big guy.'

I sat up on one elbow. 'A woman against a man? You're only as good as your weapon. Surprise being the best one. OK?'

'I wanted to know.'

Actually, surprise is the second-best weapon a woman can use. But I wasn't going to tell da Silva that.

PART TWO

GROUNDING

9

My face aroused no attention at Tangier airport, but the passport official at Naples looked fairly horrified when I obeyed his request to remove the scarf. For a moment I thought he might try to arrest da Silva for trafficking, but a flash of the *Guardia* badge and a matey explanation got me through. I reckoned once I got to my Eight Hour cream it might not look too bad, perhaps might even lend a certain piratical air. Dashing. Anyway, I had other things to think about. Now that we had the panel, Li was almost ready to start work on the piece.

In a letter written during his first visit to Tahiti, Gauguin had described 'a pretty piece of painting', a severed head whose form he had drawn from the grains and whorls he had seen within a pine board. 'When marble or wood draws a head for you, it's very tempting to steal it,' he had claimed. If I could get the provenances right, I planned that Li's painting would appear to take its form from the panel. In 1899, just before he left Tahiti for the Marquesas Islands, Gauguin had made what was believed to be his last Tahitian piece, *And the Gold of Their Bodies*. In 1902, after he had changed location, he had produced *Woman with a Fan*, a seated, topless girl, modelled by the wife of his cook, holding a white feather fan with the cockade of the French flag in its handle. I was going to posit our piece as a last, 'lost' work from Tahiti, with a supposed date of around 1900, cross-referencing the double portrait to produce an earlier version of the fan picture.

I explained the idea to da Silva once we were in the car on the last stage of our journey back to Siderno.

'So we'll need to go to Essen.'

'Christ, don't you ever stop? Where the hell is Essen?'

'Germany. The known version of the fan picture is at a museum there. The Folkwang. Has Li got a passport?'

Da Silva banged his head lightly on the steering wheel, a move which only an Italian could have pulled off, since we were doing 140 kilometres per hour on the autostrada.

'No. Obviously. I can fix him one of those temporary ones. They last a year.'

'Excellent. Because he needs to come with us to look at a picture.'

'What's wrong with – I don't know – those flowers? The nutter who cut his ear off? Why can't you get Li to do something like that?'

'You mean van Gogh?'

'That's the one. He's worth a fortune, isn't he?'

'I pity you, Romero. Just keep driving.'

We were skirting the foothills of the Aspromonte, the famous 'Mafia mountain', almost the toe tip of Italy. I had heard about the meetings the 'Ndrangheta bosses held there, an ingenious form of torture for soldiers whose loyalty to the clan was suspected. Mutton was the traditional dinner menu. Not to attend meant certain death, instantly proving a man untrustworthy, but attending held out the chance of being garrotted over the boiled sheep.

'Did you ever go to a *schiticchio*? A banquet?'

'That's Sicilian. We don't call it that.'

'So you admit there's a "we", then?'

'I thought I told you to shut up? Jesus, what did I do to deserve this?'

I stared out at the landscape. Grey winter fields, blotch-veined earth rotted with illegal pesticides. Half-finished buildings whose purpose couldn't be guessed from their sagging concrete skeletons. Outlet malls, blowsy amusement arcades, despairing medieval churches, tattered publicity hoardings every fifty metres, all blending into a seamless dinginess brightened only by random swamps of rubbish, blooming by the roadside like sweating, exotic orchids. Italy.

I was thinking about da Silva's suggestion. They had been friends, Gauguin and van Gogh. Everyone knows van Gogh's Sunflowers. *It's reproduced on calendars and notebooks and fridge magnets, a pleasing, cheery picture of a nice, under-standable bunch of flowers. Yet, in a sense, the canvas is as bloody as anything Artemisia Gentileschi ever painted. Van Gogh intended the* Sunflowers *to flank an 'altarpiece' he was planning for the Yellow House in Arles, the home he shared with Gauguin for nine weeks in the winter of 1888. In London, Jack the Ripper was slashing his way to immortality, matched only for celebrity in the French press by a home-grown version, a murderer named Prado, the brutal killer of a prosti-tute, whose trial began in Paris in November that year. Like the rest of the country, in between painting and drinking and paying 'hygienic' visits to the nearby brothel, van Gogh and Gauguin were captivated and horrified by Prado's crime. Nine days after his trial began, Prado was condemned to the guillo-tine. At the time, van Gogh was working on* La Berceuse, *'The Cradle-Rocker' for which he used his regular model, Augustine, the wife of the postmaster at the station in Arles. He planned to make as many as nine versions of the picture, the soothing mother wrapped in the silence of the night, and hang them between the* Sunflowers, *whose joyous, radiant petals would act as 'candelabra', like the votive candles mounted next to the tiny statues of the Madonna he had seen at the street corners of the mist-enveloped southern town.*

The papers reported that Prado was turning mad in his prison cell, while Gauguin was concerned that his friend, too, was losing his reason – either drunk or painting in a frenzy. The colours of La Berceuse, *which van Gogh believed to be the finest arrangement he had ever devised, are sinister when compared with the clarity of the* Sunflowers. *At first they seem fixed, a ground of red containing Augustine's stolidly seated body in its green dress, but as the eye moves up to the garish flowered wallpaper, they swirl and meld, orange swelling against the flesh tones, the vicious malachite of the sitter's eyes seeming to wink, horribly, from the greedy pistils of the flowers. The paint crawls and shivers, making delirium of serenity. Gauguin couldn't take it, the sweating and the singing, the wild declamations. He informed van Gogh that he was leaving Arles. Van Gogh silently handed him a newspaper cutting, an account of another, anonymous killing in the capital – 'and the murderer took flight', it said.*

It was nearly Christmas. Gauguin left the house, but van Gogh followed him into the little square where the oleanders were in bloom, an open razor in his hand. Or so Gauguin said, fifteen years later. He ran, left van Gogh there, took a room at a hotel, and when he returned to the Yellow House the next day, he found the floors soiled with bloody linens. Van Gogh had sliced off his own left ear, wrapped it carefully in another piece of the newspaper and delivered it to the brothel, as a gift for a whore named Rachel.

Gauguin left on Christmas Night. He never saw his friend again. Two days later, he waited amongst the crowds on Rue de la Roquette to see the condemned Prado guillotined. He claimed to have been near enough to the prisoner to hear him ask 'What is that?' 'The basket for your head,' the gaoler replied. Exceptionally, as the blade fell and the crowd roared in release, Madame Guillotine missed her mark. Prado's face was sliced, rather than his neck, and two blood-spattered constables had to wrench him back into position. One month later, Gauguin made a vase, dully glazed in blood-red, in the form of a self-portrait of his own severed head, both ears sliced away. That spring, he left for Tahiti.

We had been driving for two hours in silence. I relented, dismissing the drift of images, the colours, the blood.

'Look, you don't have to come to Germany. We'll only be gone overnight. You could go home, see your family?'

'I have to stay with you,' da Silva answered wearily.

'There's stuff you can work on here – I told you, I have a list.'

'No.'

'Suit yourself. But then . . . um, we may have to go to Palermo.'

'*Madre di Dio.*'

So, three days later, we touched down at Dusseldorf. Despite the abrupt drop in temperature, Li looked pretty jacked to be out of Italy. I had no sense of the terms of his employment, but I wondered whether da Silva's insistence on accompanying us might have had more to do with the odds on the forger's defection. Not that da Silva hadn't been faithfully, indeed relentlessly, by my side. Even had I been in with a chance at the Siderno nightlife with an eye like a fried egg, there hadn't been a moment for any further visits to the *castello* dive bar during the short time we had been back in Italy. For a start, da Silva and I had set up home together. Our new pad was a converted farmhouse not far from where da Silva had banged me up in the shed, let in the tourist season to the kind of people who imagined that a shower in an olive press and a five-kilometre drive to the baker's constituted the 'real' Italy. No Calabrian would have holidayed there for money, but I had asked da Silva to find somewhere secluded, with a workspace where I could lay out my plans for the provenances away from inquisitive hotel staff.

A small man in a sturdy overcoat and a flat cap had arrived at the President to help us transfer our things. It wasn't until he bent over to help me lift my suitcase into the car boot and I caught a whiff of him that I realised this was Fish-Breath. Having grown into such a chimera during my days in the shed, it was odd to see my mysterious captor was as commonplace as any other of the middle-aged men who sip away their days in espresso cups in every Italian town. Da Silva didn't seem to feel the need to reintroduce us, and the brief conversation they exchanged during the drive took place in the same impenetrable dialect I had heard the night we arrived on the beach. Fish-Breath unloaded several boxes of provisions from the supermarket before he drove away from the farmhouse, and when we were sitting down to our first domestic evening (artichoke ravioli courtesy of Signor Rana, which da Silva insisted on boiling himself as he refused to believe a foreigner could be trusted with pasta), I asked him how he had managed to conjure Fish-Breath out of nowhere to play Cerberus.

'Does it matter?'

'I'm curious.'

'You don't say.'

'I mean, is that guy one of – your people?'

'I don't have "people". I'm an inspector in the *Guardia* in Rome. I don't work down here.'

'But that business at the docks? The stuff you move?'

'It's not like I'm loading it personally. I don't have anything to do with it. Salvatore is a friend – a family friend – he helped me out.'

'In the middle of the night, landing a prisoner and keeping her, feeding her, for days, without asking questions? Some friend.'

'Ask him yourself. He's just outside.'

I unfolded the grey-washed shutter at the kitchen window and looked out onto what had once been the farm's threshing floor. There was old Salvatore, sitting on a white plastic garden chair, with a shotgun broken across his knees.

'Are you for real? So this is a house arrest?'

'You said you wanted somewhere quiet to work – you have it.' He rubbed his temples with his thumbs. 'Leave it, will you? You don't need to know anything more than what you're working on. Just get on with that, for the love of God.' He got up from the table and marched into the sitting room, snapping on the TV.

'You're a dickhead, you know that?' I called after him.

'Fuck off.' Really, we might have been happily married.

I cleared the plates. It was chilly in the kitchen. I fetched another sweater from the bedroom I had chosen at the end of the low house and went to work.

First, I needed Gentileschi to be back in business, which meant resuscitating Elisabeth Teerlinc. I sent out a few emails explaining that though the gallery space in Venice was temporarily closed I would still be buying for private clients, and that a shipment of new pieces would shortly be available on the website. I hadn't thought I'd need to be Elisabeth ever again, but obviously I couldn't enter a painting in an auction at the House as Judith Rashleigh. That part I hadn't quite got round to mentioning to da Silva yet. Ever since I had heard Raznatovic's ultimatum, I had known where I wanted to sell the piece. Partly it was a practical decision, in that there were only two auctioneers in the world who could command the type of client able to raise the sort of money the Serbian was demanding, but I didn't bother pretending to myself that was my motivation. From a distance, I had kept track of the career of my former boss, Rupert. The House had undergone a bit of a corporate shake-up by the look of its website. My old enemy Laura Belvoir had retired, while her god-daughter Angelica, who had taken my job when I was fired, was nowhere to be seen. Probably designing jewellery, like every other thick heiress I'd ever met. Rupert had been promoted – probably out of despair – from Head of British Pictures to Chief Coordinator, European Paintings. There was a photo of him, bulging out of his Savile Row suit, with an oleaginous, unnatural smile. I didn't imagine the new title had made much difference to his daily routine of lunching and bullying the juniors, but it would be Rupert who decided if 'my' Gauguin was fit for sale. Once I'd re-established Gentileschi as a viable presence, we could begin the game.

The next question was where the 'Gauguin' had suddenly emerged from. Provenance is a tricky thing. For a masterpiece to be 'found', ideally there needed to be a paper trail that buyers could follow, clearly showing that the painting had a consistent timeline, but equally, I would have to invent a story in which none of its 'owners' had suspected what they had.

I took a pad of paper and began to tear off leaves, giving each one a title and laying them out in front of me. When the painter returned from his first expedition to Tahiti in 1893, over forty of his works had been exhibited at the Paul Durand-Ruel gallery in Paris, and Gauguin continued to send pictures back to France after he left for good in 1895. The real version of *Woman with a Fan* was produced in 1902, but usefully, Gauguin himself had never directly referred to the picture in any of his own extensive writing on his work. There was a photograph, taken from Gauguin's home at Hiva Oa and recovered after his death, which showed his model in a similar pose. Conceivably, then, if there were two versions, then 'my' picture could have travelled with him from Tahiti to the Marquesas Islands and then been shipped back to Marseille. Unlike the real original though, my version would never travel north. I imagined a young officer, exhausted and excited after the sixty-day voyage, arriving in port with a picture given him by some crazy old drunk in a battered cowboy hat who reckoned he was an artist. By that point in Gauguin's career, the booze and the syphilis as well as his own careful and disingenuous cultivation of his image as an outlaw made it plausible that he would have given a picture away, or lost it at cards, or sold it for a song.

So, my officer arrives at Marseille, does what sailors do when they come home, finds himself short of cash, pawns the picture. Li would make a suitably period receipt from the pawnshop that would be pasted to the back of the panel. The pawnshop, unfortunately, would be destroyed when the Nazis dynamited the old town north of the port of Marseille in 1943. However, the canny 'uncle' had taken the picture with him when he fled the city along with 20,000 other refugees. I'd have to choose a name for him. It might be more realistic to choose a Jewish name, as many of the persecuted Marseillaises had been Jewish, but I reflected that this could cause complications. It wouldn't do to have the picture classified as one of the looted art objects which the Nazis' specialised 'cultural plunder' division, the Einsatzstab Reichsleiter Rosenberg, might have got their hands on, as this could cause legal disputes over its ownership. No, he'd better be only French.

My supposition would then suggest that the pawnbroker sold the picture, again with no idea of its worth, to an Italian partisan returning over the Alps at the end of the war. After the Nazis left Italy, many soldiers in the Italian army had been shipped to prisoner of war camps in Germany, making their way home as best they could through the chaos of Europe after peace was declared. I made a note to myself to check the names of the ranks of different soldiers to describe my imagined partisan on the label. Another receipt to add to the panel, another invented name.

And then, the painting would disappear for thirty years, only to turn up as a lot in a sale of miscellaneous objects abandoned in the left luggage of the Rome railway terminal. Such sales periodically took place. After the sale, the Gauguin would travel south to Palermo, where it would hang for a decade in the kitchen of a modest apartment. The owner of the modest apartment would then have taken out a mortgage, on which he would default, leaving his home and its contents to be repossessed by the bank. In the inventory, the owner would also state that he had picked up the painting at the railway sale. I would then 'examine' the records of that sale and insert

a document into the original price list, where the dismiss-
ive description 'Painting of a woman', could then be found
amongst the genuine items. Inserting details of fake paintings
in real sales was a trick that had been used by a forger named
John Drewe who had succeeded in selling fake Giacomettis,
many of which still hung in museums, their authenticity in
abeyance.

And the bank in question would be the Società Mutuale di
Palermo. As I had discovered from when I was tracking down
the fake Caravaggio, the Sicilian organisation owned a large
collection of art assets – some genuine, some less so. The pictures were held at the main headquarters in Palermo, but the
bank had small branches in Rome, Naples and Milan. Both
Moncada and then Kazbich had flipped paintings through
the Società Mutuale, which meant that it was, at least in
part, used as a cover for the art-for-arms operations which
had been conducted for at least twenty years. Officially, I
would pose as a disinterested private dealer who had 'discovered' the Gauguin while looking to acquire pieces from the
Società Mutuale's holdings. I would buy a couple on behalf
of the gallery and stick them up on the website, and in the
meantime the bank would then engage me, as Gentileschi, to
research the Gauguin and broker any potential sale. I would
then 'investigate' the backstory I had already prepared. The
bank would be my client, with the proceeds going to them,
after which it would be da Silva's responsibility to see that any
money reached its destination, with the surplus profit taken
by Gentileschi as a fee.

If I 'acquired' the picture for Gentileschi fairly soon, then
the time it took Li to actually make it would cover the period
of my supposed research into its provenance.

Presumably the Società Mutuale would be able to provide the paperwork for the mortgage, the default on the loan and the repossession of the picture, all suitably backdated. I'd need to work on a third identity, this time of the last owner who had bought the picture at the railway sale in the seventies, and then lost it to the bank in the eighties, all conveniently pre-computer database. The unfortunate mortgage defaulter would pass away shortly afterwards, I decided, leaving no living descendants. I looked at the sheets in front of me, now filled with scribbles and underlinings, added a note that we would need period paper from the forties, seventies and eighties. And a couple of old phone books. Da Silva would have to arrange a meeting in Palermo. It could do. It could just do.

It was nearly midnight, but Salvatore remained in place, upright and staring out into the lights of Siderno twenty min-utes below us. Indoors, da Silva was still glaring at the TV news, a report about fresh migrant routes into Western Europe from Romania. I was going to offer him a glass of wine, but there was already a three-quarters empty bottle of red open in the kitchen. I poured out the last of it and joined him, staring at the screen.

'Romero?'

'What now?'

'When you took me to the port that day, you said that the refugees mostly ended up in the camp. What did you mean, "mostly"?'

'I meant accidents happen.'

The report switched to an ad break, the usual showgirl in a micro-bikini. This one was ecstatically washing a car, mostly with her breasts.

'Go on.'

'Sometimes they need to make space for the stuff. So the boats have to unload their cargo first.'

'That being the people? You mean they just dump them in the sea? On purpose?'

His eyes were still fixed on the glow of the screen. He nodded and reached for the remote, zapping through the channels until he arrived halfway through Clint Eastwood facing down a saloon full of outlaws.

'You want to watch this?'

'No thanks.' I chucked back the remains of my wine in one and went to bed. I didn't lock the bedroom door, in case he heard the latch over Clint's last stand. I didn't want him to think I was locking him out, because that would have implied I was thinking about him in my bedroom. Which of course I wasn't. The air tingled with ice as I opened the window to reach for the shutter. Salvatore was standing, watching the firework display crackling above the sea. I went back downstairs.

'Do you know what day it is?'

'Of course.'

'Happy New Year, then.'

10

The Folkwang Museum in Essen was once described as 'the most beautiful museum in the world' but that was presumably before the construction of its three modern extensions. Even the snow that had, to Li's delight, greeted us at the airport, couldn't prettify the greenish concrete boxes plonked dispiritingly by the highway. We'd taken three rooms at the Dusseldorf airport Sheraton, where da Silva and I ate *currywurst* in the atrium while upstairs Li changed into the warm jacket I'd insisted da Silva buy him and assembled his kit. We couldn't afford to use anything too professional in case it attracted attention, but I'd suggested Li buy an LED clip-on magnifier for his smartphone to get the best possible image of the brushstrokes. Gauguin had usually drawn out his compositions in Prussian blue, then covered them with a base ground of colour before adding further layers of pigment with regular vertical or diagonal strokes. Li was already equipped with period sable-tipped brushes, but I wanted him to practise laying the colour in until the supple gestures of Gauguin's tools had become part of his own muscle memory.

It was already getting dark by the time we entered the transparent-walled corridors of the museum. There were only a few other visitors – Essen wasn't exactly a Christmas holiday destination. Li put his palm wonderingly to the glass, as though he was absorbing the snow's coldness through the pane. We made a tour of the collection, pausing before works by Renoir and Macke before approaching *Woman with a Fan*.

For a moment, we none of us moved, even da Silva hypnotised by the still intensity of the colours. The model is seated on an ornate carved chair, the folds of her simple white wrap framing the ostrich plume fan erect in her hand. She looks solid, densely fleshed, the weight of her body apparent in the shadow beneath her fingers, and yet she might be floating on a sunlit cloud, so delicately do the infinite shades of the ground play out around her. A blue patch diagonal left, the suggestion of a flower against a glimpse of sky conducts the eye up and around her body, its journey enclosing her in the looping magnetism of the painter's gaze. Very much a girl, she might equally, in this endless captured moment, be a goddess, poised serenely between two worlds. The veined feathers of the fan are laid in flat, reducing the perspective between living skin and lifeless object, yet their tips have just left off quivering, as though moved by the warm beat of her heart. She was entrancing.

I broke the spell, hustled the guys together and we wrapped our arms around one another for a selfie, just like the majority of other visitors, because isn't that what museums are for? We take a selfie to show that we have been in the presence of something amazing, something extraordinary, when what we are actually doing is pushing ourselves into the foreground of the artwork, this marvellous thing on which we are literally turning our backs. It doesn't matter whether we're giving the cold shoulder to a Michelangelo, because our own banality is the real subject, degrading the piece to a frame for our own egos even as the need to take the photo subverts our intentions. It made me want to puke, even as I gurned for the camera. Our normality established, I sent da Silva off to the coffee shop and took out a heavy *catalogue raisonné* – the compendium of all an artist's known works – while Li photographed the painting from every angle. I was hoping we'd pass for students, or just particularly eager fans, should anyone be watching.

'Look at this one,' I suggested when I'd found the illustration I wanted. *And the Gold of Their Bodies*, from the Musée d'Orsay in Paris. Two girls, one subject nude, the other wearing just a white hip cloth, both of them gazing out at the viewer from what might be the edge of a forest, a blaze of orange flowers centring their heads in a formless halo. The pose of the nude sitter echoed that of the woman in the painting before us, leaning forward slightly on the left shoulder, hand splayed flat from the wrist, the crook of the bicep pushing the exposed breast slightly forward. I traced Li's hand over the book as he looked up at the painting, echoing the line of the composition.

'We'll put the fan here, in her right hand,' I whispered in Italian. Li nodded, captivated, his eyes darting between the two images.

'Ah mean, it's really disgusting!' A loud, forceful voice broke our vigil. A tiny woman in black was advancing along the gallery, swathed in a huge down coat that covered her so completely it seemed that she moved on wheels. Heavy black sunglasses covered most of her face, beneath the severe fringe of a bright-red bob. *Fuck*. I buried my face in the catalogue. MacKenzie Pratt was an instantly recognisable art world harpy, an heiress from Virginia who fancied herself as a latter day Peggy Guggenheim. I'd glimpsed her in person at the Venice and Kiev Biennales, but her photo popped up everywhere from the Met Gala to Frieze Art Fair. She owned a significant nineteenth-century collection that she leveraged with loans to museums to get herself onto every board and prestigious junket going. She was giving the benefit of her opinions to a harassed-looking young man with a clipboard trailing in her wake.

'Ah mean, I'm not having my Monet hanging next to him. He was a day-generate!' she continued, planting herself between Li and the Gauguin. 'What he did to those girls – sheer exploit-ation! They were teenagers. No, you'll have to move it.'

'That might be –a bit – difficult?' ventured the young man.

'Ah don't care. Ah think it's a disgrace that he should be displayed and Ah intend to take a stand.'

I turned away, but she moved at the same moment, planting a spiked boot heel into my sneaker.

'Oh. Excuse me,' she murmured disdainfully, as though her clumsiness was my fault. Then she glimpsed the book in my hand. 'You like Gauguin?' she demanded.

I gave her a blank look. 'Yes.'

It was impossible to tell from behind the glasses but I sensed she was glaring at up me. Beneath a strained, Botoxed fore-head, her face was shot through with fine wrinkles like a piece of crumpled cling film. Bright poppy lipstick had bled into the corners of her mouth, giving her the look of a junior ghoul.

'Well you should think again, honey. He was no more than a payed-o-fyle.' Her companion made an apologetic face as she marched off.

'What was she on about?' asked Li.

'Nothing. It's too boring to explain. They're closing in a few minutes, see if you can get really close now.'

Gauguin painted a whole lot of other subjects aside from naked brown-skinned young women, but it's the Polyne-sian babes that everyone recognises. Not the rich tensions of *Self-Portrait with Halo and Snake*, not the disquieting, rural *Yellow Christ*. The complex, elusive iconography, the perfervid brilliance of the colour aren't worth considering when we can tut instead about the poor colonials, exploited by the old white pervert, as though his paintings could be explained by the vulgarities of psychology. No one ever asks whether our prurient obsession with Gauguin's sex life says more about us than it ever could about him.

A bell rang and a tannoyed voice informed us in German and then English that the museum would be closed in five minutes.

'Quick,' I whispered to Li, 'get a few shots of the borders, where the frame meets the canvas.'

The finish at the rim of a piece is often a weak point for spotting forgeries. He knelt down as near to *Woman with a Fan* as he could, positioning himself carefully. Major pictures are usually alarmed to prevent curious visitors from getting too close. An echoing tap of heels sounded in the direction of the lobby. I moved in front of Li and opened the book again, trying to conceal him as much as possible. Mackenzie Pratt appeared again, peering into the gallery from the corridor. She lifted her sunglasses and stared at me once more. Her exposed irises were almost colourless inside their jagged clumps of mascara, miniature poisonous flowers.

'My, aren't we studious?' she remarked.

I gave her a blank nod and turned my eyes to the book. I didn't look up again, but as Li shot I could feel those suspicious, malevolent eyes absorbing us across the wide space.

Li planned to return to the museum in the morning, but he was already eager to try out the composition. Working from the pictures and the illustrations in the catalogue, he quickly sketched out version after version in pencil on an A2 pad, shifting the angle of the pose slightly each time. His line was clean, unhesitating, so much so that after a few attempts I could almost believe I was looking at a Gauguin. He was astonishing.

'Li,' I asked when we paused for a lukewarm Lipton tea. 'Why don't you work for yourself? You're an amazing artist. This stuff – it's not all you could do.'

He shrugged, tucking his pencil behind his ear.

'It pays well. And what else would I do? I can paint, sure, I can paint pretty much anything. But no one's interested in painting any more.'

'But—'

'I'm used to it. No sweat!' he added endearingly in English, his hand moving deftly across the paper. *Too right*, I thought. *I'm the one who should be sweating.*

We ordered dinner in da Silva's room, where I ran through my suggestions for the provenances, explaining what I would need at each stage of the backstory I had concocted. Li mentioned that he'd need some wax to mix with the paint, showing da Silva the close-ups from the museum, the thin layers built up for sheen in the colour, but da Silva barely glanced at *Woman with a Fan*. He was distracted, endlessly checking his phone, fiddling with the gold Dupont. Li cleared his plate efficiently, folded his napkin and excused himself to go back to work. All his movements were quiet and precise, as clean as his hand when he drew.

'Want a smoke?' I offered.

'It's too cold out there.'

'Drink?'

'Sure.'

I found the minibar and made him a gin and tonic, took a brandy for myself.

'What's the matter? Nervous?'

'I should be getting back to Rome.'

'I thought you had leave?'

'Until July, yes. It's not that.'

'The wife?'

'Yes.'

I was half minded to ask him if he fancied a screw. It seemed like there was eff-all else to do on a cold night in Essen. And isn't that what people do on business trips – empty the minibar and fumble away the loneliness in anonymous hotel rooms? I realised I was admitting to myself that I fancied him after all, but that was hardly news. I'd fancied him ever since I first saw him that summer on Lake Como. I could still remember the way the muscles of his chest had stood out beneath his shirt. In between thinking up ways to kill him, that is. There was a coldness to him, a detachment from anything but the next thing. He was quick at reading people, situations – the gunman on the dock, the boy in Tangier. And I'd watched his eyes when he shot the man in Albania. I couldn't stop remembering it.

'Romero?'

'What now?'

'When you have to . . . you know. How does it feel?'

'You already asked me that.'

'I didn't mean emotional shit. I meant physically. How does it feel to you? Your . . . body?'

He thought. 'My eyes. My eyes feel different. And I hear really well. As though the volume's been turned up. I've never really thought about it.'

I wanted to say, you *are* like me. I felt your heart, after you killed the Moroccan boy. But maybe we weren't that special. *Maybe all we had in common is that we did what other people only think about.*

'What about you?' he asked. I didn't answer at first, went to the window and looked out at the dirty banks of snow four floors below.

The Picton Library closed at eight, so it would have been about nine when I got to the bus stop nearest our flat. I used to go there from school most days, not only because it was warm and quiet, but for the grand columns on the curved façade, the orbs of gold-green light along the polished rows of Victorian desks, the dusty, lulling shuffle of the librarians' feet as they pushed trolleys of books between the stacks. As soon as I was inside, I was someone different, serious, important.

I must have been about sixteen then, the year before I left for good. The Tesco was already shut, bundles of homeless wadded down for the night on their cardboard pallets. I usually crossed the road to avoid them – sometimes a hand would snarl out from one of the rancid heaps, or a rearing figure, slurring a demand for change. A ginnel ran between the supermarket and the first of the blocks, round the car park at the back, a shortcut past the bins to the pub. That night, I heard a woman's weak wailing and a tinny thud as though something had fallen against the wheelie bin. At first I thought it was just the pissheads scrapping, but then I recognised the whine of my mother's voice.

'Giv' iback! Don'be a bastard. Giv'iback.'

She was trapped between two of the big metal containers, three lads in hoodies blocking her way. They were just ratty-limbed kids, no more than twelve or thirteen. Messing with her.

One of them had her bag, taunting her as she lurched forward to grab at it, but she missed and fell over, hauling herself pathetically forward over the wet dirt.

'What'll you give us, missus?'

They weren't trying to mug her, just taking the mick, but once she was on the ground, they got scared and vicious. The biggest of them kicked her hard in the face. She shied back, hitting her jaw on the corner of the bin, curling up with her hands clutched to her face.

'There you go! There's your stuff.' They emptied the bag on the ground; I heard a few coins fall and the heavier weight of her pink umbrella.

'Fuck off, you little gobshites!'

They shot off at that, trainers pounding down the alley, but I was fast, much faster than them. I kept my eyes on the pink nylon brolly as I shot across the road, scooping it up without breaking my stride, and had the last of them by the back of his neck before he reached the open space of the car park. I kicked his legs out from under him and the other two turned round.

'Ar ay, it's Rashers.'

They closed in, scabby shaved heads shrouded by their hoods, the light from the lamp post catching the greyed crumble of their last baby teeth.

'Fuck off, you fucking no-marks.'

'Or what?'

'How about this?'

I had the boy on the ground, his trainers scrabbling on the slimy tarmac. Using the umbrella as a truncheon I started battering his face, so hard I felt the stem inside the rolled fabric snap. I beat him until his grey hoodie was dark then pushed him onto his back and brought the thick heel of my school shoe down on his balls, once, twice, again and again until he was clutched up, whimpering.

'You fucking bitch. You're fucking mental.' But they were backing away. I brandished the umbrella at them. A spike had come loose. It looked sharp.

'Want some? Want some of what your mate's got? Not the big men now, are we? Now fuck off.'

They ran. It had only taken a minute. I gave the kid on the ground one last kick and went to find my mother. She was still on all fours, rooting blearily for her possessions.

'Get up.'

There was blood on her chin and a cut under one eye. He'd taken a tooth out.

'Look at you. Look at the fucking state of you.' There was dog shit in her hair.

'I'm, I'm sorry, love.' Shorry. She was a fucking disgrace.

'Just get up, Mum.'

I reached out a hand to haul her to her feet but she flinched back, toppled over again. Her eyes were huge in the neon glow of the Tesco sign. Wide and white and suddenly sober, brimming with fear.

'Nothing. It feels like nothing,' I said finally.

We were silent again.

'You were right about my wife.' He offered it in the same voice he had used in the dark at the riad, quite different from the exasperated contempt of his usual tone towards me.

'How so?'

'That it was . . . an arrangement. We were together for years before we got married, from when we were teenagers. I lived in her family's apartment while I was at the university. Separate rooms of course.' He finished his drink.

'So you didn't?'

'Not until the wedding night.'

'Jesus. And . . . since then?'

'We don't like . . . waywardness. Even now, a divorce – impossible. So, I don't mess around.'

I thought about that one. *Did he really mean he'd never slept with anyone else?*

'You want another?' he asked.

'Better not. Li and I have a lot to think about.'

I was almost at the door when he spoke again.

'Cleret. He told me about you.'

'What?'

'Where you met him. That stuff you're into.'

'That wasn't very gentlemanly of him. And?'

Romero da Silva was actually blushing. 'I just thought.'

'What? What did you think?'

So da Silva knew about my taste for the night. Did it excite him? Or disgust him?

The silence stretched out like the lozenges on the hideous Sheraton carpet.

'Nothing. Sorry.'

'Good night, then.'

'Good night, Judith.'

In the corridor, I waited a moment, listening. I heard the compressed rubbery squeak of the fridge and the sound of liquid hitting the bottom of a glass. *Like the volume's been turned up.* So much so that I could also hear da Silva's ears, casting for the stagger of my breath as I leaned against the wall.

11

'Tomato sauce.'

'You what?'

'Li needs some tomato sauce. Can you make some?'

'Can't you we just buy some?'

'We need Sicilian tomatoes.'

Da Silva and I were smoking on the deck of the ferry between Reggio Calabria and Messina. We were the only passengers outside – the few other travellers today, the feast of Epiphany, were downstairs, many of them vomiting unselfconsciously into paper bags. The straits were so choppy that the first departure had been cancelled. It was also freezing and pouring with sleet, but at least up here we didn't have to inhale the stench of regurgitated New Year *zampone*. Da Silva was in uniform, accessorised with a cane for his 'injured' leg. I couldn't see why he was being arsed to keep up appearances, but then much of the logic of his façade was still beyond me.

'You can buy some in Palermo.'

'How far is it?'

'About three hours, round the coast. They're sending someone to meet us.'

'You got your gun?'

He whipped round to face me from the rail, sheltering his eyes against the slicing wind.

'Always. Why?'

'I just thought – you know, venturing into enemy territory.'

'Funny.'

I was only half teasing. All the books I had studied on organised crime in Italy divided the clans into three primary groups: the Sicilian Cosa Nostra, the Neapolitan Camorra and the Calabrian 'Ndrangheta. At one point or another in the last thirty years, each had been at war with the other. I had read about the murdered public officials, the mass trials, the Kalashnikov shoot-outs. But then those were the kind of details that sold books. Da Silva was a public official, and he stood for a different kind of symbiosis. Ultimately, it seemed that the state had no real interest in crushing the Mafia, because the Mafia was already part of the state; the politicians were as scared of the *pentiti* – the Mafia informers – as their bosses were. If you slash open a shark's belly it will feed on its own innards, but it will keep on swimming.

'Were you here a few years ago, then? The Greek case?'

The anti-Mafia squads were made up of police divisions from all over Italy, including several units from the *Guardia di Finanza* in Rome. Da Silva had worked on an operation involving fake Greek antiquities being used for money laundering. It had never been solved, in large part because the café where most of the team had been having their breakfast had been blown to pieces one morning.

'Yes, I was here.'

'But not in the bar that morning? Lucky.'

'I was having a cigarette outside when it happened.'

'And there was me thinking that smoking damages your health.'

Da Silva gripped the rail until his knuckles went white.

'Sorry. I didn't mean to be flippant. They were your colleagues, weren't they? The men who were murdered.'

For a second I thought that he was going to slap me, but he turned and stalked as best he could to the other side of the pitching deck, where he remained for the last twenty minutes of our voyage.

The suburbs of Palermo looked even more wretched than I'd imagined under the deluge of mud – coloured rain that had accompanied us from Messina. Everywhere that wasn't motorway seemed to be contorted, squalid tower block or lightless ruin. The old city was meant to be very beautiful, but it was hard to picture. Why does Italy's ugliness seem so perverse? It wasn't that Palermo was much worse than, say, Birmingham, but it had no business looking like Birmingham. Perhaps the dissonance comes from the contrast with Italy's abundant, careless loveliness, the sense that there is so much beauty to spare that it can be despoiled and wasted.

I was carrying a set of photos Li and I had collated on his laptop, a melange of *Woman with a Fan* and *And the Gold of Their Bodies* that gave an idea of what the eventual Gauguin would look like. I would be visiting the bank's archive of holdings alone the next day, where I would in theory see the picture for the first time among the other lots Gentileschi intended to purchase. In the boot of the car was a pre-wrapped plywood panel the same size as the miro wood we had taken from Tangier, to be transported to the archive that evening. I would then sign for it and leave with it, after which a chain of emails between me and the bank would report on my progress with the 'research'. Which was where the tomato sauce came in.

I'd found a restorer in Reggio to whom I could take Li's picture to have the varnish stripped, a process I would report on to the bank. The relative proximity of the two cities, Reggio and Palermo, would add another element of plausibility to the provenances. Gentileschi was officially still based in Venice, where it might have seemed natural for me to take the picture, but if it really was a Gauguin then the bank might be reluctant to have it travel such a distance. Security, insurance, possible damage in transit. Maybe a guard from the bank to witness the cleaning process? That would be a nice touch. Given that the picture had supposedly spent thirty years in a kitchen, traces of tomato sauce on the varnish would add another small, essential detail.

Our meeting with the bank's representative at the Grand Hotel et des Palmes was set for seven, in a two-bedroomed suite I had booked under Gentileschi's name. Da Silva had set it up, as I had requested, with the same mysterious smoothness with which he had magicked away the remains of Alvin Spencer. He had shown me a news item a few days before on his phone, a couple of lines from the international edition of the *New York Times*. Italian police had identified the remains of a corpse found in an underground car park in Trieste as Alvin Spencer, a twenty-three-year-old American who had been reported missing by his family the previous summer. The death was not being treated as suspicious, as Spencer had apparently become a heavy drug user during his period in Europe and post-mortem evidence suggested an overdose. The body had been released to his family for burial. All nice and tidy.

I still had no idea how da Silva's double life worked, who he reported to, who gave him instructions. Raznatovic was a colleague, of sorts, but not a boss. Given that notoriety in organised crime is conventionally in inverse proportion to power,

I didn't imagine da Silva saluting some diamond-ringed comedian in a room full of white fur rugs, but nor could I see him checking in with a smelly old peasant, which was what the Sicilian bosses turned out to be on the rare occasions that one was arrested. Probably a dentist or a mid-level lawyer in a bland air-conditioned office in Rome. I'd never know.

Dottore di Matteo was shown in at seven on the dot, which was more than could be said for the tea I'd ordered. We made awkward small talk while da Silva cursed down the service phone in his bedroom, and more of it while a blond-haired young waiter rattled it in on an enormous silver trolley. We were presented with three chipped cups, a pot of lukewarm water and a plastic box containing transparent sachets of tea. No milk. Only once the squeaking trolley had departed down the corridor could we get down to business. Di Matteo was a slight man in a tan suit, who ceremoniously presented me with a card with his title 'Director of Material Assets'. I thought that was quite good.

Wordlessly, di Matteo slid an A4 sheet of paper across our depressing tea table. I read over a set of instructions explained as 'essential preliminaries' to our conversation. The picture was to be referred to as 'the object'. I was not to speak the name of the artist. I was to refer to the backstory of the mortgage as though it were an actual event at all times. I was not to address the *dottore* directly by name. Courteously, the instructions were also printed in English. I went along with it – at least it could be practice for the tale I was going to have to give at the House – until I reached the last item on the list, which stated that Gentileschi would receive a brokerage fee of ten per cent on any price reached by the object over and above the reserve as stated in the catalogue of the institution which sold it. That wasn't what I'd agreed with Raznatovic. The bank was a cover, nothing more. It would just have seemed too unlikely for the picture to belong to me, not to mention if it reached the price I'd hoped, the figure would make me far too conspicuous. I shook my head. Whoever was bugging this conversation was having a dull night of it. I took out my Mont Blanc and wrote '100% of extra-reserve price to Gentileschi, as agreed'. Di Matteo shook his head. *Fuck, were we going to conduct this entire negotiation in pantomime?*

'More tea?' I asked, to break the silence.

I gestured to da Silva to follow me into my bedroom. I spoke, or rather hissed, in English.

'I'm not having this bollocks. Did you cook it up with him? Ten per cent? You can piss off, the pair of you. Or are you planning to split the cash with our Serbian friend?'

'Calm down. It's just, there are ways of doing things. Umm . . . conventions.'

'Like, screw the woman? That convention? You heard me in Albania. Fifty-fifty anything over the reserve. So the bank pays me first. Less expenses, fair and square. You can melt me down in acid and dump me in the reservoir, but I'm not moving.'

'Judith, you know what . . . what our Serbian friend said.'

'Yes. He'll kill you if you don't pay him.'

'And you.'

'So call the *Corriere* and tell them to hold the front page.'

'This is not to do with me – or the . . . gentleman we met in Durres. It's to do with them. What they expect from us.'

I held up my hands. 'Us. Them. I don't know who the fuck any of you are anyway. Your mess, you sort it. Or make Franci a widow. Whatever.'

He went to the window, struggled with the double louvres and let in a gust of January air as he lit up. Maybe he thought the Befana was going to fly in on her broomstick and give him the answer. The Befana is a witch-like character who brings Italian children presents on the Feast of Kings. Naughty ones get a lump of coal, though the coal is really made of delicious black-dyed sugar. I was fond of the Befana. And then I realised something. Da Silva was ignorant of what a Gauguin could actually be worth.

'You silly fuck. You have no idea, do you? Wait, give this to the old man.'

I took a sheet from the notepad by the service phone and scribbled 'Any sale price exceeding one hundred and fifty million pounds sterling to be paid exclusively to Gentileschi. Ten per cent of any remainder on the price exceeding the stated reserve fee but less than one hundred and fifty million pounds sterling to be received as brokerage by Gentileschi.'

His eyes widened when he saw the figures, but he carried the paper through. After that, the *dottore* became quite cordial.

'Do you want to order some food?' da Silva asked an hour later when, after a great many '*grazie*', di Matteo had finally left with the dummy panel.

'I doubt I'll live long enough for it to arrive.' My appointment the next day was not until noon. Palermo isn't an early town. 'Do you know what I feel like? *Penne alla Norma*. And lots of red wine.'

'Done. There's a place near the Arsenale. We can walk if you're not too cold.'

We skirted the Borgo Vecchio and made our way towards the seafront, leaning into the wind. A hook-nosed Befana was picked out in fairy lights over the street, her broomstick trailing a banner for the Esselunga supermarket chain. Da Silva pointed up to the left with his stupid walking stick.

'That's the Ucciardone up there.'

The old prison, built when the Bourbons ruled Sicily, a part of which was notoriously reserved for 'men of honour'. It's where the gangster films get their ideas from – deliveries of champagne to the cellblocks, bosses holding court in luxuriously furnished cells. There was probably a gift shop nowadays, selling homemade tomato sauce, light on the sliced garlic.

'Have you been inside?'

'Often. Section Seven.'

Seven was the part of the prison reserved for the bosses.

'Police business, then?'

'Sometimes.'

'Was I police business?'

'Not any more.' There was something in his voice that sounded like regret.

'Would you really have done it? On the beach? Before Raznatovic's eager mate turned up?'

Huddled together against the rain under the coloured blur of the lights, I felt that this conversation was something intimate, one that we had both been having, or trying to have for quite some time, without ever finding the words.

'No. Maybe no. You weren't going to be any use to me dead.'

'Thanks.' Nothing I hadn't known already.

'I'm sorry. I didn't mean . . .'

He twisted to look at me, both our faces wet, the few inches of air between our mouths suddenly poignant. I could have leaned forward, but – *what was I thinking*? I'd already made arrangements for the evening. And then a crowd of kids ran past, heavy coats pulled on over ragged black witch costumes and crooked pointed hats. Da Silva said good evening to the patient father, huddled under an umbrella, and we walked on.

I took a hot bath after dinner and poured out a couple more glasses of red wine. Beyond two closed doors, I faintly heard da Silva's shower running, picturing him naked, the water streaming down his thighs, the musk of his armpits as he soaped them. I put my right middle finger between the lips of my cunt, brought it glistening to my mouth. Eleven p.m. There was a discreet tap from outside, the corridor side. I opened it and put the finger to my lips again. 'Shhh.' The blond waiter who'd brought the tea trolley came in, his white uniform jacket folded over his arm. He looked a bit nervous.

'Judith?' called da Silva through the locked door to the sitting room. 'Everything OK?'

We were going to have to be very quiet.

'Fine. It's nothing. Just room service.'

12

Morning in Palermo was all the colours of the baroque, pinks and golds and ivories and periwinkle blues. Even the red Ultra football supporters' graffiti dripping down the palazzi at the marketplace seemed tinged with the delicacy of a Caracci dawn. Piazza San Domenico was already busy at seven a.m. I'd bounced out of my bed of sin at six to run and worked out where the market was from the noise. I picked up three kilos of fresh tomatoes, a jar of paste and a bottle with a string-tied cork full of tiny fruits, almost berries, under oil. Maybe Salvatore would have a good recipe. The fish stalls reminded me of the Rialto in Venice – jaunty mackerel and buckets of chattering crabs, heaps of strange whorled shellfish, crates of alien deep-sea plunder I couldn't name. I picked up two cappuccini in takeaway cups and a pair of fat brioches oozing vanilla custard.

'Breakfast!'

Da Silva was still under the blankets. He reached out to check the time on his phone and groaned.

'Why have you woken me up?'

'Because it's going to be a beautiful day! Here, I got these. You don't want to get involved with the buffet downstairs. It's sunny out. Can I come in?' I drew the heavy velveteen drapes. Da Silva cowered beneath the bedclothes like a startled vampire.

'What's got into you?'

I thought it was best not to answer that.

'Do you fancy a walk before I have to be at the bank?' I wiped custard off my chin.

'I have paperwork to do.'

'It'll wait, surely? Please?' I'd never thought I'd catch myself soliciting da Silva's company, but being away from the farmhouse made me feel giddy, as though we were sagging off school.

'OK, then.' He gave me the first genuine smile I thought I had seen on his face, a broad flash of square white teeth that hit me just about where last night's waiter had done.

'I'll just grab a shower.'

Da Silva tapped on my bathroom door just as I was elegantly wrestling off my sports bra.

'I'm sorry, I just need to send an email, but my laptop won't switch on – I'll have to take it downstairs. Sorry.'

'Mine's just there – wait a second.' I threw on a robe, scuttled across my bedroom and tapped in my password.

'Are you sure?'

'It's no problem. Believe me, there's nothing for you to find. Go ahead, I'll be with you in a minute.'

The Società Mutuale's archive was held, not in the grand Spanish-era main premises of the bank, but in the basement of a six-storey seventies block two streets away. After a bright, blowy walk along the Conca d'Oro, da Silva accompanied me as far as the street corner where Dottore di Matteo was waiting. He signed me in and we took a lift three floors down before handing our IDs to a guard who wrestled with a combination-wheel on a reinforced steel door to admit us. The pictures – perhaps a hundred in total – were wrapped in thick cotton covers, arranged in racks according to period, then alphabetically by artist. There was also a large 'unknown' section in which I'd instructed di Matteo to leave the panel

the previous evening. The Società possessed a fairly impressive range of Renaissance works, as well as twentieth-century
pieces. I was looking for five pictures to advertise for sale on
the Gentileschi site in order to convince the House that my
gallery was still a viable concern – nothing too flamboyant,
around the 100k mark. Working through the rack, I picked
out a rather unusual Lina Bryans, a portrait of a woman in
a jaunty red cloche, two William Kentridge scribbles and a
grey-on-white Lucio Fontana, a design of thick oil bands and
pricked out dots, for old time's sake. Fontana had been the
first painter Gentileschi had ever bought. Di Matteo checked
off the prices against a flyblown list, and I asked him if he
could make out receipts for all of them, though the pictures
weren't going anywhere. It only needed to look as if I owned
them. But then a small canvas caught my eye.

'May I see that, please?'

It was a Kees van Dongen, a luscious scene from a Paris cab-
aret. A narrow woman in an absinthe-coloured evening dress,
with a swollen red mouth and huge tubercular eyes framed in
the lurid gold leaf of a cramped proscenium. I looked at that
one for a long time.

'Well, Dottore. Are we ready to find the Gauguin?'

He glared at me.

'Sorry. Well, I'll just remove this very interesting panel here.'
I sorted through a selection of nasty fifties acrylic abstracts
until I got to the dummy and hauled it out. 'I'll need your
authorisation to research it, as we said.'

He handed me a stamped paper with the flourishing crest
of the bank.

'And what about this one? If I wanted to buy it?'

'A receipt, as before?

'No, I mean really buy it. How much?'

'Let me see. A million.'

It was ridiculously cheap. Van Dongens were selling at between five and seven in London. And I could afford it, though it would take about a third of all the money I still had. Silly, really. But I wanted it. There was something about the woman's face, brassy and pleading at the same time, the eyes so vivid in their chalky surround of powder. The whimsicality of Chagall and the brutal clarity of Lautrec.

'Done. We can do a transfer upstairs?'

Di Matteo looked confused. 'But I didn't realise – that is . . .' He was tongue tied by his own rules, that we were to make no verbal reference to what was taking place.

'This is for me. I can give you the address of where I want it sent.' I still had that storage box in the depository at Vincennes.

'And then I'll need the photocopies of the mortgage agreement and repossession order. Are we ready?'

13

Li began *Woman with a Fan II* the day after we returned from Palermo. Da Silva vanished up to Rome soon after. He was gone three weeks. He called every afternoon, but I knew he was also calling Fish-Breath, to check up on me. Aside from brief shopping trips, Salvatore had effectively moved in, setting up camp without apparent discomfort on a blow-up mattress in the garage. Outbuildings were maybe his thing. I hadn't investigated where or if he washed. In the mornings I ran and worked on the provenances, in the afternoons Fish-Breath drove me to the studio. We were polite to one another, but it was mostly nods and greetings. I wondered if he ever slept – no matter how late I stayed up reading and thinking and sipping wine he was there in the courtyard with the gun, and he was still in position no matter how early I woke. At least he didn't attempt to follow me when I went running.

I wasn't bored, or lonely. There's only one kind of group fun I go in for and there wasn't much chance of that with Fish-Breath about. As Li worked painstakingly on the panel, I was deep in its backstory, the characters I had dreamed up becoming so vivid I almost believed in them. I was going to have to believe in them, when I presented at the House.

And then one morning I opened the shutters to find the countryside had exploded. The Italian spring had come overnight, as though someone had shaken confetti over the landscape. I dragged on a sweater and ran outside in my knickers. Fish-Breath watched me silently as I climbed over the fence at the back of the farmhouse into the patch of meadow that sloped uphill to where the woods began. The grass was full of pink campions and blue borage flowers, the hedgerows alight in yellow and orange; I could smell almond and peach blossom from along the valley towards the town. Fish-Breath came up to the fence and watched me capering about in the wet grass.

'*Ti piace?*' *Do you like it?*

'*Bellissimo!*' I beamed. It was the longest conversation we'd had. He obviously thought I was mental, or maybe just English. The grape hyacinth around the farmhouse door had come into bud. Later I picked a little bunch and put it in a water glass next to his mattress.

I found myself telling da Silva about the flowers when he called that day.

'It is beautiful, isn't it, the spring down there?' he agreed. I could hear a smile in his voice. 'How come you know all those names?'

'Oh, just art stuff.'

A particularly dreary week at the House making slides for a sale of Victorian watercolours. I find being able to tell hawthorn from blackberry blossom such a relevant skill. Fond as I was of a bloom, William 'Bird's Nest' Hunt was never going to make my list of fantasy painters.

'Listen, how soon can you get back? I need you to let the bank know we're ready to take the varnish off, and you'll want to be there.'

'Why did you put the varnish on if you're going to just take it off again?'

'*Madre di Dio*. Why can't you stop asking me questions?'

'Friday. I'll be home on Friday.'

After we hung up, I stood gazing at the meadow with what I imagine was a pretty dopey smile on my face. And then I experienced an overpowering urge to find a hairdresser in Siderno. *Home*. He'd said 'home'.

Mariangela Lucchini, the restorer in Reggio, had been delighted to receive my call. Much of her work had been for the Ministry of Culture, restoring artworks for the south's innumerable churches, and she said she'd be thrilled to have the chance to clean up something exciting.

'Mostly, it's varnish they want. And all the decent stuff gets sent north, anyway. Like the oranges.'

The Società Mutuale was sending a guard to witness the restoration; Li, da Silva and I met him at the port before driving to the studio in the basement of Mariangela's apartment block. Li was agitated, anxious about the effects of the de-varnishing on his work, especially since he couldn't be in the room as the process was begun. I tried to reassure him by promising to send a photo every five minutes to the bar where he would wait. Mariangela was about forty, in canvas dungarees with a bushy topknot of hennaed hair. A baby was crying as she let us in.

'I'm really sorry, the babysitter called in sick. Would you hold him for a second?' She thrust the baby into my arms. The shrieks grew louder as I jogged it nervously.

'Here,' offered da Silva, 'give him to me. *Ciao, piccolino, ciao*.' He was practised, tender; I had a sudden image of him with his own children. Giulia and Giovanni. I'd never thought about them much. The baby stopped crying and reached out a questing hand for da Silva's face, tiny fingers uncurling like the fronds of an anemone.

'He'll go down in a minute,' said Mariangela, 'he's used to me working. There was a crib with a mobile of yellow rabbits above it in a corner of the low-ceilinged windowless room. The rest of the space was given over to a long formica-topped workbench and a large easel positioned between an array of different lights, similar to the viewing benches at the House. Da Silva set the baby down and offered to go out for coffees.

'Right,' said Mariangela, putting on her glasses, 'let's have a look at her.'

I helped the guard, who had introduced himself as Giuliano, to unwrap *Woman with a Fan II*. Mariangela gave it a long, appraising stare.

'Well,' was all she said. 'Well.'

She knew what she was doing. I asked her if she objected to my filming the first passes at the varnish and she shook her head, pulling on her latex gloves, already absorbed in her work.

'Right. I'm going to get the gloss off with a three per cent dilute of Relgarez 1094. Shell D38. It's a non-aromatic mineral spirit,' she explained for Giuliano's benefit. He nodded gravely as though he had a clue what she was on about. The baby chuckled.

'Just pick him up if he starts off again. Now, I'm going to use a badger-hair brush' – she held it up for the camera – 'to take off the fluid after I've applied it with a sponge. Like this.' She began dabbing at a small patch in the bottom left corner of the panel. I could practically feel Li's tension through my phone as I sent the first screenshot. As Mariangela brushed, the colour laid in over the Prussian blue, a deep magenta brown, seemed to deepen.

'OK. OK. You see, the varnish had blanched it out. We can see the saturation level much better now.'

'What about varnish residue remaining on the surface?' I asked.

'The spirit will take care of that. Anything stronger will soften the matte.'

I moved around her as she worked, shooting the process from every angle. An hour later, the baby was asleep and we had cleaned about ten square centimetres of the panel. Giuliano spent the time playing Candy Crush.

'What's this?' asked Mariangela suddenly.

'I think it might be *sugo*. The painting was hung in a family home for some time. I didn't like to try to get it off myself.'

Mariangela took a little wallet which looked like a nail kit from a drawer and removed a tiny palette knife with a filed blade.

'This should do it. Do you want it on a slide.'

'Yes, please.'

Getting the sauce off took another thirty minutes, Mariangela delicately scraping the residue onto a glass slide. Another little piece of the jigsaw.

'I still don't see why we had to bother with all that,' Da Silva bitched after we had finally seen Giuliano off on the ferry.

'Do you really want me to explain?'

'Sure.'

'The thing is, Gauguin loathed varnish. It stood for everything he wanted to set his art against – rich, smooth, glossy, a veneer between the painter and the viewer. So he shortened his paint.'

'What?'

'Sorry. He drained it, through blotting paper, and then he diluted it with turpentine. He wanted it to look like the Italian

Primitives – pictures that were five hundred years old. Sort of chalky, caked on. And it might not sound like much of a revolution, but when he chose not to varnish his pictures, Gauguin was rejecting a whole tradition, replacing polished veneer with rawness. He wanted people to look at paintings again, to see beyond the surface of a lazy sophistication. He didn't care if people found his work ugly, or mad. He wanted them to *see*. Do you get it?'

I trailed off, aware that I had been speaking too long. I sounded like a total geek.

'Not exactly. So who's supposed to have varnished it?'

'Could have been any one of the supposed owners. People like shiny pictures. More classy. The point is, removing the varnish to see if the pigments stand up makes it look more authentic. A real Gauguin wouldn't rely on varnish to smooth out the light. So naturally I'd check.'

'You really care about this stuff, don't you?' Da Silva didn't sound bored.

'Yes. I do. I mean, I have to, don't I? Sorry for droning on.'

'Don't be.'

That evening, I began to assemble the file to send to the House. An overview of how I had come across the picture, my recognition of Gauguin's technique, my research into its background, the months of work. The receipts were prepared, the sale book from the railway station in Rome, the story I had constructed carefully outlined. Photographs of every stage, the paint samples and the slide, the papers from the Società Mutuale. I had to admit, it all looked pretty convincing. But the papers, the provenances, the picture itself, could only be as convincing as I was. And sure, it wasn't the first time I'd had to lie because my life depended on it. In a way, my whole life, the life I had constructed, had always depended on my capacity to lie, to make myself into what I was not, to observe and imitate and pretend, until whatever mask circumstance made necessary adhered so seamlessly that it became my face. I had often relished that, been proud of it even. Mostly, though, I didn't even notice. Whatever self I had was only ever a case of good or bad performances. Yet this time, if the mask slipped by so much as a millimetre, I was looking at the endgame, and it just didn't feel like a game any more.

14

Rupert emailed on 19 March. It was eleven a.m., ten in London. Things had obviously changed at the House if he was actually in the office. Leaning out of my bedroom window to get the best signal I called the front desk, asking to be put through to Rupert.

'European Paintings.'

I repeated my request.

'I'm afraid Rupert's just in a meeting,' answered the girl automatically.

'Please tell him this is Elisabeth Teerlinc speaking.'

'I'm afraid I can't disturb him.'

'Just tell him.'

It was a cheap thrill, but it thrilled me anyway when I heard Rupert bounding to the phone. Well, lumbering. After delighted noises from both parties, we agreed that I would bring the picture in as soon as I could secure its passage, to remain in the safekeeping of the House until they had completed their evaluation.

I bounced down the stairs to tell da Silva.

'He's dancing!'

'What?'

'I mean, he wants to see the picture. You'd better get on to Raznatovic, call him or send a carrier pigeon or whatever spooky shit you two do and tell him he can put the pliers away. And we'll need two tickets to London, business class.'

'We?'

'Me and the picture, you idiot.'

The slightest ripple of disappointment crossed that blandly handsome face, followed by an ugly twist of childish spite.

'You must be pretty excited, getting to play art dealer again. You'll be wanting your passport, then? The Teerlinc one?'

'For sure.'

He left the room and returned a moment later with his precious brown envelope, shoving it at me sulkily.

Was he actually jealous that he wasn't coming with me?

'Thanks,' I answered briskly, ignoring his reaction. 'So . . . I have to send a condition report before I take the picture, and you'll have to let the airline know. Bulkhead seats and permission for me to go through with it on the forklift. Li's blokes have done us a t-frame already.'

'T-frame?'

'Transit frame. It keeps the painting at the right angle in the air. We have to soft-package it, rough-frame it and crate it, so you'll have to deal with airport security on that too. It's all got to look super-official. The more we treat it as though it's priceless the more chance there is the House will. I'll keep the passport for now, then. Will you take me down to the workshop?'

'What am I, your bloody chauffeur?'

'That's about right.'

Fish-Breath was lurking about in the courtyard as usual. He raised a paper bag at da Silva.

'*San Giuseppe. Ho portato le zeppole.*'

Da Silva translated – I could still barely make out a word of what Fish-Breath said.

'It's St Joseph's day. He's brought cakes.'

'We should celebrate!'

'San Giuseppe?'

'No, you idiot! The picture. Let's buy some champagne for later, make dinner. We should ask Li.'

'Li? *Il cinese?*'

'You know, this casual racism thing is really unappealing. Yes, the Chinese guy who might just have saved your life. I thought we'd buy him a present.'

An hour later, Li and I stood in front of *Woman with a Fan II*. I closed my eyes and opened them, trying to trick myself into seeing the panel for the first time. Li had taken the pose from the version we had viewed in Essen, but altered the line of the head to echo the uptilted, more knowing gaze of *And the Gold of Their Bodies*. Our model was nude to the waist, but her wrap was a radiant scarlet, flowing into a darker, plum-grey ground that melded into magenta and dark greens at the edge of the panel. Her skin and hair were darker than those of the Essen picture and instead of the circular emblem of the *tricolore*, her white feather fan was embossed with a curling silver snake. Throughout his career, Gauguin had reworked stories from the Bible – even his Tahitian women could be seen as a series of exotic Eves or Madonnas. Instead of the carved chair, we had given her a wooden stool set with a black and white mosaic pattern, and above her shoulder, where the patch of blue in the Essen picture suggested a captured fragment of sky, floated a cloud-coloured asphodel, the petals faintly tinged with pink. Another symbol, the flowers of the meadows of Hades. I was quite proud of that suggestion. Gauguin was never interested in realism – the likes of MacKenzie Pratt, who thought they were clever to point out the 'inaccuracies' of his depictions of Polynesia, entirely missed his point. All of Gauguin's painted objects are deformed and reformed by the gaze of the subject, hence the incongruity of the flower was entirely correct for a man who disdained the duty to reproduce nature as a 'shackle' to his vision. At least, that was what I hoped the House was going to explain in the catalogue.

We watched the colours for a long time, letting our eyes melt into the panel.

'Are you pleased?' I asked Li eventually.

'I think she is the most beautiful thing I have ever made.'

There was no need to say anything else, because I thought so too.

Moët was the best Siderno's supermarket could offer, but Fish-Breath enjoyed it. We made an odd company at dinner that evening, but with the help of the three bottles of what Fish-Breath called '*monsciando*' it was quite jolly. He even left his shotgun outside. Li appeared in a dark suit with white shirt and beautifully knotted tie and a bunch of creamy narcissi, which he presented to me. I gave him a return ticket to Amsterdam that I'd bought in the travel agent's that afternoon. It was about time he saw the Rijksmuseum. Da Silva had raised an eyebrow at that, but I told him I was sure Li would be back.

'We might even go into business if this one works out! I wouldn't mind moving the gallery down here. He's amazing.'

Da Silva had given me a blank look.

'Afterwards, I mean. When you go back to Rome.'

'Sure. Yes. Great idea.'

He was very polite to Li at dinner. We ate chickpea pasta and the *zeppole*, ridged fried doughnuts dusted with sugar to celebrate St Joseph's day, though he'd never struck me as being a saint who had much to celebrate. Fish-Breath didn't say much, except to repeat his name for the champagne every time he took a sip, but that only made the conversation easier. Mostly we talked about food, the Italian conversational catch-all, but I learned a little more about Li. He had been in Italy thirty years, but aside from our trip to Essen, he had never left the country, though he had travelled all over, seeing every artwork he could. Later, when Li had left and Fish-Breath had resumed his usual place in the yard, da Silva opened a bottle of Barolo and we smoked at the kitchen table.

'Thanks for this. I can't stand Moët.'

'Snob.'

'I'm not a snob. I just like things to be good of their kind.'

'Yes. I saw your flat in Venice. It was . . . elegant.'

I could have said that I was touched that he'd taken time off from arranging Alvin Spencer's skeleton to notice the décor, but the wisecracks were getting to feel a bit old, so I just thanked him.

'Do you like it? Having money?'

'Yes. It means I can do what I want. Most of the time, anyway.'

'I'd like to know what that feels like.'

'What, money? I'd have thought you were taking off any minute for your luxury retirement in Venezuela. You and Franci.'

'I didn't mean that. I meant . . . doing what you want.'

'What did you want? If you hadn't gone into the *Guardia*?'

He dragged deeply on his cigarette. 'Down there, in town? My dad used to have drinks with the cops in the bar all the time. Kept everything quiet. So it was natural for me to join. Either that or they said I had to be a civil engineer.'

'Ugh. There you go again with "they" . . . And if there hadn't been a "they"? What then?'

'It never occurred to me to think about it. That's just not how things are.'

Travelling behind the House van in the car Rupert had sent to City Airport, London seemed vast and strange as we came in from the flatlands of the docks, the skyline ragged with cranes and ever-taller buildings, rookeries of new apartments and block-towered containers. Only when we came past Smithfield into the centre did it begin to seem familiar again, though much brisker and shinier than I remembered. I'd obviously been holed up in the sticks too long. As we crawled along Shaftesbury Avenue I found myself checking and rechecking my face in the driver's mirror. When I had met Rupert briefly at the Biennale just after I launched Gentileschi in Venice he had certainly not recognised me, but we had been passing in a crowd. Might propinquity stir a memory in him? On the evening when he fired me from the House, I'd been fairly forthright with my opinion of him. If someone had called me a talentless overprivileged cunt I was pretty sure I'd remember them, but then I wasn't a talentless overprivileged cunt.

Yet Rupert hadn't recognised Judith Rashleigh in Venice simply because he didn't expect to find Judith Rashleigh there. Memory can be a matter of context, of association – you might think you remember the features of the guy who makes your skinny latte every morning, but without his barista's uniform and the jaunty name badge, chances are you'd walk past him on the street. I'd considered the porters, obviously, but there I was relying on the strict hierarchies of the House. Clients came and went all the time, and if one of the porters saw a resemblance between one of them and a latter-day employee, it certainly wasn't their place to mention it. That left the girls on the front desk – the 'Spice Rack' as they were sometimes called – but they had been virtually interchangeable to me when I worked there, those glossy-maned Euro-princesses who handed out catalogues in between skiing holidays. Besides, they had been far too beadily focused on husband-hunting to pay the slightest attention to a scruffy junior. Back then, I hadn't even looked like competition.

I settled the lapels of my jacket. Siderno didn't offer much in the way of luxury brands, but inevitably there was an outlet store and I'd picked up a slouchy Céline suit in French navy that I'd put with a soft grey T and plain brogues. Unassuming but confident. I already had the story of my discovery by heart, but I repeated it over as the van pulled into the yard behind the House. And there was Rupert, large as life and twice as repulsive. *OK, Judith. Showtime.*

He gave me a meaty handshake as we watched the porters lower the back ramp of the truck and load the picture onto a trolley, as carefully as if they were disembarking an ambulance. He affected to recall our last encounter in Venice, but it was plain he discerned no connection between Elisabeth Teerlinc and Judith Rashleigh, or 'Er' as he'd usually preferred to address me. We progressed ceremoniously behind the trolley into the basement. Tracing the once familiar route through the complex warren of passages that led to the warehouse, we passed a lovely, arrogant Bronzino portrait and a sedan chair with a stuffed Minion toy seated inside. One of the porters' gags. Smiling to myself, I remembered how lucky I had once felt to come down here, to move amongst so many beautiful things. A bench had been prepared and Rupert leaned forward eagerly as the wrappings were slowly removed.

'I must say, I can't wait to see her!' he boomed. The two porters stood back respectfully. I hadn't seen either of them before.

'I'm Elisabeth,' I said firmly, offering my hand.

'Sorry!' said Rupert. 'This is Jim and this is, er . . .'

'Malcolm, sir,' the older of the two supplied.

Rupert made a show of adjusting the UV light and running his eyes over the panel, first with a large old-fashioned magnifying glass and then with a loupe. He made little panting noises of appreciation. I'd heard those before, though this time I tried not to shudder.

'Very pretty. Very pretty indeed.'

'I think so.'

'What do you think, Jim?'

Rupert smiled patiently, the expression an adult makes when a fond parent asks their child's opinion.

'Looks pretty straight to me, miss.'

The tension in my nerves slackened a notch. The porters had always had the best eyes in the House.

'Well, if you're willing, Miss Teerlinc, I'll have the chaps get started straight away.'

'Of course.'

'There's a bit of bumph for you to sign, I'm afraid. I'll get someone down from the department and then I'm sure you'd like a spot of tea?'

The affected nonchalance was a good sign. A very good sign. If Rupert *hadn't* been acting as though I'd just dropped off a fruit cake for the church bazaar it would mean he wasn't convinced. He sent a message on his phone and in a surprisingly short time a young woman appeared – a young woman in a cheap black suit that was working hard without convincing anyone and a striking mop of red-gold Pre-Raphaelite curls. She would have looked very pretty had she not recently applied too much powder to her lovely pale complexion, but the UV glowing from the bench behind us showed what the make-up would otherwise have concealed, that she had recently been crying. Not that she gave any indication of this to Rupert.

'Is this it, then?' she asked in a broad Yorkshire accent. She turned to me and offered her hand firmly.

'I'm Pandora Smith, Rupert's junior. Pleased to meet you, Miss Teerlinc.'

Yorkshire accent? 'Pleased to meet you'? What the hell had happened to the House?

'I've brought the permissions, Rupes. If you'd just look them over, Miss Teerlinc, and then sign here and here and . . . here, please.'

Rupes? I was so flabbergasted I almost signed my real name on the paperwork that consigned the Gauguin to the House and authorised their investigation into its authenticity. Pandora waited respectfully while I fiddled with the fountain pen, then stepped forward for a look at the canvas.

'Late,' she said, after a long but unselfconscious pause. 'The saturation from the chalk is really high in the ground. The lean technique.'

'Which recalls?' asked Rupert genially.

'Italian Primitivists, change in application marking transition from Naturalism to Symbolism between 1886 and 1889.'

'Bravo. Isn't she marvellous? A real asset to the department.'

'Spot on,' I muttered. *What the fuck was happening here? Rupert encouraging a junior? Asking her to display her knowledge?*

Pandora made a sort of half bob and disappeared back through the warehouse.

'First from Edinburgh,' Rupert remarked, 'Super girl. Now, about that tea. I'm sure you must be dropping after such a fraught journey.'

What was left of my disdainful composure collapsed entirely when we arrived in the lobby on Prince Street. The ornate carved staircase remained, but the House I recognised had vanished completely. The Spice Rack were still in evidence, but they actually appeared to be working instead of booking salon appointments and keeping their eyes out for passing billionaires. What had once been a gloomy waiting area furnished with heavy Victorian sofas had been transformed into a café, which was actually Open To The Street, serving what seemed suspiciously like green smoothies in bright coloured Murano beakers to several people who looked quite normal. There were even tables outside on the pavement. Rupert asked a young, bearded waiter in skinny trousers and braces showing under a witty House tailcoat for a pot of Earl Grey and a plate of cinnamon biscuits, which came dusted with the company logo in icing sugar.

'Awfully good,' he munched, spraying crumbs. At least some things never changed. 'We bake them here, you know, all in-house. Organic.'

'Yummy. I remember them from the last time I was here,' I lied. 'I popped in to the Old Masters sale last summer.'

'Oh – you ought to have called me.'

'It was just a flying visit. You know how it is, the travelling.'

'Quite. I was in Maastricht and Miami in a week myself last month,' Rupert divulged proudly. 'Well, may I say, Miss Teerlinc, that we're delighted, just delighted, that you have decided to go with us. And if we have a Gauguin – well!' For a moment I caught a glimpse of the old Rupert peering acquisitively from behind those fat-cushioned eyes. Eyes that had no idea what I had planned for them.

'Do call me Elisabeth. I'd love to see around the department, if I may, before I present?'

'Of course, of course! I thought we'd start about five.' Rupert gallantly took my briefcase and ushered me towards the stairs. 'How long are you staying in London?'

'Oh, just until this evening. I need to get back to the gallery. But of course, in a month or so, we'll need to meet again?'

'With something stronger, hopefully? By way of a celebration?'

'I'm sure my client will be delighted to provide the champagne!' I enthused.

The café had prepared me for what to expect as we reached the European Painting department on the first floor, and sure enough the torpid dustiness I remembered from British Pictures had been well and truly swept away. Most of the experts were working at shiny Macs with headphones in, occasionally whizzing backwards on their chairs to consult on a price or a detail.

'Hot-desking,' explained Rupert. 'We introduced it last year. Keeps things dynamic.'

'Is this the catalogue for the July sale?' I asked, pointing to a layout of Impressionist works on one of the screens.

'Just so. Huge sale – our first collaboration with American twentieth century. We're very excited about the de Kooning.'

'Which one?'

'Weeell, as a matter of fact, we've got *Intersection* coming in.'

I whistled. 'Impressive.' De Kooning currently held the record as the world's most expensive artist, with a price tag of three hundred million pounds at a recent sale.

'We're finding that our clients prefer to bid across a wider geographical range – period too. That's why we're mixing up the sales.'

'You're so right, Rupert.' I twinkled. 'Those old categories just don't feel *current* any more.' Not to mention that if you include all the most fashionable artists in a single sale, buyers are more likely to compete for works and drive the prices up.

'Perhaps you'd like to see my office, Elisabeth?' Hot-desking clearly didn't include the boss's chair. Health and safety wouldn't have allowed it, for a start.

There was a knock at Rupert's leather-padded door.

'And this will be Charlie. Charles Eagles, our chief auctioneer.' Rupert still had his corporate smile firmly pasted on, but I could hear the loathing in his voice.

'So you're the girl who found the Gauguin!' The deep, drawling voice belonged to a man about my age with thick coffee-coloured hair just touching the collar of his tailored Turnbull and Asser shirt. He was tall and slim and tieless with a tennis tan and Arctic-blue eyes that ran over me with all the warmth of a rattlesnake being introduced to a rabbit.

'Elisabeth Teerlinc. I believe we've met,' I said as I offered him my hand. He took it and leaned in for an expert double-cheekbone brush. We hadn't actually met, but Eagles wouldn't care either way. He had been poached by the House from New

York after several seasons of racking up record sales for what we had always called the Other Place. A profile in *Vogue* had described his 'uniquely insouciant blend of uptown chic and downtown cool'. He modelled for Mr Porter, dated actresses famous enough to land him in *Heat* and had two million followers on Instagram. I almost found myself feeling sorry for Rupert. Eagles was obviously a total twat, but I still would have done him.

'Well, now Charlie has joined us,' Rupert said, pointedly looking at his watch, 'we might begin?'

'Sorry, Rupes,' Charles's tone was briskly insolent. 'Lunch at Isabel. You know how it is.' He gave me a little cool-kids-together eye roll as Rupert waddled to the door and clapped his hands.

'Everyone! If we could all gather round? This is Elisabeth Teerlinc from Gentileschi. I'm very much hoping – that is, *we* are very much hoping, that she's brought us a Gauguin!'

I flipped open my laptop while the members of the department formed a group in Rupert's office, noticing that Pandora wasn't amongst them. I waited until they were silent and then a moment more, allowing their expectancy to build. Charles was lounging against the wall, reading a message on his phone.

'If we're ready? Thank you. So – I'm an independent gallerist with a space in Venice. Last year I spent some time looking into the archive holdings of the Banca di Società Mutuale in Palermo, and one of the pieces I took out for consideration was this.' I clicked onto the first screen of my presentation, a simple shot Li and I had taken of the picture against a white background. They leaned forward, even Charles. 'Immediately, I noticed . . .'

I didn't describe a moment of thrilling discovery, the exhilaration of recognising a potential masterpiece. That kind of stuff was for amateurs, or PR releases. We were professionals concerned with the intricate details of our merchandise, no more. Clear, practical, impassionate, that was how I needed to seem.

So I went through the background, the research, the provenances. I outlined the work Mariangela had done, adding that she had used the same de-varnishing technique employed by the Getty Museum in New York on Gauguin's *Arii Matamoe*. They laughed politely at the tomato sauce, nodded sagely at the dendrochronological confirmation. I explained the pigment analysis, the correlations with Gauguin's process. Fluent, precise, confident – all the things I had dreamed of being once, in this place, with people just like this, attentive, respectful. And as I watched their faces, I saw in each one of them the moment of epiphany, the seizure of the possible, the crucial transformation of hope to faith, of that desire which is the most important of all, the need of the art lover to believe. The last screen was a quotation from Gauguin himself:

My artistic centre is in my brain and nowhere else, and I am strong because I am never thrown off course by other people, and because I do what is in me.

'Of course,' I added in conclusion, giving Rupert the most Madonna-like look of humility I could conjure, 'the real knowledge is yours, and that knowledge will determine whether my . . . suggestions are correct. I hope, for all of us, that they will prove concrete. Thank you.'

I kept my eyes modestly on my shoes as they applauded. For a few magical seconds, I almost believed it myself. The strings picked up on the soundtrack and, outside, a rainbow danced over St James's Square. Here I was, triumphant, vindicated. *Except, as with most things in your life, it's all the most terrible crock.*

I excused myself to go to the bathroom, remembering to ask the way. I'd half been expecting a water wall and a gender-neutral Japanese loo, but the Ladies was still furnished with the same row of reassuring old thunderboxes. From behind a closed door, I heard someone crying. Muffled, snorting tears, stifled and then jerking out again in short bursts. Angry tears. It had to be Pandora. I'd spent enough time suppressing my rage in these stalls to recognise the sound of a woman who'd been fucked over by Rupert.

I lingered at the basin until she unlocked the door.

'Man trouble?' I asked, keeping my eyes on my reflection in the mirror. She started.

'Oh, Miss Teerlinc. I'm so sorry, have I missed – I had no idea. Oh shit!' The tears welled up again and she turned her face away, rubbing furiously at her eyes.

'Would you like a cup of tea? I've got a few minutes. We could go to Crown Passage, out the back stairs?'

She looked at me, smeared and bloodshot. 'Thanks. Yes, I would.'

I ran some cold water over a paper towel. 'Put that on your eyes first. I'll just say goodbye and meet you there.'

Rupert gave me a warm double handshake on the steps of the House. Warm as in sweaty liver.

'That was a very impressive presentation. We'll go through it all, of course, and then it'll be time to let the boffins get to work!'

* * *

The greasy spoon across the road in Crown Passage was fuggy with fat and coagulated London sunshine. I bought two thick white china mugs of tea and a Chelsea bun. Pandora picked at one of the burnt currants in the crust, then pushed the plate aside.

'Smart move. They've been on the counter since Rupert was a junior.'

'Rupert . . . '

'Not a boyfriend, then? Or a girlfriend?'

'No. Just something that happened this morning.'

'I don't want to pry. It's just you seemed so upset.' I let the implied question hover sympathetically.

She pushed her untidy hair defiantly out of her face and took a swig of tea.

'I'm fine, thanks. Sorry, I don't even know you. You must think I'm a right pillock.'

'I can keep a secret.'

'Miss Teerlinc.'

'Elisabeth.'

'Elisabeth. You have your own gallery, right?'

'Yes. Gentileschi.'

'You see, that's what I want – one day, you know. After I've been at the House a bit longer. But this morning . . .' I could see her wanting to tell me, to confide, just as her need to seem professional was holding her back. The black suit had a tear on the collar, ineptly mended. It made me ache for her.

'How old are you, Pandora?'

'Twenty-five.'

There were only four years between us, but I felt ancient.

'So, when I was about your age' – *God, I sounded ancient too* – 'I had a bit of bother with a client. Was it something like that?'

'Yes. Rupert asked me to go – well, on a call.'

I knew exactly where Pandora had gone. To a white stuccoed house in St John's Wood where a valuable collection waited behind heavy closed drapes, and the man who owned it waited for Rupert to send a pretty one. Colonel Morris, who'd tried to rape me and who knew how many others. I nodded, waited for her to give in to the silence.

'So this bloke – he had a real go at me. Nasty. Not just a bit of touching.'

'Did you tell Rupert?'

'Of course! I came straight back and asked him to call the police.' Pandora belonged to a different world from me, I thought. A world where safety was a right, not a negotiation. At least, she'd believed that.

'And what did Rupert say?'

'That I should consider my future seriously before bringing any complaint against Col— against the client.'

'Ah.'

'I'm sorry, I shouldn't be telling you this: it's completely inappropriate. Please forget I said anything.'

'He's right.'

'What?'

'Pandora. You seem really smart. Bright, ambitious. I could tell by what you said in the warehouse. This man – he didn't actually . . . ?'

'No. His cleaning lady arrived early and I got away.'

'So you're fine. Shaken up, but fine. You have to take it. You're strong enough, I bet you are. And one day you'll have your own place and that bastard – both those bastards – will be specks. Fleas in your memory. Don't fuck it all up because you've got some righteous ideas about justice. There's no safe space at the House. I'm sorry, really sorry about what happened, but you have to be practical, love. Of course, you could start a campaign online – get your hashtag viral . . . '

'You really think so?'

'Why not? And then when a million people have written "UgoGurl!" on your page, you'll still find yourself unemployed.'

'Oh.'

'It depends. Do you want some attention, a few days of affirmation, or do you want a career? What's the best way to win? Lose your job, drag yourself through a court case that you'll also lose or suck it up and achieve the success you deserve?'

'I hadn't thought of it like that. I'm just so angry.'

'Good. Angry is good. Rage can take you places.' *Didn't I know?*

Pandora sat up a bit straighter. 'Just – leave it, then?'

'I didn't say that. What I meant was, finish your tea, go and wash your face and stay the fuck away from St John's Wood. It's a useful maxim in general.'

'St John's . . . how did you know?'

At that moment, the tea urn let out a hiss like a dragon's fart and we both started. Maybe I jumped rather higher than Pandora. I'd never said anything about what happened at Colonel Morris's flat, but Rupert had sent me there. *Pandora had complained to him – if she now let slip that the new client . . . No, just finesse it. Act like you're on the powerful squad.*

I raised an eyebrow. 'It's a small place, the art world. Let's just say gossip gets around. You'll be fine. Just fine. And if the sale of the Gauguin goes ahead, I'll put in a word for you.'

'Really?' her eyes were bright again, and not with tears.

''Course. Now,' I gathered my things, 'I have a plane to catch. Good luck.'

I glanced back at her as I left the Victorian alleyway. She was still sitting straight, determined. But that didn't mean that she wasn't still vulnerable, or that part of me wasn't still angry.

So, after that, there was nothing to do but return to the farm-house and wait. The House would treat such a potentially important picture as a priority, but still it would take at least four weeks for the evaluation to come through. As art fraud becomes increasingly sophisticated, so the big sellers use ever more complex technologies to keep pace with them. Li had given me a pretty thorough grounding in the latest laboratory techniques. Emission spectroscopy, which used lasers to break down pigment, and X-ray photoelectron spectroscopy which could detect and date the oxidation states of metallic com-pounds used in paint, were able to date materials with extra-ordinary precision. But we had used nothing that wasn't from the correct period, no compounds that Gauguin couldn't have obtained. In that sense, I was pretty confident that *Woman with a Fan II* would get past Rupert's 'boffins'.

What concerned me more was just how good Li's technique was. The finish we had taken care of with the varnish, the col-our choice exactly matched Gauguin's other Tahitian works, but the danger point was the brushwork. In the past, paint-ers had strived to replicate the methods of the great masters, but by Gauguin's time a unique manner of laying on paint had become a sign of originality. Brushwork had become like handwriting – individual – and an expert with a good eye would be able to detect the most minute deviation from an artist's known manner. Making a Gauguin *look* like a Gau-guin was the easy part: it was *how* precisely the picture had been built up that would be crucial. Practically, I had nothing to fear from the rigour of the House inspections – if they discovered *Woman with a Fan II* to be a fake, or surmised it to be a copy of a lost picture there was no disgrace in it. I had come to them with a theory and they had proved my theory wrong; it happened frequently. That Raznatovic would kill me if it didn't pass wasn't the House's problem. It was all mine. And after I'd been back in Italy a few weeks, I confirmed that my other problem was that Raznatovic was going to kill me anyway.

The attempt to play hardball with the bank in Palermo had been no more than a feint. Only an idiot would have expected to see a penny of the money from the sale, whatever had been agreed. I was vulnerable, anonymous, dispensable, and moreover I knew far too much, not only about how the picture had been made, but about the business with the refugee boats at Siderno docks, about da Silva, about Raznatovic, about everything. They would see to me, no question. I predicted it would be what the Sicilians call a *lupara bianca*, a 'white shotgun', a corpse that is simply made to disappear. No body, no crime. It wasn't as though there was anyone who'd be wondering what had happened to me, except maybe Dave. The question was, *when*? If the House took the Gauguin, I'd be safe until the sale, I reckoned – I was necessary to make sure everything went through correctly. That meant I'd have to go back to London. Perhaps they'd try to lure me back to Italy, some promise of the money being signed off, and then dump me on the Aspromonte. That could be avoided easily enough, but on the other hand Raznatovic's scare tactics with the photos of my mother had shown me that he had people in England.

After what I had paid for the van Dongen, there would be just under two million remaining in my Gentileschi account with Klein Fenyves in Panama. Plenty of money by most peoples' standards, but using any of my bank cards would throw up a trail that someone in da Silva's position would have no trouble following. I would have to open another account, move the funds, get myself yet another set of false papers if I wanted to realise the painting's value in the future. The flat in Venice was owned outright by Elisabeth Teerlinc, so shifting that would require yet more identity shuffling so long as Raznatovic was looking for me. And then? Continue in the art world? Fuck off to Polynesia? Elope with Li? None of it seemed terribly appealing.

Once I was securely returned after consigning the piece, da Silva went back once more to Rome, taking the envelope of IDs with him. With no next thing, the days dragged. It wouldn't have been that hard to escape – as it got hotter and I sunbathed in the garden with a book, I went over all the ways I could imagine doing just that. I might as well have been back in the shed. I didn't have papers, but I had money, enough to buy the time to get them, maybe. I went back and forth on the risks endlessly, but it was more of a diversion from my temporary lassitude than an attempt to construct a serious plan. I wasn't motivated to run for two reasons. First, I wanted to win. And second, and it took me quite a while to get round to admitting this, I wanted da Silva to be safe.

Four weeks passed, then six. Da Silva still called each day, but our conversations had dwindled to monosyllables. I didn't care to ask him about his life in Rome. A couple of times I went down to the workshop, but Li was busy on another piece, a legit reproduction of Botticelli's *Primavera* to hang in some vile nouveau riche villa. I took to accompanying Fish-Breath on his shopping trips for our daily supplies, just to get away from the farmhouse. As the season turned, the scruffy town beach slowly started to fill up, first with old people down for the summer, then mothers and young children. Sometimes we passed groups of young men from the camp, kicking round bus shelters, smoking joints in the drab heat of the super-market car park. I asked Fish-Breath what they did all day.

'*Un cazzo*. Spend our money.'

They weren't allowed to work, though some of them volun-teered for free to pass the time. Unlike mine, their limbo was endless.

Even reading da Silva's emails was proving pretty dull. It really ought to have been more difficult to get his password. The only challenge had been getting the battery out of his lap-top. After our snarky chat on the Messina ferry, I'd sneaked back into the car and removed it, not the easiest of jobs in a force-six wind. When he couldn't boot his computer up in the hotel, I'd let him use mine, but it hadn't occurred to the silly bugger that I'd installed Key Tracker. I'd taken an extra-long time in the shower to allow him to have a snoop, and he'd certainly taken advantage of it, but why didn't people *think*? Da Silva had used three accounts that day in Palermo. The first had been a personal one from which he'd sent a mes-sage to Franci reminding her to get someone to look at the radiator in the bathroom. Domestic bliss. The second was his official *Guardia* one, and trawling through that would have been enough to make Gandhi crack out the Doritos. The third had given me a moment's trouble – an email address 'rusti-cosiderno1' from which he'd apparently sent nothing. Then I had a look in the draft folder. I'd often wondered how da Silva kept Raznatovic up to date on the Gauguin, and they were using a sophisticated, if dated method. Each had the other's log-in password, but all messages were filed in draft, so they could be read by the other but not intercepted by a third party unless they too had the password. Raznatovic's was in trans-literated Cyrillic, *icon lover*. Da Silva's was Italian, *custode*, but they wrote in English. Their brief correspondence was *en clair*, that is in innocuously coded language, good old Mafia style. I was referred to as 'the asset', the farmhouse as 'the let', the picture as 'the lady'. The last drafts were dated 19 March, when the asset had been sent to London to show the lady, followed that night by a confirmation of the asset's return. I checked the emails every day, but spying on Franci had somewhat lost its appeal, while Raznatovic was apparently waiting patiently enough. He knew how the art world worked, after all.

I did notice that sometimes, when I got back from my run in the relative cool of the mornings, Fish-Breath wasn't there. Naturally the first thing I had done was check the car, but wherever he'd gone he'd taken the keys with him. Two days later, I set off as usual, then doubled back to the other side of the house, waiting until I saw him set off up the track I usually took into the trees. *Had he been following me after all?* I kept about a hundred metres between us as I stalked him into the forest. He climbed for about a kilometre without pause, pretty fit for an old guy, then turned off to the left onto a narrow path I'd never taken. I continued past, further up the hill until the trees broke into rocky ground. I sat on a boulder and listened.

Faintly, over the breeze and the sound of birds, I could hear him whistling. I set off straight into the woods towards the sound, wishing I wasn't wearing my running shorts as twigs and briars snagged at my legs. The whistling stopped. Then I heard a swish and a soft thump, as though he was throwing something. I didn't get closer; I didn't want him to know I had followed him. I scrambled back up the hill and jogged to the farm, lingering over my stretches in the courtyard until he came back.

The next day I took the hill in a series of sprints, turning off at the path he had taken. I balanced along the edge of the dry depression in the soil, so as not to leave footprints. After about thirty metres there was a clearing, a cleft in the high rocks where I had waited the day before. It was very green and very quiet. To one side, the rocks closed over a passage, which came out into a narrow, steep-walled space. There was something lying on the ground, wrapped in a tarpaulin. I kicked at it. A shovel. I took another step and I saw a shallow depression about a foot deep, effortfully carved out of the hardening summer ground. *Super.* Fish-Breath was digging a grave.

And, naturally, that was also the day when Rupert's second email finally arrived. He wrote that he was delighted to confirm that after extensive research on the part of the House experts, they were pleased to confirm my attribution, and invited me on behalf of my client to include the Gauguin, *Woman with a Fan II*, in their July sale. If it was convenient, the House would like to invite me to stay as their guest at Claridge's for several weeks before the sale, in order that I could attend various events they had organised for buyers as well as the auction itself. I called da Silva immediately.

'I'll need my passport back. I have to leave for London. It passed.'

'You don't sound pleased. I thought you'd be excited?'

'Yeah, well, six weeks in this fucking dump would knock the *joie de vivre* out of Pollyanna.'

'What?'

'Forget it. How soon can you have it here?'

'I'll bring it myself.'

There was no need for him to come all the way south. We'd agreed that if necessary I should go to London alone – it was more discreet – and Fish-Breath could drive me to the airport.

'Judith? I said, I'll bring it myself. I can be there tomorrow.'

'Whatever. I need to see Li now.' I cut the call without saying *ciao*. I think what I minded most was how obvious it was. Da Silva didn't even think I was worth a proper send-off. A bullet in the back in the woods and rolled into the ground without a coffin? The *cheek*.

Li had finished his Botticelli. The buyer had wanted it double the size of the original in the Uffizi; it took up the whole of one wall in the workshop.

'What's with the colours?'

The delicate tempera of the *Primavera* had been substituted with glaring acrylics. Li shrugged.

'It's what the client wanted.'

'It's a crime.'

'I know.'

'Li, you know what I said, in Essen? You could do other stuff, you know. You don't have to rot down here. You're a brilliant painter. Genius, really. The House just said so.'

Li looked uncomfortable. 'It's not as simple as that.' He looked around warily. Fish-Breath was outside in the car park, there was no one but the assistants to hear us.

'They won't let me leave.' *Always with the 'they'*.

'Li, you're not a slave, for goodness sake. You have your passport now. Did you look at the date on the Amsterdam ticket?' I'd bought his flight for 6 July, the day after the Gauguin would come under the hammer. I wondered if Li knew anything about the grave in the woods. *Of course he did*. That was what he was afraid of.

'I put down a few useful addresses in Amsterdam. Take a look in the envelope. Think about it. You'll keep up with the sale?'

'Of course!' We hugged goodbye.

Da Silva appeared early next morning, crumpled and sweaty. He'd driven through the night. I was waiting for him at the door of the farmhouse, underneath the browning leaves of the hyacinth. I'd packed the best of my Venice clothes, though the first thing I planned to do when I got to London was some serious shopping. Elisabeth Teerlinc was going to have a *fantastic* wardrobe for her last hurrah.

'Judith! Isn't this amazing!'

'Don't bother. Shall we go?'

I didn't say a word all the way to Reggio. Da Silva looked more crushed than ever. We pulled up outside Departures underneath a sign that read 'Kiss and Fly'.

'So, I'll see you for the sale. You can phone me as usual if you want.'

'Of course I want. And then, er . . . you'll come back here with me?'

'I don't see any reason to. The financial stuff can be done from London.' *Where it would be much more difficult to off me.*

'Of course.' *What else could he say?* 'But I thought, maybe, we could . . . ?'

'Could what?'

'Nothing. Have a good flight. Good luck!'

'Bye, Romero. I wish I could say it's been nice.'

16

'It's Claridge's then, madam?'

'Thank you.'

The driver handed me into the car and went round to deal with my bags. By now, I was pretty good at acting as though I didn't notice these things, as though I accepted them graciously as my due, but for once, as we drove into Mayfair, I let myself experience the secret thrill. We had done something extraordinary, Li and I. Not just the audacity, but the skill to pull it off. We'd really fooled the House. And if I engaged in a fairly strenuous suspension of reality, the spoils felt pretty good too. The soothing creamy lemon walls of the lobby with its black and white marble floor, my second-floor suite, a huge bunch of crisp white roses with a card signed by Rupert, the quiet professional deference of the hotel staff. If only nemesis didn't arrive on the Louboutined heels of hubris with quite such predictable regularity. I'd barely had time to order a lobster sandwich before the lobby respectfully informed me that there was a Miss Belvoir expecting me downstairs.

So that was seventeen kinds of cunting hell. I only knew one Miss Belvoir – Angelica. Whose time at the House had briefly coincided with my own, but, more importantly, who had led Alvin Spencer to Venice. Most inconveniently, Alvin's sister had happened to be engaged to Angelica's brother. Angelica had apparently spotted Elisabeth Teerlinc in the background of a photograph at the Venice Biennale, and remarked on her resemblance to a certain Judith Rashleigh. She had encouraged Alvin to contact me, supposedly in the hope of some work experience in my gallery, or possibly just for snooping. I'd never had the time to ascertain which, as I'd fucked Alvin in my flat in Venice, then strangled him with a Hermès foulard as he tried to snap the moment for posterity. That was the problem which da Silva had so efficiently helped me to dispose of, and I hadn't counted on seeing Angelica again. She no longer worked at the House. So what was she doing here?

I made a few futile, frantic passes at my face and hair in the pearly gleam of the bathroom mirror. Not the moment for a quick dye job. If Angelica recognised me then the whole sale would be blown, and without that . . . The memory of Salvatore digging his pit in the hot, hard ground flashed irrationally behind my eyes. Absolutely nothing for it but to brazen things out. Buy some time, at least. I swiftly gathered my hair into a messy bun. I'd never made it to the Siderno hairdresser and, after months of neglect, it was looking distressingly like Judith's old barnet. As I twisted my head to shove the grip in, the silvered tissue of the scar on my cheek caught the light. I had got used to covering it with concealer, but I hadn't bothered with make-up for the plane. Judith Rashleigh hadn't had a scar. Using a lipstick and a cotton bud, I intensified it very slightly, just enough to make it stand out. The only other thing I could do was dial up the Euro-lilt in my accent. The backstory I had invented for Elisabeth Teerlinc had her down as Swiss. I picked up the service phone.

'Zis is Miss Teerlinc in 203? Please tell Miss Belvoir that if she'd be kind enough to wait for me in the Fumoir, I'll be down in a moment.'

It was just after seven, a decent time for a drink. The art deco opium den of the bar was dimly lit, and moreover had a strict no-photographs policy. Alvin Spencer's obsession with selfies hadn't worked out too well for him.

Angelica rose to greet me as I entered the bar. Just as tall and blonde and spikily slender as I remembered, she was wearing a witty Dolce & Gabbana maxi-dress, a print of farfalle. My own cotton shirt and jeans felt crushed and dingy with travel – Angelica's ability to make me feel awkward and irritated hadn't diminished. Good. I held out a stiff hand.

'Elizabeth Teerlinc. I'm so sorry, I wasn't expecting – you must be?'

'Angelica. Angelica Belvoir. Rupert sent me over to welcome you. We're, like, sooo excited!'

So far, so gushy, but there was an alertness in her eyes that hadn't been a big feature when she was drifting round the department.

'Rupert?'

'Oh, yah, sorry. I used to work at the House, but I'm free-lance now. I've come back to, like, maximise on their social media profiles?'

'Amazing!'

A waiter set down two glasses of champagne. We sipped, I smiled expectantly.

'So, yeah, amazing, right?'

I went right on smiling. I wasn't going to make it easy for her, although my heart was banging so loudly I was surprised she couldn't hear it over the faint tinkle of undemanding classics from the piano in the lounge. Angelica sat a little straighter. I toyed briefly with glassing her with my champagne flute and making a dash for it.

'Ooops! Nearly forgot – Rupert asked me to bring you these.'

Three catalogues for the July sale, with a glossy insert on *Woman with a Fan II*. She looked gorgeous, truly gorgeous. I flipped politely through the other pages.

'We've got the de Kooning too, of course, and some other fabulous things, a Cezanne, a Utrillo.'

'Wonderful.'

'So,' Angelica continued, scooping a handful of hair off her face in a familiar gesture, 'obviously we're really keen to get going on publicising the sale, and your fantastic discovery. It's going to be huge!' She began explaining her 'strategy' for Instagram, but I cut across her.

'Angelica,' I said, 'it sounds weird to ask this, but do you know a guy called Alvin Spencer?' *If she was suspicious, better take her by surprise.* She paused. I scanned her face. *Wrongfooted, but not astonished.*

'I'm so glad you asked that. Your name was familiar, I'd seen it on Facebook. I did try to write to you, last year, but . . .'

I'd taken down Gentileschi's social media account soon after Alvin and I got acquainted.

'I've been making some changes – buying for private clients. But I ask about Alvin because he came to see me at the gallery, in Venice. Last year, I think? Nice guy, how's he doing?' *Light and breezy as you please.*

'Oh. I'm sorry, this is really, like, awkward. He, um . . . he passed away.'

'Oh God! How terrible. Was he ill? He seemed . . .'

So then all I had to do was listen as Angelica explained the tragedy of Alvin's disappearance. I discreetly signalled for another couple of glasses, which took us up to the discovery of Alvin's body in Italy. I made the conventional noises of disinterested sympathy, keeping my eyes on her face, occasionally touching her arm.

'It's just . . . really sad,' she concluded. 'He was so sweet, and he had such a passion for art. But he couldn't . . . he just couldn't battle his addiction.'

'Devastating,' I agreed. There was an air of bewilderment about Angelica's story, of disbelief that something so actually nasty had happened in her vicinity.

'But, can I ask you something?' She leaned forward. *Here it comes.*

'When I saw you, I was sure I recognised you. Obviously I remembered the name. You don't know someone called Judith, do you? Judith, er . . . Rashford, or something?' Her casualness only showed how carefully she had planned the question.

'I'm sorry, I've never heard of her.'

'It's just, sorry, I hope you don't mind me saying, you look really like her. She used to be at the House.'

'Maybe I have a doppelganger!' I twinkled. That had been the word Alvin had used. Angelica seemed to scrutinise me in the red glow of the Fumoir lamps.

'Actually, not really. You're much prettier, Elisabeth!'

I touched my hand to my cheek, suddenly wishing the room was brighter.

'That's so sweet. I feel really self-conscious about this. Skiing accident when I was a kid!'

'Oh you poor thing – I'd never have noticed. I've got one too! On my knee. Kitzbühel when I was ten.'

Now the conversation was on the slopes, Angelica seemed much more relaxed, even convinced. And she was here to suck up to me, after all. Once we'd done five minutes of various Alpine resorts, she explained about a planned photo shoot, which would then be 'dripped out' on social media to encourage interest in the sale. Sky News wanted an interview and there had been enquiries from several weekly magazines. Which meant I was going to have to call my mother. *Fabulous.* I'd been out of England too long; the changes at the House should have warned me to expect an all-singing, all-dancing media fest, but then I'd had other things to think about. Now I was supposed to be doing an effing podcast about Gauguin. When I had been working at the House, it was expected that sellers would wish to remain anonymous – 'Property of Lady' or the name of a dealer was sufficient information for the catalogue. In the past, sales had been relatively discreet affairs – the big money might have attracted attention, sure, but only after the fact. Now, however, everyone was famous, everyone was singing desperately into the bedroom mirror, wanting to be chosen, wanting to make it to the final. Angelica, who, she proudly informed me, had 33k followers on her own Insta account, was clearly much more evolved in this respect than I was. I told myself it was nice that she'd finally found her niche, if you could call taking selfies at charity fashion shows a career, but even to me that sounded bitter. What was it about her that made me feel so . . . provincial?

At least we'd called a truce on the identity parade for the moment. Still, when I finally left the Fumoir, longing wearily for a cup of proper English tea and my bed, I felt her eyes on me as I crossed the lobby, and my spine felt cold.

'All right, love! How are things?'

My mother and I went through the regular routine of our irregular conversations – the weather (crap) what she'd been up to (nothing much) what was going on round the estate (the usual).

'Listen, Mum. I'm in London.'

'That's nice, then.'

'Yeah. Look, there's something I probably should have told you earlier.' I heard her breathe in sharply.

'Nothing serious. It's just . . . well – I'm here to sell a painting. Through my gallery.'

'That's good, isn't it?'

'It's going great. It's just, when I set it up, I changed my name. Ages ago now. And there's going to be some stuff in the newspapers about the sale. I didn't want you to be shocked.'

She paused.

'Mum? Are you there?'

'Sorry, I was just putting the kettle on. Look, I understand. It's best. What with . . . with what happened.'

What happened being that Judith Rashleigh's biggest claim to fame in Liverpool was being found with the dead body of her five-month-old baby sister in her arms.

'OK, then. Thanks.'

Another feature of our little chats was the terrible hiatus at the end.

'Take care, Mum.'

'Tara then, Judy. Love you.'

'No you don't,' I whispered after she'd hung up.

After the makeshift arrangements at the farmhouse, the slip of the Pratesi bed linen on my skin felt wonderful, but even an astronomical thread count couldn't soothe Angelica's image from my brain. What were my options? Disposing of her might not be difficult, but it would be stupid. Some sort of blackmail? Da Silva had arranged the discovery of Alvin's body convincingly – Angelica appeared to swallow the overdose story without question, but might there be something else da Silva could do, some secret we could invent to compromise the family? Yet why would Elisabeth Teerlinc be concerning herself with such things? To attack Angelica would be to expose myself.

I rolled over yet again and stared at the ceiling. At least my mother had made no fuss. She had always been the weakest point in the rickety bridge between my past and my presents. The practical thing would have been to get rid of her years ago, but I'd somehow never found the time. I doubted she'd talk, and even if she did it would only be to a load of pissheads in the pub. Yet, with social media, it would only take one twattering busybody to connect the long-forgotten piece in the *Liverpool Echo* with the face that was sharing a joke with Eamonn Holmes on the sofa and Judith Rashleigh's cover would be worth less than her 'Gauguin'.

What were the odds? I seemed to have spent most of the past five years asking myself that question. Refusing Angelica's planned publicity could look suspiciously shady. But I'd spent a long time burying my old self – I didn't look very much like her and I sounded nothing like her, so as long as my dear old ma kept her trap shut, I reckoned the odds were pretty good. Angelica had nothing to go on but a coincidental resemblance, diminished perhaps by the scar. All I could do, all I had to do, was appear serene.

I closed my eyes serenely for a few moments. Then I flicked on the light and grabbed the catalogue. *Woman with a Fan II* had a full page in the centre, the other half of which was occupied by the other star picture, de Kooning's *Intersection*. The abstract work seemed dull and rickety next to Li's radiant colours, though the photo couldn't capture their subtlety, the infinitesimal shifts in their depth. My fingertips circled over the page like a medium reading a tarot card, harder and faster until I caught a nail and the thick paper shred a sliver of its surface in the bottom left corner, where the model's wrap flowed into the frame. It recalled the moment in Essen, Li stooped over, trying to get a shot of the original canvas edge, that bloody midget interrupting us. And then I sat bolt upright. MacKenzie

Pratt. Angelica had mentioned a picture by Maurice Utrillo. The Pratt collection was comprised primarily of Impressionists and Post-Impressionists. Very slowly, I turned the pages. My fingers left smears of sweat on their thick pale margins. I found the Utrillo, quite average, one of his innumerable Montmartre street scenes. Though I knew what I was going to see, I forced myself to read the name of the seller. 'Property of Ms Mackenzie S. Pratt.' S for spy, S for spite, S for sabotage. Mackenzie had a picture in the sale, which meant Mackenzie would be in town. And I knew that the little scrape I had made in the paper was at precisely the point of the Gauguin's weakness. The brushwork. The only thing I had ever doubted. The House had missed it, taking the brushwork as a whole, seeing what they dearly desired to see. But if there was a flaw, it was there. Waiting for the dissenter, the someone who didn't want to believe. As she had made clear, Mackenzie hated Gauguin. And she had seen us.

17

My instinct was to run over to the House first thing the next morning and check the Gauguin, but after a night of fitful sleep and roiling dreams I thought better of it. Especially if Angelica's beady eye was on me, any suggestion of uncertainty could alert suspicion. The pieces for the July sale were to be displayed over a three-day viewing the following week: Mackenzie Pratt would doubtless attend the cocktail party the House had arranged for the opening night, so until then my doubts about her and Li's brushwork would have to wait. Instead, I spent the morning on Bond Street, giving my Gentileschi credit card the most vigorous workout it had seen for a year. As I made my way methodically through the boutiques, I couldn't quite brush away the feeling that I was arming myself for a last stand, but then if the fat lady was going to sing, she might as well do it in Saint Laurent. Swinging into the Claridge's lobby around noon, my phone rang. A helpful concierge dashed forward to catch my bags as I struggled to answer it.

'Elisabeth? It's Rupert. How *are* you? Are they making you comfortable?'

I'd managed to get my head around Rupert's newfound bonhomie, but I didn't think I'd ever get used to being anyone but 'Er'.

'Wonderful, thank you. And you?'

'Well, things are moving – there's been some press already today. Angelica Belvoir said the two of you had had a nice chat?'

'She's super, isn't she?' I chirruped grimly.

'So, I wondered if you might be free for supper with me at my club this evening?'

'Of course, Rupert.'

I wondered which of the Establishment strongholds on Pall Mall it would be – the Athenaeum, the Travellers, with its famous library? Or maybe Brooks's, which I remembered Rupert used to favour for his afternoon nap?

'Super. It's, er . . . Soho House, actually.' Rupert was clearly pretty chuffed about that. He was really moving with the times.

'Lovely.'

'So, 76 Dean Street at eight?'

'I'll look forward to seeing you.'

The story of the discovery of *Woman with a Fan II* had made three nationals as well as the early edition of the *London Evening Standard*. I read through them in the pedicure chair at the Elemis spa that afternoon. The Gauguin was described as being the property of an Italian bank, but Elisabeth Teerlinc and Gentileschi were mentioned in each, along with prices for previous Gauguin pictures, the details of the upcoming sale and speculation about the reserve, the basic price set for the picture. It was a curious feeling, to see something I had invented, both the picture and the person, in black and white. Five hours later, steamed and creamed and waxed and trimmed, Elisabeth Teerlinc emerged as poised and polished as the woman Judith Rashleigh had once dreamed of becoming. I had forgotten how *long* that shit took. As I was shopping, I had tried to remember what Judith Rashleigh might once have worn. After I'd stopped cringing at the recollection of my own immature taste, I considered that Rupert and Angelica had only ever seen me in my old black work suit, so I kept my new purchases to a range of tasteful neutrals. I'd had a few inches lopped off my hair, which I was going to wear pinned back at all times, the better to show off the little scar. It wasn't much, but as I examined myself in the mirror before meeting Rupert, the woman in the scarf-necked white Gucci blouse, with her austerely bare face, bore only a marginal resemblance to the shabby junior expert I had once been.

Arriving first, I took a table under the heaters on the ground-floor terrace of the Georgian building to get a fag in before Rupert appeared. The club felt huge, floor after floor of restaurant spaces and drawing rooms, each of them an artfully painted distillation of matcha-sipping hipster cliché. A guy at the next table in Nudie jeans and George Michael frosted flicks was grumbling to the waiter about the 'no Macs after seven' rule. Rupert's concession to another club policy – no suits – consisted of removing his jacket and tie, which produced an unpleasant billowing effect around his flanks as he squeezed himself between the group of unique individuals at the bar.

'Just signed up for this place,' he gloated as he handed me a glass of champagne. 'Got them all over now – Istanbul, Mumbai.'

'It's . . . pretty cool, yes.'

'So,' he leaned forward and I grabbed the stem of my glass before his gut sent the table sideways.

'You'll be pleased to know we've agreed the reserve for our girl. Two hundred.'

'That's good,' I said, as calmly as though I made ten per cent of two hundred million every day.

'And we've been sending out some fluffers.'

'Fluffers?'

'Little joke in the department. You know, teasers, for the major clients.'

I did know. I'd written a few teasers in my time – lavish descriptions of the investment value of paintings to encourage serious buyers to sign up for paddles. What I didn't know was if Rupert knew where the term 'fluffer' came from, but then, looking at his expectant leer, I had a sinking feeling that he did.

'And we've had a pretty impressive response. Including a request from Heydar Zulfugarly.' He leaned back to enjoy my reaction.

'The oil guy?'

'The very same.'

Ever since I'd started Gentileschi, I'd kept an eye on the industry magazines as well as the social pages, updating my index of who was buying what, and where. I'd seen Zulfugarly pictured a few times, though I hadn't had the impression that art was really his thing. He was more the type to name his boats after women's secondary sexual characteristics. He was certainly rich – a '*kryshaliq*' oligarch from Azerbaijan, one of the generation who had made fortunes from transforming state assets into private capital.

'Since when has he been a client?'

'Apparently he's setting up some kind of cultural foundation in the city. Wonderful, really, you know, giving something back to the Azeri people.' Even Rupert had the decency to look shifty as he came out with that guff.

'So if Zulfugarly's interested, that could set up some pretty . . . competitive bids?'

'I've put the word out. Discreetly of course. But we've already had enquiries from . . .' With some difficulty, Rupert extracted his phone from his pocket and scrolled through a list of names.

Many I knew already, but I had to gulp back my astonishment when I saw that the Folkwang in Essen was on the list. *Li's painting, hung next to the real thing . . .*

'And you have the photographs tomorrow, Angelica's thing? She's a real whizz on all that Facegram stuff.'

'I'm looking forward to it.'

'Wonderful, wonderful. Now, you must be hungry. They do a wicked rib of beef upstairs.'

Wicked? Oh, Rupert.

'Would you mind if I had a cigarette first?' I reached for the packet on the table and lit up, dipping my eyes as I guarded the flame of my lighter. When I looked up, Rupert was staring at me. I was still holding the lighter, a cheap orange plastic one from a newsagent. I'd always used them – I thought smart ones like da Silva's Dupont were a bit naff. Rupert looked oddly startled. And then I remembered.

Dave and I, huddled outside the warehouse, my hand cupped around a quivering match. Rupert giving me a disapproving look for consorting with menials. The association between object, gesture, my face. Fuck.

Quickly, I stubbed it out.

'On second thoughts, let's go up. Filthy habit.'

Rupert blinked rapidly and looked blankly round the terrace.

'Sorry, Elisabeth. Had a bit of déjà vu. Do finish it if you want to.'

'No, please. I don't really smoke, anyway. Let's go up.'

If I'd ever had any desire to be famous, I might have enjoyed the next few days. During the quiet summer news cycle, the idea of a priceless masterpiece hanging unnoticed for years on a kitchen wall was thrilling. As 'the girl who found the Gauguin', Elisabeth Teerlinc was having her moment in the sun. She was interviewed for Sky News, made small talk in make-up artists' chairs while her face was powdered and contoured, posed obligingly on the front steps of the House and at a charity luncheon at the White Cube Gallery for something called Artists for Unity. Gentileschi's mailbox filled up with invitations to openings, parties, conferences. Elisabeth gave two interviews to Italian newspapers and one to *Pravda*, and she smiled and she smiled and she smiled.

Since Angelica Belvoir couldn't be eliminated, I did my best to neutralise her by becoming her new best friend. At first, as we floated on a foam of amazing from drinks party to photo op to drinks party, I'd catch her glancing at me with a ripple of doubt crumpling those prettily vacant features. But confusion was no stranger to someone with Angelica's IQ, and it was much less strenuous for her to believe that Elisabeth, who just happened to love all the same things she did, was exactly who she seemed to be. The more frequently Angelica saw 'Elisabeth', I figured, the less room there would be in her memory for Judith. I created an Instagram account, @gauguingirl, just so I could follow her, not letting a post pass without a 'swoon' or a 'soooo adorable'. We made plans to party in Ibiza in the summer, after the sale; Angelica even suggested I meet up with her brother and his now wife next time I was in Manhattan. I wasn't sure that Emily Post had much to say about the correct way to introduce yourself to someone when you've murdered one of their family members, but I wasn't troubling about it. The vague plans I had turned over back in Calabria had begun to coalesce.

Da Silva would be in London for the auction, but I figured he would try to persuade me to return to Italy as soon as it was over. That still left a window. He was unfamiliar with the way the House worked – if I could invent a meeting, some documents that needed signing to transfer the fee to the Società Mutuale, its official destination, I reckoned I could give him the slip for four or five hours, long enough to get the Eurostar to Paris. No more – he could use his *Guardia* status to have me stopped at the border if he grew suspicious. But he didn't know about the Van Dongen, safely waiting in the depository outside the city. That would be my security. I took myself to St Pancras and bought a one-way ticket for cash, first class, then used the left luggage service to store it in a nearby shop (380 metres away, according to the helpful website), to be recovered the day after the sale. I couldn't risk da Silva finding it among my things if he went snooping. And then?

I didn't think much about that, since as the date of the viewing drew closer, my thoughts returned obsessively to that slumping corpse in Albania, to Salvatore digging my grave. Mackenzie Pratt's lipsticked mouth reared like the maw of a praying mantis through my dreams. But all I could do was carry on until the sale. As for Rupert, he was so busy rubbing his hands over all the lovely money coming the House's way that he seemed to have forgotten his own twinge of doubt, though I made sure never to light a fag in his sightline again.

Yet I had been right in my instinctive fear of Mackenzie Pratt. Her first broadside came in the form of an opinion piece that appeared in the *Guardian* two days before the viewing. Pratt was described as a 'distinguished international art critic', and the substance of her piece was that the House had no business selling a painting 'alleged' to be by Gauguin, on the grounds that he was an exploitative racist colonialist who had abused young Polynesian women. Within about five seconds the online bottom-feeders were shrieking for the picture to be withdrawn. There were suggestions that the sale be boycotted, though as Charles Eagles pointed out to me over an affable old-fashioned in the Ivy Club that evening, this was hardly a worry, since the type of people who Twittered about the House being a disgusting bastion of elitist privilege couldn't afford to buy anything there anyway. In Charles's view, anything that generated controversy could only be good for the sale.

But Mackenzie's plan to take *Woman with a Fan II* down didn't stop at op-eds. Rupert called me as I was laying out wardrobe options for the viewing on my bed at Claridge's.

'Elisabeth? Sorry to disturb you, but can you come over to my office? Something rather serious, I'm afraid.'

I was trying to choose between a backless Tibi midi-dress and a full-on Roland Mouret gown, both ivory. The Mouret looked a bit bridal, perhaps. I forced myself to continue smoothing out its skirt as I spoke.

'Whatever's the matter? Is there a problem?'

'You could say that. But I'd rather speak in person.'

'So mysterious, Rupert,' I flirted, but there was no warm glow in his voice as he told me he'd be at the House in fifteen minutes.

'I had a call from Solomon Mathis first thing this morning.'

'Why?'

Mathis was serious, a curator at the Reina Sofia museum in Madrid, where he had held a major Gauguin retrospective two years ago.

'He said he had been contacted by Mackenzie Pratt.'

The old cold fist around the heart.

'Go on.'

'Solomon told me she had been in touch not only with him but with several other experts. She said she wanted to warn them that your picture was a fake.'

Your picture. Not *our* picture any more. The missing consonant the first splash of a diving rat.

'I don't quite understand, Rupert. Miss Pratt has never seen the picture.'

'Quite. But she said she had seen you. At the Folkwang in Essen, photographing *Woman with a Fan*. In the company of a, um . . . Chinese colleague.'

'You were quite aware that I had visited the Folkwang, it was in my original notes. Obviously seeing the only known version of the picture was a crucial part of my research. I think we both know what Miss Pratt is implying, Rupert.'

That China – specifically Beijing – was a major centre for talented art forgers. Spot on, Mackenzie.

'Leaving aside Miss Pratt's appallingly unprofessional meddling – she's a collector, not an expert – I brought the picture to you in good faith. I gave you my reasons for believing that it was a genuine Gauguin and left it to you and the House's experts to ascertain whether or not I was correct. The assertion of its authenticity is yours, not mine.'

'Of course, of course, Elisabeth, I didn't mean—'

I cut him off.

'Miss Pratt has made her ideological objections to Gauguin public. So if you seriously believe her disgraceful allegations carry more weight than the opinion of your own professionals, you have only one option. Withdraw the picture.'

'I never suggested—'

'Just withdraw it. My reputation as a dealer is hardly as serious as the House's, but I nonetheless have to consider it. I'm sure my client would agree that if there is the slightest doubt as to the validity of the picture's status, it ought to be removed from the sale immediately.'

I was certain Rupert had no intention of following my suggestion. There was simply too much potential money involved, not to mention the public loss of face for the House. My willingness to step back from the sale could only cement his resolve. I softened my tone.

'Look. This Pratt woman is on a witch-hunt. Is that what the House is coming to? Judging works by the private lives of their artists? I know she has her Utrillo in the show. He's an important artist for you. So fine – she's entitled to her point of view. But just because she's got a bee in her bonnet about Gauguin being a reprobate – he was a drunk, he had syphilis, his wife was thirteen, whatever . . . The picture is the picture.'

'She'll be attending the view tonight,' he replied thoughtfully.

'All the better. Everyone's a grown-up here. She's not talking about withdrawing her piece, is she? I think we can see where her principles end. So if you don't want to remove *Woman with a Fan II*, just don't.'

18

In the end, I went for the Mouret. Demure, unimpeachable. I planned to arrive at the view on the dot of six, hoping to get my first look at the Gauguin since I had been in London, but before I left, I called da Silva in Rome. I had kept up our custom of a daily conversation, not to mention a regular check of his emails to Raznatovic, though there had been no updates on 'the asset' lately. I had mailed him a link to Mackenzie Pratt's anti-Gauguin diatribe in the newspaper.

'So everything's OK?' he asked. 'The sale's still going ahead?'

Even knowing how little he actually cared about me, it was somehow galling to be reminded that the sale was all he did care about.

'Why shouldn't it?'

'And you, you are OK?'

'Why shouldn't I be?'

'I wish I could be with you this evening.'

'As I said, it's all fine. It'll sell. We have nothing to worry about.'

Pandora Smith greeted me eagerly in the lobby. She was looking much better than when I'd last seen her, though her black sheath dress was spoiled by an awkward fumble of thick tights under its fitted skirt.

'It's lovely to see you. And I hope you'll be pleased with the hang.'

The Gauguin had been given a whole wall in the gallery space off the lobby. The mount had been backed in a deep green felt, which emphasised the richness of its shadows.

'Perfect choice. Well done.'

Stepping back, as though to study the effect, I let my eyes hover over that bottom left corner. I couldn't see anything wrong with the brushwork, but then I was no Gauguin expert. Pandora was already hard at work, pointing out aspects of the piece to an older Australian couple.

'It's a superlative example of his late style,' she was saying. 'The fluidity of the brushwork really makes it extraordinary. We can *feel* his liberation.' The couple nodded seriously, earnestly glancing between their catalogues and the picture. Bless her.

'Ah saw you.' The voice came from somewhere behind my elbow. I took several beats to turn around and look down at Mackenzie Pratt.

'I'm sorry, I don't believe we've been introduced?' I said coldly.

'In Essen. With your Chinese friend?'

'Of course. You must be Mackenzie. How do you do? I'm Elisabeth. I read your little piece. Quite . . . stimulating.'

'Do you know what he did to those girls?' she spat. 'The ones he painted? He infected them with syphilis! They were thirteen, fourteen. Did you know that? Syphilis!'

The Australian couple moved quietly away.

'It's an interesting question, isn't it? How ready we are to judge the artist rather than the art? Utrillo, for example, a chronic alcoholic. Didn't he get into trouble for exposing himself to schoolgirls? And yet the work . . .' I droned on, long enough for the room to fill with chattering visitors, trapping Pratt in the pretence that this was a civilised exchange of views. I couldn't see her eyes behind the perpetual sunglasses, but as I showed no sign of letting up she began to flap the wide sleeves of her Etro kimono like a frustrated penguin.

'Elisabeth!'

It was Angelica, phone at the ready. 'Can we do a few pictures, darling?'

I gave her a little wave and an eye roll that went above Mackenzie's bobbed head.

'So lovely to have met you at last, Mackenzie. Good luck at the sale!'

The space was crowded by then, and I didn't see Mackenzie for the rest of the evening. Rupert puffed up to me as I was fetching my coat.

'Everything OK, Elisabeth? I saw you speaking to Mackenzie?'

'Absolutely.'

'The thing is – this is rather awkward. That chap over there? Willy Novak.'

He indicated a skinny old party in tight purple jeans, a careful shock of white hair arranged over his forehead.

'He's hosting a pre-sale dinner for us down in Sussex next week. We were very much hoping you'd attend. The thing is, apparently he's asked the Pratt woman.'

'I don't think that's a problem, Rupert. I can handle her.'

It was still early when I stepped out onto Prince Street, and though the evening was typical for a London June – grey and raw – I thought I'd walk back to the hotel. I'd reached St James's Street, moving rather slowly on my heels, when Charles Eagles jogged up behind me.

'Elisabeth? Where are you off to?'

'Nowhere special.'

'Feel like grabbing a bite? Chuc's in Dover Street?'

I turned to look at him. He was ridiculously handsome. And it would be so easy. Not quite professional perhaps, but then no one would have to know. That huge empty bed in my hotel room . . . It would be so good, to be nowhere but the present for a few minutes, to scour myself out on his body. I hesitated.

'No thanks. School night and all.'

He gave me a boyish shrug. 'Oh well. Annabel's for me, then. Another time?'

'Maybe. Goodnight, Charles.'

He crossed the road with a jaunty bounce in his step. He wasn't hurting. I had other things to think about anyway. Not da Silva, who had said he wished he could be with me. No. I had to think about just how I was going to handle Mackenzie Pratt.

Who wasn't letting up in her campaign against *Woman with a Fan II*. The next morning's *Mail* had an item on the gossip page about our encounter at the view. 'Glamorous gallerists in Gauguin spat'. I thought 'glamorous' was stretching it a bit in Mackenzie's case. The BBC obviously agreed that she had the perfect face for radio, because next she turned up on *Woman's Hour*, spouting about Gauguin's 'gross personal conduct' and his 'abhorrently patriarchal perspective'. The House was obliged to put out a statement and the @gauguingirl account was swiftly filled with trolls denouncing Elisabeth Teerlinc as a disgrace to the sisterhood. Rupert suggested getting Pratt disinvited from the client dinner, but I persuaded him it would only fuel her animosity. The best policy was just being English – we should simply act as though Mackenzie's unpleasantness didn't exist.

So, as planned, Rupert and I caught a train to Arundel from Victoria five days later. I'd packed my snazzy new Bottega Veneta turquoise suitcase with overnight things and a sequinned Emilia Wickstead gown I'd ordered from Pont Street, a liquid flash of a dress that was so wrong for the country I knew it would look just perfect. It gave me a certain pleasure to watch

Rupert hoiking the case into the rack of the first-class carriage. Willy Novak, Rupert explained, was a contemporary collector who let his house, Lancing Park, for events. The aim of dinner was to schmooze some of the House's major clients, as well as attract the attention of 'influencers'.

'Whatever they think they are,' Rupert added with disgust.

'What kind of people are the clients?'

'Oh, financial chaps mostly. Hedge funds. You know.'

I gave him a sympathetic look. 'Yes, I know.'

We were met at the station by a white soft-top Rolls-Royce that transported us with absurd solemnity along the narrow, bramble-thick lanes to Lancing Park. After being so long in Calabria I had forgotten just how *green* England was in summer, the tumult of leaf tones from cyan to viridian, but even had I been inclined to draw Rupert's attention to the beauty of the flora, he was engaged in polite conversation with the third passenger, who to our intense mutual displeasure naturally turned out to be Mackenzie Pratt.

'Remind me, honey,' she growled as we drove off. 'Who was your little Chinese friend?'

'A colleague from Paris,' I smoothed, wishing one of the thorny branches would whip into the car and take her beady eye out. 'He worked on the 798 show at the Vuitton Foundation last year. The Beijing artists. Did you catch it?'

That kept things going as we crunched over the gravel drive to the house, but I could feel her glaring at me even as we were bustled into the hallway by a collection of fully liveried footmen. Rupert was doing pretty well at the breezy denial act, but increasingly, I knew this was personal. I had no idea why Mackenzie disliked me so much, but I wasn't planning on giving her much more time to explain.

* * *

Lancing turned out to be a severely lovely eighteenth-century house in softly lichened grey stone, a pedimented central block flanked by two high-windowed pavilions. The footmen introduced themselves, which gave Rupert a bit of a turn as we followed them along the shallow curve of the wing to an orangery. The fruits on the trees had been replaced with little disco balls, twinkling over the pastel fifties frocks of a gaggle of tea-pouring maids. The place had more staff than Downton fucking Abbey.

'Isn't it ghastly?' whispered Rupert cheerfully as he helped himself to half a Victoria sponge bulging with whipped cream and raspberries. I took a cup of Earl Grey and a caramel éclair. There was very little one could have done to spoil the exquisite spare lines of that room, but our host had certainly tried his utmost. The panelling along the closed wall had been white-washed and a stuffed rhino wearing a Yankees cap was positioned by the window, flanked by urns of silver-dyed ostrich feathers. The lozenges in the orangery panes were filled with more taxidermy – a mounted giraffe's head, a gaping turbot, a zebra, each wittily adorned with clashing headgear. A hidden sound system wafted soft Ibiza beats and the huge fireplace had been turned into a gleaming chrome and silver bar.

'Revolting,' I whispered back.

'The clients love it though. Ah, here's Willy!' Rupert did an impressive switch from contempt to beaming pleasure as we greeted Novak and the room began to fill with guests. Novak dragged me enthusiastically from one group to another, presenting me yet again as 'the girl who found the Gauguin'.

'And this is Larry Kincardine.'

'Hello, Lawrence. Fancy seeing you here.'

'Hello, darling.'

I could see Rupert watching me approvingly as I laid down that particular trump in the name game. Lawrence was an old acquaintance from my party days in London, where he'd run a bit of a speakeasy from his place in Chester Square. Back then, he'd been languid and epicene; now he was pudgy and belligerent-looking, but then I've never met anyone who actually looked better for ditching the smack. I wasn't remotely concerned that he'd identify me – even if he'd ever known my name we had always called one another 'darling', according to the rules of the night.

'I haven't seen you around,' Lawrence managed, between urgent drags on a violet-scented vape.

'I've been . . . travelling. Fancy a proper fag?'

We slipped out through the orangery doors to the steam-ironed lawn where a family of white deer were disporting picturesquely by the ha-ha. I gave him my packet of Marlboro Golds and he lit up gratefully.

'What's with the knees-up, then?'

'My pa made me come. Reckoned it would be good for me. I'm mostly up in Scotland these days, don't get to London much.'

'Bit of a snore?'

'Yah, kept the place though. Old Kevin's still there.'

'I remember Kevin.'

'In fact I was thinking of going on somewhere else after this dinner. Waldgrave?'

I shrugged. 'Don't know it.'

'Might be a bit more up our alley.' He was sniffing slightly and looking a bit agitated; maybe he'd replaced the heroin with something less mellow.

A gong sounded from inside the house.

'I suppose that means we'd better go and change. I'll see you later, Lawrence.'

'I was thinking of ditching about eleven? It's not that far. We can get back in time for church.'

That sounded good. In fact, that sounded perfect.

The guest rooms on the first floor were arranged along a central gallery with Edwardian-style name cards in a silver slot outside each, a reminder of the good old days when bed-hopping was a rural sport. Between each doorway stood an oversized plaster reproduction of a classical statue, after which the rooms were named. I was Venus de Milo. Mackenzie Pratt, two doors along, was Laocoon. Whatever wasn't white or dead at Lancing seemed to be made of marble; after a slither around the Carrara tiles of my bathroom I hauled on the sequins and tapped lightly at her door.

'Sorry, Mackenzie. I was just wondering if you had a Nurofen? I've got a splitting head.'

'Really, honey? You have a headache? Well, come right in.'

Mackenzie was inserting her tiny figure into a stiffened black Issey Miyake column – her head was lost in one of its three sleeves. 'Just in the bathroom,' she muttered through the crepe.

'Thanks so much. Sorry to disturb you.'

I crossed the leopard-skin rug to find the bathroom. My room had ocelot; likewise Mackenzie's marble was veering towards fuchsia as opposed to my black and gold. A neat black leather *necessaire* was open on the mount of the sink, containing the usual face creams, a silk eye mask and a packet of painkillers.

'Got them!' I called brightly. I ran water into the tooth glass while I opened the bathroom cupboard. Valium, Zoloft,

Lexapro. *So Mackenzie had depression issues. Interesting.* A diminutive pair of black silk pyjamas hung on the back of the door next to a thick white dressing gown with 'Lancing Park' embroidered over the pocket in silver, identical to the one in my room.

Mackenzie had emerged from the Miyake, her sunglasses still attached. I nodded at her and made for the door, but one tiny foot in a black patent Mary Jane shot out and kicked it shut.

'So. Here we are, Elisabeth.'

19

'Quite the place isn't it?'

'You can cut that shit out, honey. I don't like you and you don't like me.'

'That's not quite how I see it.'

'And you've convinced them all you've got the first version of *Woman with a Fan*?'

'It belongs to my client at present. Are you planning to bid on it?' I asked lightly.

'I very much doubt it.' She came closer, laid a ligneous hand on my arm. The glasses goggled up at me malevolently but her voice retained its Southern softness. 'I don't buy fakes.'

'I don't believe it's a fake. Nor does the House.'

'It's as much a fake as you are. I saw you there. "Research" my ass. I know what you were doing. I might not be able to prove it, but that doesn't mean I don't know.'

I was beginning to rather warm to Mackenzie. She might have looked like a cartoon but she was the only person connected with the Gauguin so far who wasn't yearning to believe in its authenticity.

'I have no idea what you're talking about. Thank you for the pills, but I'm afraid you're being rather rude. I'll see you at dinner.' I stared down at her. Slowly, she removed her foot and let me pass.

Dinner was served in another white-panelled room, twenty places set along a white marble table with a silver crepe runner and piles of silver-sprayed fruit. I rather envied Mackenzie her sunglasses. A catalogue of the July sale at the House lay beside each placement. Novak had given me the seat of honour on his right; we discussed his renovations at Lancing over the first course, a chilled cucumber soup with oyster and horseradish toasts. I turned to my left as the footmen, who were now sporting white velvet dinner jackets, served a venison carpaccio with sour cherry compote.

'I'm Elisabeth. How do you do? I don't think we've met before.'

'Ned.'

My neighbour was very tall, so tall that he had to stoop deeply over his plate. The dress code on the invitation Rupert had given me had said 'Fabulous'. Most of the men around the table had made an effort – there were quite a few garishly coloured waistcoats and even a pair of orange cowboy boots, but Ned clearly hadn't got the memo. His height and his greening dinner jacket gave him a lugubrious air, which his conversation did nothing to leaven. After receiving monosyllabic answers to my increasingly desperate questions, I clutched at the ignominious life raft of the conversationally marooned and asked him what he did.

'I . . .'

I leaned towards him encouragingly. 'You . . . ?'

There was a pause in which several square miles were lopped off the Amazon forest and Greece got a new prime minister.

'I . . . hunt.'

'Oh. Who do you go out with?'

'In' – Ned made a superlative social effort – 'Shropshire.'

He sat back, overwhelmed with his contribution to the entertainment. I spent some time carving the last of the translucent strips of venison into tiny strips then stared despairingly at the table decorations. Our mutual silence was interrupted by Novak tapping a glass and introducing Rupert to talk everyone through the sale.

Rupert hauled himself to his feet, clutching his glass of '71 Pomerol. Novak may have had the taste of a pikey prizefighter, but no one could say he was stingy with the plonk. 'Fabulous' for Rupert had turned out to be a vast shantung Favourbrook smoking jacket in a print of pineapples which clashed revoltingly with the deepening puce of his complexion. He made a few sycophantic remarks about the company, who if it was to be believed were single-handedly keeping the art market afloat, then launched into the highlights of the auction. The finale was me, to talk about the discovery of the Gauguin. I got to my feet as Rupert led a round of applause, feeling Mackenzie's shaded glare from the other end of the table. Lawrence's place, between her and a Swedish model married to yet another hedge-funder, was empty. I presumed he'd popped out for a toot on the molly. I ran through an abbreviated version of the presentation I had given at the House, emphasising the agreement of Rupert and his team on the provenances and being sure to credit them, rather than myself, with the attribution. Rupert watched me approvingly, smiling and nodding along, and despite myself I experienced a similar wave of the pleasure I had felt when I had first given the speech, the sense of affirmation and belonging which was all I had ever sought from him. It could all have been so different, really.

'And what if you're wrong?' Mackenzie's voice interrupted me before I had finished, which at least provided a moment of interest for the table. The women had been watching earnestly, showing how knowledgeable and cultured they were, but the men hadn't felt the need for the pretence and were most of them checking their phones.

'What if you're all wrong? What if it's a fake?'

MacKenzie had clearly been having a good go on the Bordeaux, more than was advisable, perhaps, for an elderly midget. Nonetheless, the word 'fake' was taboo, the art-speak equivalent of the 'N-word'. It fell into a silence which thickened as the footmen exchanged the plates for truffled guinea fowl poached in yellow Jura wine. Rupert and I exchanged a sudden look of camaraderie, both of us standing, exposed.

'I don't think any of us would be here this evening if we didn't rely unconditionally on the credentials of Rupert and his team,' I replied eventually. 'There is no other institution in the art world which has such a reputation for probity. That's why I wanted to sell the picture there, so that I could be absolutely assured of its authenticity. As such a serious collector yourself, I'm sure you agree, Mackenzie?'

'Phooey,' she spat.

'Steady on, old girl.' The voice at my elbow was Ned's. Perhaps he was sentient after all.

'I saw her.' She pointed a blood-tipped nail through the candlelight. 'I saw her with a Chink! In Essen. And what are Chinks famous for?'

'Well,' I smiled, making my effort to keep my temper conspicuous, 'there's Ai Weiwei. Or perhaps you were thinking of another Chinese artist?'

I cast a pleading look at Rupert. *Please rescue me. Please don't let the bad fairy spoil my pretty dream.* It had the desired effect. He straightened his shoulders, lifted his chins and sallied forth on the billows of the pineapples.

'Mackenzie, Elisabeth is here as my client and my guest and I will not have her offended. Moreover, I think your remarks are racist and extremely inappropriate. Perhaps you're rather tired? Maybe you should go and lie down. In the meantime' – he raised his glass – 'a toast to Willy for this wonderful dinner, for such wonderful connoisseurs of such outstanding works.' He stressed the word *connoisseur* just enough to let Mackenzie know it didn't include her.

Show over, the company dutifully scraped back their chairs and bobbed up to toast Willy. Rupert came round to embrace me as Mackenzie stalked from the room. She hadn't reached the door before one of the velvet footmen had cleared her place.

'I'm sorry, Elisabeth' – Rupert's voice was sweetly coaxing – 'she should never have been asked. Terribly set in her ways. All that silly business with Gauguin's life – it's obviously a fixation. I hope she didn't upset you?'

'Not in the least, thank you.' I was all molten gratitude in his big strong arms. The other guests were making that extra noise that groups do when something embarrassing has happened. The Swedish model swayed round the table and informed me that Mackenzie was a bitch.

I hadn't worn my watch to dinner, as naturally a lady should never need to know the time, but I heard a clock striking the quarter hour and looked around for Lawrence. His offer of a party had really been an excellent idea. Novak got to his feet and crossed the room to a concealed door, from which an enticing pink light emerged. He announced that dessert would be served in the 'secret' cellar, and everyone trooped down a spiral staircase into the hectic welcome of El'se Massoni from a DJ booth contrived from a giant barrel. More disco balls hung from the ceiling around a small dance floor that was soon mostly occupied by Rupert. Gauging his crowd, the DJ flipped resignedly from Berlin underground to 'Blurred

Lines'. I'd never seen Rupert in party mode before and, after being briefly mesmerised by him attempting the nae nae in the general direction of the Swedish model, I hoped that I never would again.

'Are you still up for going out?' Lawrence was already installed with a fag on a silver velvet loveseat.

'Definitely.'

'I've got my car in the stables. Whenever you're ready.'

'Give it a bit, maybe. I need to change my shoes. About half an hour?'

'Sure. Go out the front, then left past the garden door.'

Bracing myself, I took a turn on the dance floor opposite Novak, who was giving it an Ibiza hand pump. I endured until the footmen carried in a Methuselah of Krug and then slipped up to my room, carrying my slim Stuart Weitzman sandals. I set down a pair of flat boots near the door and took the dressing gown cord from my bathroom just in case. Then I moved slowly along towards Mackenzie's room, listening as the party amplified two storeys below.

First I switched out the light on the corridor, then tried the handle very slowly. If this hadn't been an imitation country house it would have creaked or stuck, but the latch slid out quietly. The room was in darkness except for the light of a single candle on the leopard-skin covered floor – Diptyque Feu de Bois – and the upwards beam of a phone screen which caught the shimmer of Mackenzie's black silk pyjamas. She was seated cross-legged, with ear buds in, humming softly to herself. She didn't move as the noise of the party wafted in briefly before I closed the door. I couldn't sense anyone else nearby on the guest floor. Meditation and a massage to the vagus nerve, very calming. She didn't react until I was behind her with her body clamped between my knees, and in the first swift gasp of her fear I twisted her head round into the cotton-padded crook of my shoulder, straining her neck to the right while my left hand felt for the sweet spot under her ear. I forced my thumb into the little hollow and began to squeeze. She struggled, but I had her too tight, and she was so small, so horribly small, her flailings only exhausted her even as the first twitch of her stopping heart momentarily stiffened her resistance. I counted out a minute until her head drooped more gently against my arm. The stable yard clock struck eleven as we sat there, a black and silver *pietà*, and I counted another minute before relaxing the muscles of my thighs. Strong antidepressants can have an ageing effect on the carotid arteries. A heart attack. I'd originally thought of hanging her from the shower rail with a dressing gown cord, but she was so old and tiny it wasn't worth the bother. She fell forward softly, her sunglasses landing on the rug. Something rustled, sudden and repulsively alive around my knees and I nearly dropped her before I realised that the vivid red bob was a wig. The head sagging level with my hipbones was bare and flaking, crossed with a few wisps of colourless hair. I shuddered, but it gave me an idea. A heart attack was good, but a full on house fire was even better. Everyone else was awake, they'd have time to get out, but here in the country, with luck she'd be ashes before the fire engines arrived.

When I left the room, MacKenzie was arranged on the skin, the headphone from her left ear pressing into her neck where her weight against it would bruise her just so. It seemed a kindness to replace the sunglasses, but the tip of her dislodged wig just touched the naked flame of the candle. After I had washed my hands two doors down I paused a moment before the closed door of her room. Beneath the soft fragrance of woodsmoke from the candle there was a definite high, bitter smell, the singe of burning hair. A floor below, the black and white tiles of the hallway were pearly in the light of the sconces, bouncing a high shine off the smooth wood of the banister. Irresistible. I hitched up my dress, got astride and let go.

Rosemary from the walled beds, leaf mould, the incense murmur of old stone, all the sharp scents of night. Lawrence was waiting for me in the stable yard, smoking. In the dark, he looked much more like his old self. I hadn't been so much in the mood for a party as an alibi, but his slouching long-legged silhouette recalled other nights, the scent of lilacs outside the house in Chester Square, and I felt a current of anticipation sear through me so harshly that I gasped. Lawrence shoved his ancient Volvo into gear and offered me a line of coke from two cut out ready on the wide dashboard.

'I'm OK, thanks.'

'Suit yourself, darling. Jam today and jam tomorrow, then. Hold this.' I steered us lopsidedly around a bend as he ducked under my arms to snort.

'Whoa. Perking up!' He shook himself back into place.

'So what's going on at . . . Waldgrave?'

'French bird. Used to come round to the Square. Rents the house for parties – you know the sort of thing. Fuck, it's as black as a miner's arse. I hate the country. Where's the satnav, darling?'

It took us an hour to cover the five miles to the house, mostly because Lawrence was engaged in a domestic with the satnav lady. When we found the gates of a drive at the edge of a village, Lawrence insisted on another line, several ciggies and a confidential rant about his father's unreasonable stinginess before remembering we needed to message an entry code to the hostess, which he had cleverly written down somewhere. Somewhere was a crumpled receipt from 5 Hertford Street lurking deep within the archaeological strata of the Volvo's boot, so it was well after midnight before the gates opened to admit us.

'You're going to love this,' Lawrence beamed as we were shown to a parking spot by a fully booted security guard. 'Estelle's gigs are really smart.'

'Lawrence. Before we go in?'

'What, darling?'

'You might want to take the fiver out of your nose.'

Purcell's 'Hark, my Damilcar, hark!' poured over us as another guard relieved us of our phones at the door. I smoothed out the sequins and wished irritably for some chewing gum. I like to clean my teeth before a party, but that interfering midget had distracted me.

'My dears! You're the last! Come in, come in and let's get you out of those wet clothes. Now who's this, Laurence?' Her accent was comically French.

'Just another slave to love,' I answered. She clapped little hands in black lace mittens.

'Oh, I like you! Come along, come along!'

I was super glad I hadn't taken Lawrence up on the coke or I might have had a heart attack myself. The woman in front of us could have been Mackenzie's twin. Equally tiny and wizened, sunglasses, shapelessly contrived black smock. The only difference was that the bob was black and that Estelle was holding an ebony handled whip which trailed behind her as she led the way along the hallway and opened a pair of double doors.

The house appeared to be Victorian faux-Gothic; we were standing on a machicolated stone minstrels' gallery which overlooked a long, baronial-style hall. I blinked as my eyes grew accustomed the candlelight which was its only illumination. There was a strong, heady smell of burning perfume, something musky and old-fashioned. Two curving staircases descended from either side, each step occupied by a naked man wearing a black silk blindfold. Between them, facing out over the balcony, was a string quartet in full evening dress. Estelle fiddled with a nylon bumbag strapped round her waist and I caught a glimpse of an iPhone. The singing faded and the musicians sawed into Donizetti's 'Della crudele Isotta'. Estelle clapped her hands and the crowd of guests holding tall chased crystal glasses turned towards us. They were all fully dressed, the men in white shirts, the women in black dresses.

'You two watch from here,' murmured Estelle, indicating a recessed bench. 'I must have symmetry! Open the cage.' She cracked the whip against the shoulders of the nearest naked man, who did not flinch even as the knouted leather bit his skin. Two more men, this pair dressed in tight black trousers with red silk sashes, were opening a narrow iron cage, shaped like an upright coffin at the opposite end of the room. Once they had unfastened the doors, a small double bed draped in black satin sheets was wheeled into position in front of the cage and the men helped a woman out. She was naked except for a blindfold, her skin glowing like parchment in the soft candlelight, setting off the rouge on the nipples of her small, high breasts. She arranged herself quietly on her back, her arms coiled above her head as one of the men bent over her and fastened on a pair of cuffs. I suppressed a giggle. Estelle cracked the whip again and in unison the blindfolded men turned ninety degrees so that they were facing one another. She cracked it a third time and the bed was wheeled in between the staircases, the woman spreading her thighs slightly, arching her back in anticipation. Lawrence nudged me.

'Told you it was worth seeing.'

As the bed finished its progress, the men put their right hands to their cocks and began to masturbate, every variety of stroke, tweaking and plucking. The musicians bowed imperturbably as the first of them leaned forward and shot his cum over the waiting body of the woman, turning his back to her immediately as he did so. I counted twenty-nine remaining figures, and one by one they ejaculated and turned away, slowly covering the woman's body with a glistening sheen of sperm. The guests watched, motionless, as the woman twisted and writhed with each hot fall. Estelle was watching intently, caressing the polished handle of her whip. Finally, there remained only one figure, halfway down the opposite flight, hunched over a short, stubby cock, his hand working urgently. The musicians stopped playing abruptly, so that the only sound in the room was the man's swift, high panting. Expertly, Estelle sent the long whip down against the side of his face, slicing a red weal into his cheek which sent him over, the spray of his cum just missing the woman's gaping, seeking mouth. It was utterly absurd, yet part of me wanted to be her in that moment, abject, triumphant.

One of the guests on the floor, a woman with long blond hair, was stepping out of her dress, leaving it puddled on the floor as she emerged naked except for her heels and approached the bed. Glancing up at Estelle, who gave a nod of permission, she bent over the supine woman's body and began to drink. One by one, the other women followed her, kneeling and lapping, as the men began to unbutton their shirts. Estelle fiddled in her bumbag and above me the music swelled again from a speaker. The little woman turned to us and bowed slightly, then the doors were opened and she left the way we had come. She hesitated at the doors, then turned back.

'Give me your hand, dear.' I obeyed. She turned my wrist and bent her withered, dry lips to where the veins showed green.

'Did you enjoy my ceremony?'

'*C'était sublime.*'

'*Ah bon.*' She continued in French. 'Since you speak my language, tell me the answer to a riddle. Why does the cock take the feminine form in French?'

'Because the slave takes its name from its master.'

She laughed, a raucous high-pitched squawk. 'Very good! Now here, *ma chère.*'

She produced a black silk pad from her bag, embroidered with gold lettering.

'Which one, *Laurence*, for your pretty friend? This one?'

She drew a long, evil-looking pin from the cushion, its end tipped with what looked in the candlelight like a white sapphire set in old gold filigree and stabbed it viciously into the heel of my palm. I knew better than to react. We both watched as a fat ruby of blood bloomed on the skin. For a second I thought she was going to suck it, but she merely smiled and handed me a heavy black paste card with a number engraved on it, again in gold.

'You're one of us, now.'

'*Merci bien, madame.*'

'Anytime, dear. *Bonsoir.*'

I waited until the doors had closed behind her to wring my wrist and put my teeth to the tiny wound.

'She's pretty . . . intense.'

'I think she liked you, darling,' said Lawrence. 'She doesn't give many of those out. Now, what do you reckon?'

'You and me?'

'Nah, sweetheart, I'm too high. Go and have fun.'

It surprised me that for a moment I couldn't remember the last time I'd got laid. I'd turned down the best-looking man in London the other night. For what? The promise that some no-mark Italian cop missed me? What had I been thinking?

I scanned the crowd, morphing now into one mass of softly entwining bodies. One woman stood a little to the edge of the mêlée of flesh, slowly unbuttoning a long, off the shoulder sheath. She pushed it down to her waist, her hands sliding over her broad hips and the full pale gourd of her belly. Just my type.

'Unzip me, then?'

He did. I stood naked for a moment then walked tall down the stairs in my boots to find her.

20

The fire brigade had arrived by the time Lawrence and I found our way back to Lancing at about 2 a.m., along with a squad car, an ambulance and a scrum of gawking neighbours in dressing gowns. Novak's guests had obviously still been up when the flames broke out, and they were still in their party clothes. The footmen were ferrying movables into a bizarre rummage sale display on the drive, directed by their squeaking boss.

'Fuck,' hissed Lawrence. 'What's happening? I've got three grams of gear in the car.'

'I don't think anyone's too bothered about that. Oh, what a pity!'

The central part of the roof above the ladies' guest rooms had collapsed. The firemen were grimly directing their hoses at the snaggle of blackened beams, silhouetted against the country starlight in the engine's powerful headlights. The turbot had made it to safety, unlike MacKenzie. Two paramedics were bending over a gurney that held a small heap of body, entirely covered with a blanket except for one child-sized foot lolling over the side. It was hard to tell from a distance but it looked promisingly charred. One of the medics was lighting a fag as the other filled in some paperwork: there was obviously no hope. A high-pitched screaming rose above the crackle of the police radio and Novak's desperate instructions. Two firemen were holding back the Swedish model, who was fighting them off furiously in an attempt to re-enter the building.

'But you don't understand!' she wailed. 'It's the *couture* next week. I've got a Ralph & Russo gown in there!'

Rupert bounded up to the Volvo as we got out, pineapples jiggling.

'Elisabeth! Thank God you're safe. They've been searching for you! They're here!' he boomed at the firemen. The assembled neighbours looked rather disappointed that Lawrence and I were not trapped somewhere in the smouldering wreckage.

'The two missing guests?' A policeman had jogged over to the Volvo.

'Yes, Miss Teerlinc and Lord Kincardine here,' confirmed Rupert.

Lawrence's panic had been hastily smoothed into an expression of shocked concern. I was quite impressed.

'What's happened? What can I do?'

'All under control, sir. We'll just need you to answer a few questions.'

'Of course,' I said, but please, tell me . . .' I faltered off, pointing to the gurney.

'I'm afraid to tell you that a body has been recovered from one of the upstairs rooms. Mr Novak has already identified it as, er . . . Ms Mackenzie Pratt.'

'Oh my God! What happened?' I gasped.

'We can't confirm anything at present, madam. Now, if you wouldn't mind telling me how long you've been away from the property?'

'Just before eleven,' I put in, before Lawrence could answer. 'Quarter to. I heard the clock.'

Lawrence nodded in agreement. Now that I'd lodged the suggestion, that was the time he would give for our meeting in the stable yard.

'We went to call on some friends of Lawrence's who were giving a party,' I added for Rupert's benefit. It was something

I had learned back on Steve's boat, the *Mandarin*, when I'd been his beard against gold-diggers for a summer. If a woman is, however nominally, the property of the alpha male in the group, the other men will behave submissively to her. I doubted that Lawrence was the richest guest at the party, but he was certainly the poshest, which made him the silverback as far as Rupert was concerned.

I fingered the skirt of my dress. There was a smooth patch of silk where one of the sequins had shed, quite possibly in MacKenzie's room. Nothing to worry about, I'd been rehearsing my statement all the way to Waldgrave and back. The sequin could have been lost when I went to her to borrow a painkiller before dinner. I'd be sure to mention the anti-depressants in the bathroom, the same brands my mother had periodically taken, hence my recognising them. That bit was even true. The fire had gone better than I'd expected, but given Mackenzie's age, a sudden heart attack – which was after all what had killed her – was perfectly plausible, assuming there was enough of her left for a post-mortem. Consistent use of serotonin boosters is associated with increased risk of cardiac arrest. Any mark from my thumb would have been covered by the pressure of the ear bud as she fell against it, towards the burning candle. If they could pinpoint a time of death Lawrence had inadvertently confirmed that I was already with him. Fingerprints? Well, poor MacKenzie had heard me on the landing as I came up to change my shoes and we'd had a little moment when she apologised for her remarks at the party. I'd given her a hug.

The white Rolls-Royces were rounded up to drive the guests all the way back to London. Lawrence had asked for a lift to

Gatwick, to take the Edinburgh plane. It was almost 7 a.m. when I said goodbye to Rupert, who had spent most of the journey messaging, occasionally laying a solicitous hand on my arm. The paramedics had wrapped me in a foil blanket, which I huddled around me even in the enveloping heat of the car, keeping up the shock. I knew how the Swedish model felt – that Bottega suitcase had only been produced in ten editions in the turquoise. Thank Christ I'd put my Vacheron back on before leaving with Lawrence.

'Fuck!' Rupert exclaimed suddenly. 'Sorry, Elisabeth.'

Charles Eagles had sent a text saying he had been woken by a call from the *Mail* diary. The tragic incident at Lancing, following the dramatic denunciation of the Gauguin by the fire's only victim. The same woman who had had the 'spat' so eagerly reported by the paper the week before. One of the guests must have called it in, Rupert thought.

'Charlie thinks we should give an interview. I'm sorry to ask, but do you think you could manage it?'

'Of course. But . . . maybe we ought to wait and see what poor Mackenzie's family want, in the States? They may not even know yet.'

'Oh, no one cares about her. It's the picture – Charlie thinks it will really add to the sensation of the sale – the dramatic story that follows the Gauguin. And then a follow-up in one of the Sundays. He's got a point.'

Rupert sounded rather rueful. Obviously not because the idea was repellently heartless – just because he hadn't thought of it first.

Finally back in my room, I was about to switch off my phone when a text came through from da Silva.

Judith. Let me know you're OK.

Everything's fine.

I saw the fire, at the house where you were staying. It was on the BBC. They said a woman died.

Not this one.

I'm so glad you're OK. Call me later.

What was da Silva worrying about? It wasn't as though I carried the sodding picture around in my handbag. I took one of the huge hotel pillows and wrapped my arms around it, burying my face in its downy softness. She had smelled of Mitsouko and tasted of sea salt and lemons.

21

Charles Eagles had certainly been busy while I slept. I woke up to two voicemails from sympathetic-sounding women at the *Mail* and the *Standard* asking if I felt able to talk about the fire, five missed calls from Rupert and an excited email from the PR department at the House asking if I was available to be interviewed on *Channel 4 News*. Rupert was clearly beside himself, as when I called him I discovered that he was already in the hotel. I took my time before coming down in a plain black linen shift, which seemed to express the right degree of respect for the dear departed. Rupert was tucking into a spot of Welsh rarebit and a Bloody Mary. I asked for a small pot of Lapsang and a saucer of orange slices.

'How are you feeling, Elisabeth?'

'Well, very shocked, of course. It must be so distressing for Mackenzie's family.'

'Heart attack,' pronounced Rupert, shaking Worcester sauce over his third slice. 'PR just heard from the police. Dreadful thing, of course, but it means this jamboree can go ahead. Fantastic boost for the sale!' He toasted me with the thick red liquid.

'I suppose so,' I answered quietly.

Rupert set down his glass.

'If you're not happy about it . . .'

'No, of course. It's just . . . I feel so dreadful for her. She was very kind, you know, when I went upstairs afterwards. Apologised for what she'd said. Of course, I told her it couldn't matter less, but still.' I risked the faint hint of a pretty sob. Rupert laid his hand on my arm, which appeared to have become his default setting.

'Look. I know it's all . . . terribly vulgar, interviews and articles and whatnot. But that's just how things are now. We have to, you know, move with the times. Accept the chainges, like.'

For a moment, I thought he'd choked on his toastie, but then I realised he was trying to impersonate Pandora's flat Yorkshire vowels.

'We know what's what, don't we, Elisabeth? And if it means paying lip service to the oiks then that's what we'll do. Adaption or extinction, that's what it comes down to.'

Of course I understood. I had always understood. That's why I had advised Pandora to say nothing about Colonel Morris, just as I had once said nothing. Because if it suits power to ape the mannerisms and beliefs of the powerless, that is what power will do. Camouflage. Let the oiks think they've won and nothing will ever have to change.

This time though, it seemed that Charles Eagles had miscalculated. Or I had. Mackenzie Pratt proved to be an even bigger pain in the arse dead than alive. Initially, the story of the fire provoked prurient sympathy, but within days, the tabloids were pushing the idea that *Woman with a Fan II* was somehow cursed, that Mackenzie had been a victim, a brave crusader who had been left to burn while heartless art buyers swigged magnums of Krug. The fact that they weren't far wrong didn't make things any better. The *Guardian* followed up with a lurid piece on Gauguin's life, portraying him as an exploitative chancer who titillated the bourgeois buyers of Paris with images of exotic eroticism to boost his prices. An online German pressure group whose name translated as 'No Air for Abuse' succeeded in pushing the Folkwang to cancel their bid, and once the museum had withdrawn, the names on Rupert's list of potential clients swiftly began to dwindle. The House was beginning to show signs of cracking; Rupert reported a board meeting in which the idea of putting the picture in a smaller, more discreet sale in the autumn had been mooted. It made sense – if serious buyers were withdrawing because of the Gauguin, it would affect the prices of the rest of the lots in the sale. But I couldn't let that happen. Raznatovic simply wouldn't wait that long. Moreover, Mackenzie's outburst at the dinner party had started rumours that the piece was dodgy. If it were re-examined, there was a possibility that it might not pass a second time.

So, about a week after the fire, I took the Tube east to Kingsland Road, diverting for a bowl of spicy pork pho at one of the cluster of Vietnamese restaurants. Much as I loved Italian food, it was great to be back in a country where they'd heard of star anise. Azerbaijan House was a shabby building in a terrace between a dry-cleaner's and an artisan coffee shop. A faded carpet was pinned up in the window in front of a broken Venetian blind that hadn't seen a dusting since Stalin captured Baku. I rang the bell without really expecting an answer, but the door was opened by a small man with round glasses, in a black suit nearly as dusty as the blind. He looked surprised when I asked if I could use the reading room, but let me into a narrow hallway papered with flyers for concerts and cultural events.

'First floor.' He disappeared into a small kitchen in the back. As I climbed the bare planks of the stairs, obstructed by boxes of more flyers, I heard a microwave ping.

There hadn't seemed much point in looking into Zulfugarly online. The official images of Azerbaijan I had called up the previous evening were glossy and progressive, at least if you thought that Bulgari outlets and Lamborghini concessions constituted progress. I couldn't read Azeri, which is Turkic, rather than Russian-rooted, and a look at the Index on Censorship site told me that even if I could there would probably be little real information in the public domain. At first glance, the two formica tables in the community library didn't look much more promising, as most of the carelessly heaped material was Azeri, though there was a small English-language section, in which I found a photostatted *samizdat*-style book in a clear plastic cover entitled *State Kidnap!* I was still reading it two hours later, when the dusty man reappeared.

Zulfugarly came up quite frequently in its pages. Described as a 'black raider', he was one of a generation of former public servants who had blithely rewritten the law on publicly owned resources. Naturally, he described himself as an 'entrepreneur'. The announcement of his planned cultural foundation was depicted by the author as 'a blatant display of disregard for national legislation', not that this had prevented many prestigious European architecture firms competing for the design project. It was a familiar pattern in the art world. Look for an oppressive military despot who controls an embarrassment of fossil fuels and there'll be a branch of the Louvre waiting to open right next to the missile launch pad. From Astana to Tashkent, nothing succeeds in polishing cosmopolitan credentials like the acquisition of art. Zulfugarly was entirely typical in posturing as a latter-day Medici – unlike any other market, art is only regulated by the size of the cheque. You could argue that it has always been so, but at least the Romanovs and the

Bourbons were tyrants with taste. The custodian looked on dolorously as I contemplated a shot of Zulfugarly on a jet ski, the repulsive aluminium canisters of the Baku Flame Towers in the background.

'You are interested in my country?'

It seemed rude to answer 'not particularly', so I pointed to the hirsute figure in the photo.

'In this man.'

'You know him?'

'I'm going to meet him tomorrow.'

The little man removed his spectacles and polished them on his shirt.

'Scum,' he pronounced decisively. 'Now I am afraid I have to close. The reading room is no longer available.'

'Scum,' I reported back to Rupert. 'Just what we need.'

We were sitting in his office. I had noticed that the experts in the department all seemed very busy as I was shown through, heads bent diligently over their screens. Rupert, surprisingly, had come out fighting. He was determined that the sale would go ahead, presumably with an eye on his bonus, and our meetings had taken on an us-against-them air. Fatman and Robin.

'I don't follow.'

'Zulfugarly. The Azeri guy. He doesn't give a stuff about Gauguin's teenage lovelies. He wants the piece for his cultural foundation. And he's still in. I think we should tour the picture to Baku.'

'Touring' was a practice whereby particularly important pieces were taken for clients to view *in situ*.

'What about insurance? We don't have much time to arrange it before the sale.'

Of course, the Gauguin was not really insured, seeing as it was worthless, but in presenting the provenances I'd been sure to include the appropriate documentation, courtesy of Li.

'I've already spoken to Palermo,' I went on. 'You're right. My client is naturally concerned about insurance. But there's a way round it. If Mr Zulfugarly will agree to view the piece at the British Embassy in Baku, then technically it remains on British soil, so my client's insurance won't be affected.'

'Transit?'

'I believe you have a plane. The House, that is.'

Rupert was smiling now.

'Indeed we do. You can travel that way.'

'I can? Wouldn't you want to come?'

I had no desire for a weekend on the Caspian Sea in Rupert's company, but I very much wanted to keep him close until the sale.

'Can't do it. We can't officially be part of the viewing. However, we have a ... strategy that's worked before in similar situations. Since the picture has been consigned to us, we can send a guard with it. We've had one of the junior experts stick on a uniform before. It's worked very well.'

'Ah. You've thought it all through, haven't you?' *Just a little more flattery and he'd think it was all his idea.* 'I'm willing to go, of course.'

For a moment, I considered asking him if I could take Pandora as the 'guard'. But then I thought it might prove a blight to her career, after the sale, not to mention that her eye was just a bit too good.

'There's just one more thing, Rupert. All this business in the press. I think we need to take back the story. You know, own it. So we need another bidder. Someone major. Then that becomes the story, the competition for the Gauguin.'

Rupert pinched the bridge of his nose. 'But we've lost so many buyers. And if Zulfugarly is bidding, who'd go against him?'

I leaned forward. 'How about if I told you I could get you Pavel Yermolov?'

PART THREE

DELAMINATING

22

Rupert had laid on the oil so thickly on the phone that I found myself leaving from City Airport three days later. Zulfugarly was apparently ecstatic that the House was showing him such exclusive attention. The Gauguin and I were accompanied on the House jet by one hired heavy from a private security firm and Hugh, a junior in Rupert's department. The heavy introduced himself as Karel in a heavy Polish accent and was roughly the size of a garden shed. Nonetheless, Hugh felt the need to inform me as we climbed the steps to the plane that it was indeed he who was the House's undercover agent. I could have maybe worked that out from his floppy fair hair and the Sebago deck shoes sticking out from below his regulation black uniform trousers. The hostess offered me a glass of Krug as we took off; I accepted, not to drink it, but just to hold as the apricot-tinted summer clouds closed in an obliging Turner skyscape over the Thames beneath us. I had sold out everything I had thought I believed in, and at that moment, with the soft leather behind my shoulders and the smell of fresh croissants from the galley, it felt really, really good.

Like all fake democracies, Azerbaijan has a super-snazzy airport. Aliyev's terminal was a wonder of cascading steel and glass, though I only got to view the exterior, as we and the Gauguin were loaded immediately into the diplomatic car waiting on the tarmac, in order to comply with the insurance.

Once the canvas and the guards were deposited, I was to go on to the Four Seasons, where Zulfugarly had provided a suite.

'Are you coming over to the hotel too?' I asked Hugh as we watched the crate containing the Gauguin being wheeled into the embassy lobby beneath the watchful gazes of Her Majesty and Karel.

'No, um, I'm staying here, actually. My godfather's brother does something at the British consulate, so I'm a guest at the residence.'

'Of course you are. Well, I'll see you here in the morning.'

'Unless you'd like me to accompany you to the dinner?' he asked hopefully.

'No, I'm sure Rupert would prefer that you stay with the picture. Wouldn't want to bust your cover!'

'Oh-er, righty-ho.'

Once I'd signed for the deposit of the canvas, I took a cab – a London cab, only it was painted bright purple – to the hotel, skirting the edge of the Icheri Sheher, the medieval town, dwarfed by its frill of skyscrapers. There was an hour to enjoy the flocculent whiteness of the Beaux Arts suite before dinner with Zulfugarly, but after laying out my dress, the same pattered Erdem silk I had worn to Carlotta's wedding the previous summer, I felt twitchy, somehow caged. The air conditioning was on at full blast and the view of the pompous Soviet cityscape from the sealed windows was more unnerving than the concrete walls of the shed in Calabria. And the room was full of lilies, parasitical de-stemmed callas. I pressed the button for the floor butler and had them taken away, but their scent lingered, suspended on the stale, gelid air.

Zulfugarly had sent an enormous Bentley to drive me the short distance to the restaurant, complete with capped chauffeur and a bodyguard who carried his gun in a dinky leather manbag. There was a black Bulgari carrier, much beribboned, waiting for me on the back seat, containing one of the horrible triple-gold bracelets inscribed with the brand name. I clipped it reluctantly over my wrist as we arrived at the Caravanserai Bukhara, where the bodyguard informed me Mr Zulfugarly was waiting in a private room. My heart sank a little at that news, but the restaurant was in the open air, stone pavilions around a courtyard with an ancient fountain, their arches hung with white silk curtains. Vines and pomegranate trees gave it the feeling of an oasis.

'Welcome to Baku, Miss Teerlinc!'

Zulfugarly was waiting outside the central pavilion, looking exactly as I expected him to: tailored shirt unbuttoned over a froth of chest hair, slightly ambitious jeans, Gucci loafers, Hermès belt, Hublot orb on his left wrist – standard uniform for the socially anxious mogul.

'What a wonderful place! I'm so delighted to be here!'

'I'm Heydar, Heydar Zulfugarly. My friends call me Hay-Z!'

There was a pause, into which we dived awkwardly for the double cheek-brush. Zulfugarly explained that the Caravanserai was really that, one of the gathering places for merchants on the Silk Road for thousands of years. After I'd recovered from the offensive capabilities of his aftershave, made suitable cooing noises about the ancient merchants and his generous gift of the bracelet, there was another pause. The bodyguard had joined his doppelganger at a wooden table set for two in the courtyard. Zulfugarly toyed with his phone.

'It's UNESCO protected,' he dropped into the silence. He sounded rather regretful about that.

Pull yourself together, Judith. This is the easy part. Why are you standing here gawking?

I gave myself a little shake and for the next two hours concentrated on making Zulfugarly feel as good as possible short of blowing him. Like most men, his favourite topic of conversation was himself, so all I had to do was wheel out a carefully researched question now and then to keep him chatting. Over drinks – Japanese whisky for him, a musky, sweetish white wine for me – we had an inventory of his real estate holdings in the city, his vision for the future of Azerbaijan, which mostly seemed to involve turning it into Dubai, his connections in Silicon Valley and his love of New York. When I'd worked as a hostess at a London bar I'd learned a trick to stop you from yawning: pressing the tongue against the roof of the mouth. I used that quite a lot.

Dinner was delicious, fat little pancakes stuffed with spinach and pumpkin, a salad of sharp white cheese spiked with tarragon and chervil and an extraordinary dish of lamb meatballs carried in on a brazier with a bucket beneath it, into which the waiter dropped a blackened horseshoe he had first heated on the coals.

'*Fisindjan*,' Zulfugarly explained as a sticky dark sauce was ladled over the meat. It tasted of plums and molasses, smoky and sweet. We ate it with little cakes of saffron and almond rice rolled in flatbread and a thick wine almost as black as the sauce.

'чернила,' I said as we raised our glasses. 'Ink.'

'You speak Russian?'

'A little. But you must tell me about your plans for the cultural institute.'

By the time he'd finished doing that, the first bottle of wine was gone and we were the best of friends. Regrettably, Zaha Hadid had passed away before Zulfugarly could engage her for the job, but he had hired a French architect who had produced a design which looked remarkably like one of the tulip-shaped glasses in which we had been served tea with cherry jam. A space had been bought on the Bulvar, the wide promenade on the Caspian waterfront, and the project, Zulfugarly told me with relish, had already cost him over a hundred million.

'And that's before I buy your Gauguin!'

'You intend to bid for it?'

'I intend to have it.'

'You're very confident,' I smiled. 'You haven't even seen it yet. Perhaps you won't care for it.'

He looked puzzled. 'But it's a Gauguin.'

A trio of musicians in embroidered tunics over pale blue shirts and baggy black trousers had set up in the courtyard. One held what looked like a four-stringed guitar between his knees, another a fat-bellied mandolin, the third a skin drum the size of a dinner plate, which he struck with the backs of his fingernails. They began a wavering tune that dipped and wandered on the edge of a major key, playfully melancholic and deceptively repetitive until you listened through each layer of sound and heard it shift, turning towards a theme that never quite arrived. It was lovely, and I wished I could understand it, which was perhaps the best that would be said by any of the benighted visitors to Zulfugarly's institute. As he droned on about his 'artistic crusade', I wondered whether he actually believed any of it, if he truly thought it was any more than a lousy PR opportunity for in-flight magazines, if there could be any connection between the strange constrained wildness of the music he was ignoring, in this ancient and extraordinary place, and a collection of canvas squares which would appear as monotonous and alien to their viewers as the repetitions of the jigsaws of a *mashrabieh* screen would seem to me. I didn't say that, of course. I widened my eyes and ran a knuckle along my jaw and nodded earnestly while I looked up at him under my lashes with my head tilted to one side, until the sum of those small, obvious gestures had shifted the power balance between us to the point where he had entirely forgotten that it was all on my side. Sometimes, they actually are that dumb.

'By the way, may I ask who you're using for the assessment at the embassy tomorrow?'

'I flew Solomon Mathis in this afternoon.'

'Wow. He's good.'

For someone who in life had been the size of a nine-year-old, Mackenzie Pratt's reach from beyond the grave was impressive. Mathis was the expert who had called Rupert to warn him of Pratt's accusations. *Had he accepted the job out of curiosity, or because he wanted to score a coup against the House?*

Zulfugarly put an arm around me and pulled me close. 'Are you worried, Miss Teerlinc? Do you think Solomon will tell me you are selling a fake? Ha ha!' He pronounced the laugh as though he'd learned to from comic books.

'If I am, then you've got the right man to spot it!' I swallowed hard. 'Hay-Z's no fool!'

What were the odds? Mathis was a leading Gauguin expert – if the picture passed, Zulfugarly would surely stay in. Possibly good. But if it didn't? I let my body rest a moment longer against Zulfugarly's odorous bulk. *If it didn't, maybe I'd just have to stay in Baku.*

Zulfugarly was all for going on to the newly opened branch of Pacha, where of course he had the best table, but there were few things I could imagine fancying less than a night on the tiles with Borat's less sophisticated brother, so I pleaded tiredness as prettily as I could manage between thinking of where I'd like to shove that horseshoe. No harm in keeping him keen. He loaded me ceremoniously into the Bentley and I asked the driver to wait while he loaded himself less ceremoniously into his waiting Ferrari. It was actually covered in black velvet. As soon as he'd roared away, I told the driver I wanted to go for a walk. The bodyguard leaped assiduously to my side, but after a few fruitless minutes of insisting that I wanted to walk back to the hotel alone I quieted his concerns with a couple of fifty-euro notes.

Locking my hands behind my back, I stretched as I crossed the wide space in front of the Caravanserai and dived into the alleys of the old city. I had no desire to go back to that white coffin of a room.

The lanes of the Icheri Sheher reminded me of the medina in Tangier, except that they were unnaturally clean and empty. It wasn't late, and the night was warm, with just a satiny coolness from the sea trailing through the recessed arches of the gateways, yet aside from the odd tourist taxi rattling over the polished cobbles, the old town seemed deserted. Not that I minded; I like remembering that I'm a cat who walks by myself. Yellow wicks in foil bowls burned at the street corners, heightening the shadows of the low doorways, and I trailed my fingers along the walls as I wandered, feeling the contained warmth of the day's sun.

Notwithstanding the quietness, it took me a few minutes to notice that someone was following me. I was wearing flat, studded Valentino sandals that made no echo on the stones, but I could hear footsteps that weren't mine. I paused, and so did they; I walked a little, and they continued. I stopped again and lit a cigarette, glancing behind me in the flare of the lighter. No one. I made a right turn, thinking to double back towards the open space near the Caravanserai, but my first pass set me against the wall of the fortress. I doubled back, went left up a steep alley. The footsteps were getting closer; I could sense that whoever was trailing me was placing their feet carefully. A man, by the weight of them. As I speeded up, the thick walls of the buildings vanished from my peripheral vision, my pupils seeking each passing pool of brightness from the candles as I flowed into a run, holding the silk of my skirt. There wasn't much of use in my small clutch – my phone, the key card from the hotel, my wallet, a tube of lip gloss. Then I remembered the thick band of gold encircling my wrist, Zulfugarly's present. At the top of the hill the alley gave into a small high-walled square. I ducked against the angle of the corner building and held my breath, unfastening the bracelet. After a few moments, the figure that had been pursuing me emerged on the flat, passing me into the square, looking from side to side, but not behind. Before he had time to turn, I stepped forward and grasped for the collar of his jacket with my left hand, bringing the bracelet as hard as I could against his temple with my right. It bounced onto the flagstones as he staggered soundlessly, groping round for me. I feinted left, then sent a right hook to his windpipe which took him down. A sensible woman would have legged it at that point, but I straddled him, taking a handful of his hair ready to smash his face down on the stones.

'Jesus! Wait! I didn't mean to frighten you.'

'You didn't frighten me. I have an abnormally low startle response to aversive stimuli, Romero. Hadn't you noticed?'

'What?'

I let up a bit, so he could turn over beneath me. I put my hand first to his heart, then along his collarbone and up to where I'd hit him.

'Judith. I came all the way from Bari. I just wanted—'

'Shut up.' I bent forward and kissed him. Gently at first, thoughtfully, a few slow, curious pads with my lips, and then more deeply, searching out his tongue, pushing deep into his mouth. His arms came around me, tighter, pulling me onto him as my hair fell around his face. I reached back, under my dress, settling on the mound of his cock.

'What are you doing?'

'Well, I thought, since we're here.'

He slapped my face. Hard enough to hurt, but I could feel he was smiling.

'*Puttana.*'

I stretched my fingers around his bruised neck, gripping harder, squeezing.

'Am I?'

'You know it.'

He ripped the sodden scrap of my knickers from me and was in me before he stood, getting to his feet in one movement which pushed him further as we came upright, my legs locked behind his back as we made an ungainly waddle for the wall where I had waited to jump him. His trousers pooled around his ankles and I dug my nails into his arse as he forced my head back with his forearm, biting at my throat.

'Harder,' I told him, but he'd read my mind, slamming me against the wall, the thick swelling of his cock finding the heat of me, stretching my cunt as I took his width.

'I said harder.'

'*Troia.*' He slapped me again, across the mouth, the report of the blow burning and tingling as he cupped both hands under my arse to ram me deeper, the bricks scouring my back as my cunt slid over him and we found a stabbing, urgent rhythm, getting closer with every push until I felt the clutch of pleasure unfold and the rush of my cum drench his hot prick as he lunged a last time and pumped out into me in three long, shuddering gouts.

My hips were spread so wide he had to lift me off him. I straightened the remains of my dress, thought of hunting for my knickers, decided it wasn't worth the bother. I concentrated instead on finding the bracelet, which might come in handy. My pulse was finally beating again; I could hear it as he rearranged himself, buckling his belt, twitching his torn collar into place.

It turned out the Caravanserai was just around the corner after all. We left the old town hand in hand.

'Why did you come?' I asked him in the cab back to the hotel.

'I wanted to see you were OK.'

'You could have called.'

'So, maybe I missed you.'

'You'll be staying, then?'

'Until you leave. If that's OK. And then I'll see you in London, for the sale.'

It was OK. There were too many echoes waiting around my bed. It would be good to have da Silva in it.

23

Solomon Mathis was waiting for me outside the embassy at 10 a.m. the next day, balding and dark-bearded in a neat, pale-blue linen suit. We introduced ourselves, then he asked if he could have a word before Zulfugarly arrived.

'I needed to tell you, Miss Teerlinc, that I had a call from Mackenzie Pratt. Some weeks ago, around the time that the sale was announced.'

'I was aware of that,' I answered carefully.

'Then you know that the, um, late Miss Pratt said she believed the work to be a fake?'

'Indeed.'

'Obviously this was long before Mr Zulfugarly asked me to advise him.'

I suddenly saw where this was going. From the studiedly bland expression on Mathis's face, I knew we both did. I waited for him to continue.

'I wanted to be the first to reassure you that I have the greatest respect for my colleagues in London and that, while of course I will act correctly on behalf of Mr Zulfugarly, I see this inspection as, on the whole, a formality. I should add,' he said hastily, 'that I am assessing the picture for him on behalf of IFAR.'

'I see.'

The International Foundation for Art Research provides an authentication service with a useful loophole in that its experts have the option to remain anonymous. Mathis had a very solid public reputation that he would be unwilling to compromise. Yet equally, Zulfugarly would be willing to pay a lot to be told what he wanted to hear. By going through IFAR, Mathis could collect his – probably enormous – fee and save his face if the picture was later exposed as a dud. Zulfugarly, meanwhile, wouldn't necessarily appreciate the distinction between an IFAR assessment and a definitive confirmation.

Mathis was watching me intently. He had told me his position, but the slightest hint of relief from me could shift it.

'It was so terrible, what happened,' I said seriously. 'You know, I was actually there that night – there was a dinner for some House clients.'

'Yes, I read about it. You must have been very shocked.'

'She'll be greatly missed.'

'Of course. Perhaps, it would be more . . . respectful to keep Miss Pratt's opinions confidential, in so far as we can?'

'I couldn't agree more. Thank you. It was very good of you to be so transparent, and of course I shan't mention it.'

It wasn't entirely clear whether we were referring to Pratt's meddling or the IFAR clause, which suited us both fine. We shook hands, like tennis players before a match.

'I hope you enjoy the picture.'

'I'm sure I shall.'

Since I wasn't allowed to be in the room during the inspection, I took a seat at a café across the road and ordered a thick, cardamom-scented coffee while I watched Zulfugarly and his bodyguards rock up in a pair of lumpen Mercedes jeeps. They disappeared into the building and a few minutes later my phone pinged with a message from Hugh.

He's here. With Solomon Mathis. I'll have my eyes peeled!

Where else did the idiot think Zulfugarly was going to be?

I lit a fag and stubbed it out again. They would be in there for hours, or at least Mathis would, Hugh and Karel standing guard the whole time. It felt odd, to have nothing particular to do. Then my phone pinged again. Da Silva.

Want to come back to bed?

I couldn't help smiling. Perhaps I did have something else to do after all.

Hugh called at just after 3 p.m. I was lying across da Silva's chest, one hand resting on his cock. He was stroking my hair as we dozed.

'Well?'

'It's good. I mean, Mathis said he had to go and write up his assessment, but I saw him giving Zulfugarly the nod. He'll bid.'

'Have you told Rupert?'

'Not yet, I thought you'd want to know first.'

Da Silva was sitting up, casting about for his trousers. They'd somehow ended up on the balcony.

'Brilliant. Give him a call now. He'll be waiting. I'll be down in an hour to sign out the picture.'

'Sure. And will I tell them to get the plane ready?' I could feel how much Hugh had been looking forward to saying that.

'You do that. Thanks.'

Da Silva pulled me back onto the tangled nest of sheets. 'You're leaving?'

'Don't you want to know what they said about the picture?'

'I don't care. Stay here.'

I pulled away. 'I can't. You know I can't. But . . .' – I couldn't believe I was doing this but the words seemed to come anyway – 'why don't you come back with me? Stay in London until the sale? I can talk you onto the plane, no problem.'

When I thought about it, I'd spent a disproportionate amount of my life waiting for da Silva. The long days by the lake after I'd killed Cameron Fitzpatrick, the long journey from Nice to Venice where he waited near Alvin Spencer's bones, the slow hours of my captivity in Calabria. But the seconds he took to answer my question then, in that hotel room that reeked of our sex, felt like the longest wait of all.

'Yes, Judith,' he said simply. 'Yes. I'd like that.'

'Baked beans,' exclaimed da Silva as the cab pulled up on Brook Street.

'What?'

'Baked beans. You know, those disgusting orange things. That's what I remember about England.'

For a double agent with Mafia connections, da Silva had travelled surprisingly little. He had visited London just once, on a day trip to do the sights, when he had been sent to England on a residential course to learn the language in Leicester.

'We lived with families,' he explained as the doorman took our bags and welcomed me back to Claridge's. 'We had dinner at six o'clock. It was always freezing. Grey, every day. I had to wear a sweater in the summer. And all the food was orange. Those – fish toes?'

'Fish fingers.'

'And the cornflakes. It was traumatic. I lost kilos.'

'Baked beans are lovely. And you'll see – it's not all like that. Come on.'

'Message for you, Miss Teerlinc,' called the concierge.

Zulfugarly had called the hotel and asked me to contact him directly. I sent da Silva up to the room for a shower and dialled Baku from the lobby. The Azeri answered on the first ring,

shouting over thumping house music. It was two in the morning there, Pacha time. The line crackled as Zulfugarly moved
outside, then his voice returned more clearly.

'So – I have spoken to Mr Mathis!'

'And you're satisfied?'

'Most satisfied. I would like to invite you to Saint-Tropez
this weekend, if you have no engagements. There's something
I would like to discuss with you.'

'Can't we speak on the phone?'

'I would prefer to see you again in person. I have a place
there, you will be my guest.'

'Ummm – let me think about it and check my diary.'

Da Silva was stretched out on the bed in a bath towel in a
cloud of Cowshed patchouli shower gel. He opened his arms,
but I dodged away and began stripping off my clothes.

'I feel disgusting after the plane. I'll have a shower and then
how about room service? No beans.'

'Perfect, *amore mio*.'

*My love. He had called me 'my love' and he didn't even have
his cock up me. That had to count.*

First thing next morning, I called Carlotta.

'Oh my God – where have you been? I'm like, five months
pregnant!'

'That's brilliant, congratulations, I'm so happy for you! Is
it—?'

'Twin girls. Franz is thrilled.'

'Are you two in Monaco for the summer?'

Carlotta sighed heavily. 'Yeah – I mean, I wanted to go to
Mykonos but Franz said it would be too stressful for me. Like,

I'm pregnant, is all. So I'm stuck in this dump until we go back to Switzerland.'

The dump being Franz's rather beautiful art deco house near the Palais des Princes.

'Fancy popping over to Saint-Trop'? If hubby will allow it?'

'Shut up! Of course – there's like, no one here right now, I'm dying of boredom. We'll go to the Byblos?'

'Great. I'll sort us some rooms.'

'It'll be my babymoon!' she squealed. 'Only, like, without Franz. By the way, what happened with that Russian guy?'

'Maybe you'll get to meet him.'

'I'd say amazing but I'm, like, really fat right now.'

'Who's him?' asked da Silva, turning over and licking the back of my neck.

'Someone I have to see. Two people, actually. I have to go to the South of France the day after tomorrow.'

'We only just got here. Can I come?'

'No. This is work, darling. I think it's worth it.'

'What about me?'

'Don't be needy, it's not sexy. You're going to stay here and go to the British Museum and the Eye or whatever. Have a holiday. If you can square it with Franci, that is,' I added nastily.

He got up and went into the bathroom. I sent a quick message to Yermolov, asking if he was on the Côte, and then replied to Zulfugarly, saying that I would make my own arrangements for accommodation and suggesting we meet for lunch at 55.

Da Silva flushed the loo and hunched back into bed. I began a trail of kisses down his body, stroking the tight muscle with my tongue.

'No sulking. I've invited a girlfriend, so I'll have a chaperone. I'll only be gone two days.'

'Two days is forever, *amore.*'

I carried on stroking my tongue over his chest, his stomach, until my lips found their destination. I don't imagine I'm the first woman to have thought about shopping while performing oral sex. I'd need some new things for the trip. *I was going on a girls' weekend and if the evidence in my mouth was anything to go by, I'd also found a boyfriend. Hark at Little Miss Normal.*

24

The first sight of the Mediterranean as the plane comes in at Nice airport always gives me a thrill. Maybe because the runway seems to be built right into the water, so there's always that delicious moment of tension when the pilot dodges the waves. It had been a long while since my first visit, all thrilled about a weekend at the Eden Roc, and I'd learned with time that it's a bit naff to love the Riviera. Overbuilt, brash, crowded as it was, it still made me feel that I'd *arrived* in a way that nowhere else quite could. Admittedly, that trip hadn't worked out too brilliantly in some ways, what with my two latter-day travelling companions ending up dead, but the bougainvillea was just as bright and the sky over Cap Ferrat was just as sparkling and this time I was paying for it myself, not with a blowjob for a fat bloke. Seeing Carlotta waiting for me at the gate made me realise how far we'd both come, in our different ways.

Aside from the bump, Carlotta looked just the same – the only fat thing about her apart from her gargantuan breasts was the massive diamond pendant nestling in the hollow of her throat.

'Push present,' she explained, after we'd done the obligatory squealing and hugging and the porter was pushing our bags to the car. 'Only, like, in advance.'

'When are the babies due?'

'Well, technically in October, but I'm booked in for the caesar in Zurich in September.'

'I suppose with twins you can't be too careful.'

'Yah, that's what I told Franz. But actually I want to make the window to put their names down for Le Rosey.'

One of the many things I admired about Carlotta, aside from her iron grip on the main chance, was her discipline. She could have been a general in another life.

'So – the Russian?' she asked as we settled down in the Mercedes for the two-hour drive to Saint-Tropez.

'His name is Pavel Yermolov. He's giving us dinner tonight. So long as you won't be too tired, of course.'

'Tired? I mean, like, all I've been doing this summer is resting. In fucking Monaco. I mean, it's like soooo lame.'

I could remember when Carlotta would have given her implants for a place in Monaco, but I let it pass.

'He's more of a friend really. Not a prospect. But I have . . . met someone, maybe? An Italian?'

I could hear my voice taking on the ringing upspeak I'd used back when Carlotta and I were girls on a boat, on the make.

'Yummy. Is he rich?'

'Poor but honest.' *At least, as I understood honest.*

'How's the sex?'

'Good. Very good. Really fucking excellent, actually.'

'Franz hasn't touched me since we got the results of the pregnancy test.'

I couldn't see that this was much of a loss, given that Franz was north of seventy with a taste for urolagnia, but I tried to say something reassuring about him being worried for the babies.

'It's illogical, but totally normal.'

'Yah. It's just after the birth I'm bothered about.'

* * *

Carlotta said she fancied a nap after all when we arrived at the Byblos, so I spent the afternoon swimming laps, reading by the pool and going over my plans for the day after the sale. The train ticket was still waiting in its locker at the St Pancras Metro Express. But maybe I wouldn't have to use it after all. Flipping on my back, I floated in the soft water, paddling my hands as I drifted, my face turned to the cobalt Mediterranean heavens. Maybe I daydreamed, just a little.

At six, I went up to dress. I was more excited than I felt I ought to be at the prospect of seeing Yermolov after seven months, so naturally the last thing I wanted was to look as though I'd made an effort. I eventually picked out a pale-grey coarse linen Caravane dress with a double-looped brown leather Isabel Marant belt and simple flat sandals. I have a theory that once a man has seen you naked you don't need to worry about heels. But I fiddled with my hair much longer than usual and made up my face for twenty minutes before wiping it all off again.

'Are you wearing that, darling?'

Carlotta was in a billowing Luisa Beccaria empire line in rag-washed white muslin. She looked vaguely as though she was sitting for Élisabeth Vigée le Brun, one half of the female artists from whom I had chosen my alias. I'd texted Yermolov to remind him to call me 'Elisabeth'; equally I'd explained to Carlotta at her wedding the previous summer that I'd switched from 'Lauren', as she'd first known me, for business reasons. God, my life was exhausting.

'I mean, you look gorgeous, but you said the Italian's like, poor? You don't want to limit your options.'

'I like him, Carlotta. We have a lot in common.'

'Like, a spiritual connection?'

'You could say that.'

'Then you have to respect it. That's just how I felt about Franz, you know.'

I regretted my dress as soon as we arrived at La Vague d'Or, where Yermolov had a table at eight. I'd supposed he had company, since he'd turned down my request to dine at his house just out of town and take another look at his pictures, but I hadn't guessed that the company would be six foot five in heels. No wonder Mackenzie Pratt's life had been so bitter. Tatiana made me feel like a gnat as she bent down to kiss a perfunctory hello. Still, there are few things more boring than a hostile woman and my badly accented Russian wasn't too rusty, so I did my best to make friendly conversation, aided by hefty swigs of a rather perfect Corton-Charlemagne. Carlotta was keeping her end up in English with Yermolov, the usual Eurochat about where everyone had been and where they were going next, the international rich version of the name game.

Tatiana informed me that she was a jewellery designer. I suppressed my commiserations and asked if she sold her work in London.

'I'd like to, but I'm just so busy, you know, travelling with Pavel.' She reached an etiolated arm across her untouched lobster tart and clutched possessively at Yermolov. I shot a look at Carlotta. I needed to speak to Yermolov alone, but Tatiana obviously had no intention of letting him out of her sight. Carlotta excused herself to go to the bathroom, Yermolov bobbed up politely as she stood and then caught her arm as she tottered sideways, her bump swinging neatly round to knock Tatiana's cosmopolitan all over her skintight

Alaia jumpsuit. Waiters rushed up with napkins, but there was nothing for Tatiana to do except retire to repair the damage, Carlotta clucking apologetically in her wake. Yermolov switched to English.

'That was mean, Judith.'

'Well, if you will associate with the kind of girl who drinks cocktails through dinner. She'll be back in a moment. I need you to come to the sale at the House on 5 July. And I want you to bid for a painting. Not to buy it, just bid. Bid high. It's a Gauguin, *Woman with a Fan II.*'

'Yes, I've seen the catalogue. And the newspapers, in fact. So why shouldn't I want to acquire such an important picture?'

'Believe me, you don't want to. But I want you to pretend you really, really do. Will you help?'

'I'm always glad to help out . . . a friend. But why so urgent?'

'Dejan Raznatovic.'

'Ah.'

Nowadays, Yermolov's billions were one hundred per cent legit, but I knew I wouldn't have to explain who Raznatovic was.

'There are other ways of avoiding Raznatovic, surely?'

'Pavel, please. I'm planning on avoiding him anyway. I'll have to. But this, first. To buy me some time?'

'And in exchange?'

'What do I have that you could possibly want?'

'You are looking very serious this evening.'

'You mean dowdy.'

'Dowdy? Yes, that word. Perhaps these will cheer you up. Open it later.'

He handed me a small package under the table.

'What are your plans – after the sale?'

'What about her?'

'Tatiana? She is . . . temporary.'

'In which case I'm open to offers. Maybe. I can't promise. I have to see how things work out in . . . in London. But I do need you to bid for that picture.'

'Then I will be in London. And then we'll see.'

'I've been dreaming of your paintings, you know, Pavel.'

Yermolov rose to his feet again just as the ladies returned to the table. Tatiana had turned her stained pants into a playsuit by cutting them off. A waiter bore the drooping tubes of fabric over his arm behind her. Even amongst the stiff professional competition in a three-star restaurant in Saint-Tropez in mid-June her legs made a temporary vacuum tunnel along the terrace as she passed. Yermolov kissed her shoulder from behind.

'We'll go shopping tomorrow, baby,' he murmured, but his eyes remained on my face. It was odd to think I had once been afraid of him.

'He's, like, totally obsessed with you!'

Carlotta and I were having a cup of camomile tea on her balcony at the Byblos. I hadn't lit up from deference to the twins.

'We've got history, but you saw Brienne of Tarth back there.'

'Nah, this place is crawling with girls exactly like her.' The mink at the very corners of her eyelashes fluttered. 'We should know.'

'He gave me something.' I chucked the little box I had concealed in my bag over to her.

'Asprey's? Bit meh. I would have expected Harry Winston at least from a Russian. Oh. Rewind. Have a look at these babies!'

The earrings were a Belle Époque design, diamond pears the size of the ball of my thumb in a triple-strut curved pendant.

'I *told* you!' shrieked Carlotta.

I turned one of the earrings upside down. The set of the stones from that angle looked like the plumes of a fan. *Pretty good, Yermolov, pretty good.*

'At least Franz is decent with jewels,' Carlotta was saying, fingering her necklace complacently. 'I mean, before I was engaged to Hermann. You remember Hermann? Before Franz?'

'The one who went to jail?'

'Yah, so him. He was a total pig. So anyway, I was seeing this guy and he got me a pair of studs from like, Tiffany's. I mean, seriously?'

'Your life is a vale of tears, Carlotta.'

'You wanna go down to Les Caves for a bit?'

'Sure.'

'Then put these on and change that sack, will you?'

Zulfugarly had informed me proudly that we had a one o'clock appointment at 55, explaining, in case I didn't know, that only regulars could get a table before 3 p.m. He'd also sent a boat to take me round to Pampelonne, a Cerri whose thirty-odd metres was a bit unnecessary to give one person a lift. Still, perched cross-legged as far along the prow as I could get, with my hair streaming in the wind and the waves doing their limpid sparkly thing as we wound between the flotilla of showboats anchored in the Ramatuelle bay, I experienced a moment of what might have been mindfulness. Hay-Z was waiting on the jetty as the 55 tender chugged up to the club. I passed him my sandals and gathered the folds of my filmy azure Prism kaftan before letting the crewman hand me out.

Underneath I was wearing a white asymmetric Eres bikini, which Zulfugarly seemed to be appreciating.

'*Bonjour*, Patrice!' The owner of 55 flinched almost imperceptibly as Zulfugarly clapped him familiarly on the back.

'*Bonjour, madame*, Monsieur Zulfugarly, what a pleasure to see you again.'

Once we were installed amongst the blue and white linen with a bottle of rosé, and an order of sea bass and ratatouille, Zulfugarly informed me that he intended to buy the Gauguin. I said I was delighted, but that I couldn't quite understand why he had invited me to Saint-Tropez to tell me, delightful though it was to see him.

'I thought that perhaps we might come to an arrangement?'

'Do you mean a private sale?'

'Exactly.'

'And how do you envisage that working? Please remember that the picture isn't mine, I'm merely acting as the dealer.'

He gave me what I thought I was meant to take as a cunning look. Black sprouts of hair had wound their way through the shoulder seams of his white Vilebrequin shirt.

'Precisely. And for a private sale, with a pre-agreed price, I would also be willing to pay your gallery a brokerage fee. Gentileschi, yes?'

I took a tiny sip of rosé, as all the other women at the tables around us were doing. Watching them toy with their grilled fish and tomato salads, raising their forks to their mouths and replacing them still full on their plates, it seemed a perverse conspiracy that all social life on the Med was arranged around endless lunches and dinners at which the women were expected to consume virtually nothing, like Scarlett O'Hara at the barbecue in *Gone With the Wind*. I took off my sunglasses and looked Zulfugarly in the eye.

'How much?'

'One hundred for the picture plus ten for you.' He didn't need to state that he meant millions either.

'Sweet. I would be very interested . . . except—'

'Fifteen.'

'Mr Zulfugarly, I wouldn't insult you by bargaining. No, as I said, I'm acting for the Società Mutuale, and they were insistent that the picture was auctioned publicly. As you know it's already consigned, so there would be a withdrawal fee to consider.'

'What's the reserve?'

'A hundred.'

'Ten per cent on that plus fifteen to you makes a hundred and thirty-five. I could—'

I cut across him. 'But there's another reason. It's my duty to see that my client receives the best possible price. And I heard just recently that there's another buyer interested. Seriously interested.'

'Who?'

'I couldn't possibly say.'

'Of course.'

We went on with our lunch, Zulfugarly trying to conceal his irritation, finishing the wine quickly and calling for another bottle. At the table nearest the water a group of Arab guys were spraying a wriggling girl with '85 Dom Perignon. Two waiters scuttled over, not to stop them but to fend off a rubber dinghy of tourists who had got too close to the jetty with their selfie sticks. Next to us, two blond children were absorbed in their iPads, ignoring their specially prepared hamburgers with the same indifference they showed to the enticing line of wet sand on the shore, an indifference affected by the whole club when a famous actress in filthy cut-offs came through from the beach.

What would they do, these people, if a boatload of refugees washed up right here amongst the effluvia of capitalism? Jump to it and get stuck in with an urgent black tie charity gala and earnest speech by Leonardo DiCaprio? *Like you give a toss, Judith.* There was one place I intended to stay, and it wasn't the section of the beach reserved for the gawping public.

'Actually,' I leaned forward naughtily to Zulfugarly, 'shall I tell you a secret? The buyer? It's Pavel Yermolov. Will you be attending the auction in person?'

'I have to be in New York.'

'What a pity.' I reached for his hand over the table. I had reluctantly brought the Bulgari bracelet with me. 'I'd hoped we might celebrate together. When you get it.'

He stroked the inside of my forearm. 'So you're turning me down?'

'I should have said the opposite.'

I sat back. *OK, let's see who's got the biggest dick after all.* Job done.

Sometimes it happens that you have been sitting indoors all afternoon, reading perhaps, and someone comes in and turns on the light, and only then do you realise that it is twilight outside, that you have been sitting in the gathering dark without noticing. That was how I felt those days with da Silva in London, that the world had taken on a patina of drabness which he had cleaned away. Like – well, like the varnish on a painting. Perhaps it was because he could actually see me, had been there, somehow, since it all began, and that there was nothing, absolutely nothing, that I had to hide. That sounds creepy, but it didn't feel creepy. It felt wonderful.

With the sale all set, there was nothing for me to do except attend the occasional drinks party with Rupert or Charles Eagles. Angelica was 'working from home', or at least someone's home on Formentera, though she would return for the sale. Rupert was terribly proud of the way he had brilliantly taken control of the Gauguin story. As he explained to the department, it was 'all about owning the media narrative'. Charles Eagles had rallied round with a call to his close personal friends at the *Tatler*, and after a piece on their website entitled 'Bid-Off!' was posted, Mackenzie's righteous concerns were dust. Newspaper profiles of Yermolov and Zulfugarly speculated on which of them would win the picture, and I sent Pandora round to William Hill with a tenner to start the betting, followed up naturally with a discreet call to the gossip columns.

* * *

Yet none of the excitement building up around the sale felt quite real to me any more. All I could see was Romero. I'd tear myself out of bed, dash to whatever event I was attending and make half an hour's distracted small talk, the white noise of my want for him booming all the time in my head, until I could escape back to him, the nest our bodies had made on the bedclothes still warm. I don't know that either of us had ever really made love before. I don't think I'd ever even thought of it. The first times we had been together, there had been a clumsiness about his desire that I found immeasurably touching. Sex was at one remove from him, something he had watched on a screen, the words and gestures what he thought he should be doing, rather than what he wanted to do. It had never interested me before – a lover had only ever been good or bad, to me – but with a combination of boldness and tenderness I had never imagined I could possess, I wanted to teach him. And I did, and in doing so I taught myself, and it was wonderful, because no one was acting any more. What we did wasn't always gentle or loving, though often it was. Under their clothes, our skins were a map of striving pleasure – his fingerprints wealed deep in the smooth inside of my thigh, a bloody quartet of stripes on his shoulder. I was swollen and bitten and bruised, and when he wasn't inside me I felt nothing but the hollow weight of his lack.

It didn't matter that he hadn't read much and didn't care about pictures, or that my Italian sometimes got tangled up when I was trying to explain something to him. We agreed that we had never doubted that we would be together, that it had only ever been a matter of when, an unspoken question that had hung between us since we first saw one another. So now our conversations were fascinating because they were about ourselves – *what did you feel that time? how did you know then?* And maybe there was something monstrous in our complicity, but it felt strange and beautiful to us, the lovers' privilege that I had never thought to claim. The only thing we didn't talk about was what was going to happen after the sale. He faceTimed his wife and children when I was out, I knew, and I appreciated that he tried to be discreet about it. And I couldn't quite bear to contemplate the awful cliché of an affair with a married man, so I did what women mostly do about it, and pretended it didn't exist.

Apart from my mother and Dave, I'd never really had any-one to buy presents for. Romero had pretty obvious taste, but it amused me to indulge it. His delight in new things reminded me of how I had been, once, and somewhere, maybe, I thought that if I dressed him for a new life he might be more inclined to want one. So when we weren't in bed, or dining at all the restaurants I'd wanted to go to when I lived in London and had never been able to afford, I took him shopping. We ordered shirts at Turnbull & Asser and shoes at Edward Green, the softest scarves and cashmere sweaters, a real English suit from Savile Row. I wanted to spoil him, to give him gifts until everything he owned was perfect. I knew it was vulgar and silly, but I didn't care.

The night before the sale we went to a small French place in Bermondsey. After the wine was poured I handed Romero a box. A Rolex Daytona – not what I would have chosen, but I knew he'd love it. I'd taken it to the silversmith's in Marylebone Lane to have the back engraved. *Sempre.* Forever. He weighed it between his hands before fastening the bracelet.

'Judith. Thank you. It's fantastic, beautiful. I wish I could give you things like this.'

'I get more pleasure out of giving them to you.'

'I won't be able to wear it,' he added sadly.

'Yes you will. Say it's part of a . . . a cunning undercover operation.'

'I'm sorry. I'm so sorry, you know, that things can't be different.'

'Please, let's not talk about it. There's nothing to say. Let's just be here.'

Later, when we had walked home first through the cobbled Victorian streets and then along under the lights of the Embankment and around St James's Park, and later still, when we had drenched the sheets, I finally asked him the question that had been humming through my mind since the spring.

I felt for his face in the dark, kissed his eyelids, the sides of his mouth, the sweet hollow under his ear.

'Can I ask you something?' My face was in his neck, my lips on the steady, familiar throb of his pulse.

'Anything, my love.'

'Just when exactly were you planning to kill me?'

His heart remained quiet. No tension, no reaction. He turned on his elbow above me and set his mouth on mine, a kiss with the warm promise of a bruise.

'Tomorrow, sweetheart. Or maybe the day after.'

I hit him with the pillow. 'You bastard!'

'How do you know I'm joking?'

I sat up and hugged the duvet round my knees. 'I don't. But I have a suggestion.'

He lay back and clicked his Dupont. Claridge's had a very civilised policy on smoking, which was strictly forbidden.

'This. This thing. Us. It doesn't have to stop. We can get away.'

'You know that's impossible, *tesoro*.'

'I know that Raznatovic wants me dead. But what if I were to come back to Calabria with you after the sale and instead of bunging me in Salvatore's pit, we just . . . disappear?' I let that sink in for a moment before I continued. 'I think the picture will go over the reserve. That guy from Baku – he's desperate to have it. Yermolov will raise him, the bid will be huge. And the money goes to the Società in the first instance – to the bank. You direct them where to send Raznatovic's cut, so you can also take out mine. A lot of money, Romero. Real money. And then we're gone.'

He lay back, locked his hands behind his head. I took the fag from between his lips and had a long drag. I'd watched him liking the way we lived, the deferential staff, the clothes, the day's biggest decision being whether to have the oysters or the *foie gras*. I didn't hate him for it – I was that way myself.

'I can't leave.'

'Yes you can. New papers, new identity, new life. I've done it, God knows.'

'I mean I can't leave the children.'

I was getting exasperated despite myself. 'I saw you. With the baby. The restorer's baby, what was her name, Mariangela? Her little boy. You *learned* it. You don't feel it. You know I know. Because we're the same.'

A long pause. Then he said in English, 'It's a fair cop.' I smiled in the dark. He'd learned the phrase from me.

'And,' I swallowed, played my last card, 'if you wanted another one? A child, I mean, then we could, I mean, I would . . .'

He reached for my hand. 'Do you mean that?'

'Yes.'

'But how?'

'I've thought it all through. We could do it. All you have to do is . . . pretend that you've got rid of me. Raznatovic will believe you. And then we'll go to Amsterdam for the documents, I know a guy there, and I know how to hide money. You'll be done. No more of "them".'

'I always said you were good.'

'Is that a yes?'

'You're crazy.'

I felt sick.

'So that's a no?'

'Crazy but good. It's a yes.'

Gently, delicately, I laid my head on his chest. I was shaking. Everything I had said had been true, but I had somehow never believed in its possibility. Yet there were his arms around me, there the infinitely precious smell of his skin. It could be real. It actually could be. Real. For me. I think we lay there for a long while, then I felt him stir and clutched at him drowsily.

'Shhh, my love. I'll be back in just a moment.'

I turned over in our bed and heard water running in the bathroom. And somehow, that sound was more intimate to me than anything our bodies had done together. I felt scrubbed, luminescent, shiny with love. He was there, and at last I could feel quiet. As my eyes closed, I could hear the carillon clock down on Piccadilly striking midnight.

Why I did it I don't know. Why I had to be sure. But later, as he slept, I slid away from his body, wrapped myself in a robe and went to the drawing room of the suite to open my laptop. I hadn't told him about the emails, that I'd been reading them. I'd been ashamed that he'd think I was prying into his relationship with Franci, that I was the kind of woman who would be possessive and jealous. I tapped in the codes, I read the last message. It had been sent at 11.57 p.m.

The asset will be disposed of in 48 hours.

The clock sounded three. When I was finished with pushing everything down inside me, compacting it like the shit it was, I went back to the bedroom and lay down beside him in the dark. I didn't cry. I read somewhere once that as soon as a woman is sad, she is ordinary. And it turned out that I wasn't quite ready to give up on special. Not just yet.

26

Today's the day! chirped my phone brightly. Rupert was already up and at 'em. As I was dressing in a neat skirt and blouse with flat loafers, I explained to a half-awake da Silva that he needed me to go over a few last details before the sale.

'Sorry, I have to run, but I'll be back this afternoon, darling. *Ti amo*.'

Naturally the sun had chosen the day of the sale to shine.

First a bureau de change on Regent Street: ten thousand pounds cashed against my credit card by 8.05 a.m. Double espresso and a cigarette outside Pret, a text with three kisses to da Silva. Cab to Belgravia, to Lawrence's house in Chester Square. A part of me registered that it felt odd to be going there in daylight, but the last of the lilac hanging over the gardens smelled the same – if I closed my eyes I might have been one of my other selves, from long ago. I had always loved that part of the city, serene and secretive at once. The door was answered by Lawrence's batman-cum-bouncer, a relic from the party days. I remembered him, arms squarely folded over his muscle-packed shirt, watching implacably as a room full of naked bodies converged and separated, their patterns forming and reforming as seamlessly as ink in water.

'Hello, Kevin.'

He was already neatly dressed in slacks and a polo shirt, I could smell his fresh aftershave.

He weighed me up politely but thoroughly. I doubted that he recognised me but the fact that I knew his name told him just how we'd met before.

'I'm afraid Lord Kincardine isn't at home today, miss.'

'I came to find you, actually. Forgive the early hour, but it's rather urgent. May I come in?'

Kevin showed me to a small morning room on the ground floor. Like the rest of Lawrence's house, it was furnished with that uniquely toff mixture of impeccable antiques and shabby, domestic practicality which no decorator has ever been able to reproduce. I perched on a faded blue IKEA armchair positioned next to an exquisite Edo screen, a relief of cranes in pale silver and blue, with a bright orange Puffa jacket hanging off one edge.

'How can I help you, miss?'

I had always had a feeling about Kevin. He was the kind of person you'd want on your side in a fight. Or if you needed someone's legs broken.

'I thought you might be the right person to help me with a bit of business,' I began.

'I see.'

The silence that fell between us was as good as a conversation. Kevin played with the chunky signet ring on his left hand. There was a blue flash tattoo in the palm.

'I need a driver. A driver with a van. Someone . . . fit. And discreet. Very discreet. All he needs to do is hire it, meet me at a certain place at a precise time and help me load it. I need him today, I can return the van tomorrow. Nothing complicated, if you understand? Three thousand cash to the driver, one thousand to the . . . broker. In advance, of course.'

'I think I can find you someone, miss. If you'll excuse me while I make a call? May I fetch you some tea?'

'I'm fine, thank you.'

I extracted a Claridge's envelope from my bag and placed it on the arm of the chair, where we both studiously ignored it.

While he was gone I made a mental list. The next thing and the next thing. Just that.

He was back in about fifteen minutes with a phone number and an address written on a sheet of Lawrence's engraved writing paper.

'Kevin, that's wonderful. I can't say how much I appreciate your help.'

'May I suggest the Tube, miss? The traffic, at this hour . . .'

'Of course, I must be going. So nice to have seen you again, Kevin.'

'And you, miss. It's always a pleasure to assist a friend of Lord Kincardine.'

The envelope watched us out of the room.

Just after ten, I arrived at the Tottenham Hale retail park to meet with Kevin's mate Elvis who had texted me to say he was up for the job. I'd wondered if I ought to carry a copy of *The Times*, but there was only one lookalike of the King waiting in McDonald's.

'All right. You Kevin's bird?'

'That's it. So, this is what we're going to do.'

The thing was, I was going to need to get something out of the warehouse directly after the sale. Fairly heavy. And the mews which gave onto the back gate of the House was a strict no-waiting zone. I couldn't risk parking a vehicle there and then having a traffic warden fuck things up, and I had to get to the warehouse as soon as the sale was over. All I needed, I explained to Elvis, was for him to hire the van, park up in advance near the Haymarket and then drive down after I'd messaged him. Three grand for ten minutes. I'd picked up an old-fashioned *A–Z* and marked up the mews and the route to it on the journey over, adding a list of the items I would need and three hundred pounds further cash for expenses. The van would need to have a full tank.

'So you'll need to be in position from ten p.m. to be on the safe side, though I imagine it will be more like eleven.'

'All right.'

'Um – there's just one thing. You look amazing, but for the collection, do you think you might wear something less . . . memorable?'

The white-fringed suede jacket with silver lacing up the back and coordinating cowboy boots was actually a kind of fabulous look, but it might stand out in St James's.

'All right.'

A cab back into town put me back in Mayfair by eleven. I've always loved the Dickensian shops around Piccadilly – the cufflink specialist in the Burlington Arcade where you can find Victorian links set with long-dead children's teeth, the watch-menders and shirt-makers, Lock's hat shop, the specialist in military regalia which displays full dress uniforms and antique tricorn hats. Before going up to St John's Wood, I popped into Trumper's, the barbers on Curzon Street, where I bought their largest size bottle of extract of lime cologne in its sugar-pink box and an old-fashioned strop razor with a polished tortoiseshell handle. Then I walked through Shepherd Market and down to Jermyn Street to New & Lingwood for a selection of silk ties, and popped into Fox the tobacco merchant. Before picking up another cab on the Haymarket at about noon I also collected a packet of Brillo pads from Tesco Metro and a pair of latex gloves from Boots.

'Colonel Morris?' The thin-lipped, greying man who opened the door of the pale-stuccoed building looked exactly the same as he had on my first visit, down to the tweed trousers and Viyella shirt. I leaned in, beyond the range of the security camera over the door and raised my huge Dior sunglasses.

'I'm from British Pictures. I'm so sorry to disturb you, but we were wondering if we could possibly take a quick snap of your Sargent? It's for a catalogue.'

'It's not for sale,' he said rudely.

'Of course, I didn't mean that, I'm so sorry.' Dim and flustered, a bit awed. 'It's just my boss – you're such an important client, he said you wouldn't mind if I came to have a look. It's for the portraiture show in the autumn . . .' I looked at him under my lashes.

'Ah. Your boss sent you?'

'That's right.'

'I hope this won't take too long, I was just about to have lunch.'

'Only a minute, thank you so much!'

He led the way into the drawing room I remembered, with its heavy pastel curtains over linen blinds to protect the pictures. The Sargent, a satiny portrait in pinks and greys of a woman on a velvet armchair, her elaborate skirts tumbling towards the frame, hung above the fireplace. I pulled on the pair of latex gloves from my pocket and ran my fingertips reverentially over the smooth surface of the painting.

'Don't touch it!' snapped the colonel.

'Sorry, sorry – I'll, um, just get the camera.'

I put my bag on the carpet and bent over from the waist, presenting my ass like a baboon, chattering away about how we had Sargent's *Après-Midi* coming in and wanted some companion pictures for the catalogue. I felt him approach with the razor ready, and when that yellow-nailed hand I remembered so well reached for me I grabbed his wrist and spun round as I slashed downwards. It worked rather better than I expected. For a millisecond we both stared in surprise at the white bone revealed in the three-inch gash across the colonel's palm before it filled with blood and he roared, staggering back towards the hallway. I was quicker: I had the dripping blade against the canvas before he could get to his security system.

'I'd sit down, if I were you, Colonel. On the sofa, that's right. Here.' I tossed him a Garrick-colours salmon-and-cucumber tie.

'You can use that as a tourniquet. Hold it in your teeth.'

There was blood all over the floor, it was seeping into the floral sofa covers, into the turn-ups of the colonel's trousers. He did as I said, knotting the silk around his wrist and gripping it, mute and furious, between the tea-coloured stumps of his teeth.

'Now, I want you to get up and fetch the book from your bedroom. The album of photographs you showed me last time I was here.' His boiled eyes flared. 'Oh good, you remember. Now, go and fetch it, or your Sargent is ribbons. Got it? Nod if you understand.'

It was perfectly possible that he'd reappear aiming his trusty service revolver, but this was England. If the colonel was a sportsman his guns would be broken and locked away in a cupboard somewhere. Besides, the risk made it more fun – I was almost disappointed when he reappeared from the back room with only the heavy album of nineteenth-century erotica awkward in his good hand. I motioned him to set it down and he obeyed as if mesmerised, his gaze fixed on the painting as though it were his child I held prisoner.

'Now, turn around, hands behind you. Slowly. Let the tie out through your teeth. That's it, keep a good grip on the end.' I kept the open razor in my fist as I knotted a grey and burgundy striped number around his wrists. Ampleforth, I think.

'Now your legs.' I leaned away a little, and when he kicked out at me from behind as I knew he would, I caught one soggy ankle and held it while the rest of the colonel pitched face forward onto the floor. The tourniquet fell from his mouth as he screamed. Gingerly, I rolled up his trouser leg, held the razor to it over his thin sock.

'Oh dear. That was silly, wasn't it? Did I hear your nose breaking? Now, I'm going to tie up your legs and help you up. Or I can slash both your Achilles tendons and good luck calling the police with your eyebrows. OK? Here we go, then.' Jaunty red and blue, Radley College. Gripping his shirt collar, I set the blade on his throat and heaved him back into a kneeling position, classic hostage pose.

'What a mess. Shall we pop the tie back?' I poked it into the bloody pancake surrounding his worm of a moustache, then gagged him with the ugly mustard and white colours of Cranleigh for good measure.

When Rupert had first sent me to the colonel's home, I'd estimated there was a good ten million's worth of pictures on the walls: the Sargent, a Kneller, a small Rembrandt cartoon, a small Gainsborough landscape. As the colonel watched, I went round, unhooking them from their mounts, wrapped the Rembrandt in a copy of the *Metro* and put it in my bag, then laid out the other canvases along the less bloody patch of the carpet.

'You really have some lovely things, Colonel. But I do wonder whether they could do with a bit of a cleaning? Maybe we need to get them out of their frames – oops!'

The razor cut right across the Sargent lady's delicately rouged face, crunching a little as it cut through the varnish. The colonel began a spot of muffled hysterics. Gainsborough's airy spring downs went next, then I decapitated Kneller's spoon-faced clergyman.

'Time for a scrub! I seem to remember this is your preferred fragrance, Colonel?' *His acrid dried sweat cut with old-fashioned astringent cologne, his body pressing heavily on my lungs.*

I poured the entire bottle of Trumper's finest over the peeling canvases and set to work with a scouring pad. It took a few moments for the alcohol to start eating into the oil, but once I got going the pictures developed satisfying puddles in about ten minutes, though the colonel had bled rather a lot by then and fallen over sideways, straining desperately at his bindings. He looked like a toppled maypole.

'Oh dear. Perhaps the House shouldn't have sent a junior? But then that's what you always requested, isn't it? Asked Rupert to send the pretty ones? Not to worry, I'll bet you they're nicely insured. That right? All you'll need to do is give them a ring, then, after I've left. We'd better get you up though. Is there a landline? I'll move the table. There, see, the cord will just stretch. Lovely.'

I had moved one of the fussy occasional tables between the sofa and the fireplace, about two metres from where I had propped the colonel up with fallen cushions. I looped another tie through the tangle of bloodied silk at his wrists and fastened it round the leg of the sofa above the metal castor.

'Where were you, by the way? Sandhurst? They didn't have that one. It shouldn't be all that difficult to undo, not for a military chappie like you. Now, like I said, I'll be ever so quick and then you can get on with your nice lunch.'

I picked up the album and turned through the laminated pages, pausing at a plump lady on all fours with feathers in her piled-up hair.

'You thought I'd enjoy this, last time? "Unusual" was the word you used, I think?'

I knelt down and ran a hand over the colonel's crotch. 'Gets you going, doesn't it? Bit of quim? Have a good look, then.'

I propped the open album in his sightline next to the chunky old telephone. I went behind him and cupped his chin in my hand, pulling his head back, pinching experimentally at the skin of his eye sockets. Then I cut off his eyelids in two neat little triangles. Well, maybe not that neat. One of the eyeballs fell out a bit.

'Enjoy the pictures, Colonel.'

At the Planet Organic in St John's Wood I ordered a turmeric latte and used the bathroom to clean up, pulping the little patches of skin in a tissue and flushing them down the loo. The used gloves were back in my pocket. I'd get rid of them later. My DNA was still probably all over the flat, but then whose DNA was it? It wasn't as if Elisabeth Teerlinc actually existed. I was beginning to come round to that. All that bother constructing a self, becoming a real person, and then you just get blamed for it. I replaced my messed-up skirt and blouse with the fresh white Alexander Wang T-shirt dress rolled up in my bag, wiped a telltale spot of blood from my ankle then took my cup of saffron-coloured foam outside, watching the mothers and children from behind my sunglasses and enjoying the limpid haze of the still July day. I once told someone I wasn't interested in revenge, but then I say a lot of shit. Maybe the colonel made it to the phone, but I wouldn't have put money on it.

27

It was a short walk from Claridge's to the House, but they had troubled to send a car. Before I left, I sent a text to Elvis, confirming the time and place of our meeting later in the evening, then I took a long look in the mirror. So many eyes to dress for. I remembered changing for my first show at Gentileschi, the unabashed pleasure I had felt then when I viewed the reflection of my own achievements. My dress that night had been black, now it was white, a Maria Grachvogel column, draped low behind and tied loosely on the hips, Yermolov's earrings my only jewellery.

Da Silva stuck his head round the bathroom door. 'Wow.'

'Don't touch! Your hands are all wet.'

'Spoilsport.'

'You'll see me at the sale? And then afterwards, in the warehouse? Eleven?'

I was planning something special. Romantic. Something I wanted him to see after the sale, to celebrate before we went back to Italy. After I had returned from St John's Wood, I had taken him down to the House to walk him through the route to the warehouse. I used the pass Rupert had given me to let us in. I remembered the bustling atmosphere of sale days, the trolleys with the carefully wrapped works being hauled through the workrooms, the porters for once giving directions to the experts. I had waved to Jim, who was boxing a small picture for transport. I noticed with pleasure that it was Mackenzie Pratt's Utrillo, withdrawn from the sale.

'Good luck tonight!' he called, and I blew him a kiss. When we'd passed him, I put my tongue in da Silva's ear and explained a bit more about my surprise. It got a positive reaction.

'You'll need this, love.' I handed him my pass. 'You'll be going in through the public entrance, I'll go straight through the lobby to the party.'

He tucked it carefully into the waistband of his towel.

'Don't be late!'

'I promise, my love. *In bocca al lupo!*'

I watched his naked back as he closed the bathroom door.

Once I heard the shower running again, I opened the wardrobe door and then the safe inside. The combination was Franci's birthday. I'd noticed it when da Silva had stowed his Caracal away when he arrived. There was no reason for him to remove the gun this evening. My bag was a Balenciaga Giant City tote in apricot lizard skin, good and roomy. There were X-ray machines for security on the public door, but it could go in just fine with me.

You know you're wearing a good dress when you walk into silence. The sunlight from the street filled the air with motes of gold. It reminded me of Calabria, of those long days of heavy heat. I'd stayed, then, because – well, it didn't matter much now why I'd stayed. The reason had proved as transient as the phosphene stars which had danced in my eyes when I rubbed them against the glare. One thing remained the same though. I still wanted to win. As I crossed the hotel lobby to the waiting driver, the only sound was the ring of my heels on the marble.

A red carpet had been unrolled from the kerbside up to the main door of the House. The crowd might have been for a movie premiere – they had even erected barriers to keep the gawkers back. I asked the driver to make a lap of St James's Square while a tall television actress in a plunging gown posed for the bunch of paps hovering on the pavement. Two media vans were parked outside the London Library and I recognised the art critic of *The Times* giving an interview to a journalist with a microphone on the steps. I waited discreetly to one side while the paps shot a pair of fluorescent reality stars hand in hand, clutching catalogues, then walked through in their wake.

Rupert was waiting in the lobby in black tie, distractedly greeting the buyers and checking his watch. Every now and then he mopped his head with a flamboyantly printed silk handkerchief. He greeted me effusively with a kiss on both cheeks and ushered me up to the boardroom, and on into the inner sanctum of the chairman's drawing room. I hadn't even got past the door when I'd worked at the place. Slender, serious-looking women holding champagne flutes hovered on eighteenth-century silk sofas talking to a mixed crowd of men, some in black tie, a few younger ones in open-collared shirts and jackets with jeans. Jeff Auerbach, the CEO of the tech company KryptoSocial, was defiant in fat sneakers and a worn polo shirt. I remembered Carlotta trying to persuade me to have a crack at him in St Moritz last winter; I nodded at him and he grinned. Rupert introduced me to a group near the door, but as I moved across the amber parquet several people greeted me. Everyone knew I was the Gauguin seller, and while no one was vulgar enough to mention the money, I might as well have had the reserve stamped across my forehead. If the House made the price, I was going to have a whole lot of new best friends.

'You look beautiful.' A soft voice at my shoulder. I turned to look at Yermolov.

'Thank you. Not as beautiful as your gift.'

'You must be very excited, Miss Teerlinc,' he added in a more social tone.

Rupert was still hovering solicitously, but the distance created by his stomach between us was driving him frantic. Pavel Yermolov was famous in the art world for never appearing in the salerooms, preferring to buy his masterpieces through anonymous intermediaries, and yet here he was, at Rupert's party, munching on a wild mushroom and white truffle tartlet. Yermolov reached round to shake hands.

'I was just complimenting Miss Teerlinc on her extraordinary eye.'

'Indeed, indeed,' spluttered Rupert.

The room was becoming more crowded. It would soon be time to move down for the sale. Protocol and avarice were at war in Rupert's face. The idea was, we were all supposed to pretend this was an agreeable social occasion, with the impending auction a mere charming formality.

'Do you have your eye on something tonight, Mr Yermolov?' asked Rupert casually, as though a representative of the House would never stoop to following his clients' intentions through the tabloids.

'Naturally.'

Rupert excused himself and scuttled as rapidly as his bulk allowed to a minion at the door. He would be getting a message down to the phone bank, to confirm Yermolov's presence to Pandora Smith. As Zulfugarly was bidding from New York, I had requested that Pandora be his representative. It was her first big auction, and she had been thrilled. Rupert's progress opened a corridor towards us, and as Yermolov was recognised, the atmosphere was twisted up a further key. It reminded me of the other parties I used to go to, back when I lived in London, the endless moment of tight anticipation before someone reached out a hand or dipped in for a kiss, everyone waiting on the brink of the action, taut with the promise of ecstasy.

'Elisabeeeeth!' Angelica was brandishing her phone for a selfie with Yermolov, but he stepped firmly out of range. We did a bit of breathy squeaking which was mercifully interrupted by the tannoy.

'Ladies and gentlemen, please take your seats. The sale will begin in five minutes.'

Yermolov offered me his arm. 'Shall we?'

Downstairs, the Spice Rack were busy checking invites, distributing paddles and assigning seats. Major buyers were seated in the middle of the room, towards the front, with the sellers ranked behind. On either side, the standing pens were jammed with gallerists, students, journalists and a few curious tourists. Auctions are public affairs – in theory, anyone can attend for free. At the back, still in their brown coveralls, were the porters. I checked to see if Jim was amongst them. For minor sales, the porters themselves carried the works to the rostrum, but tonight the House had selected a pair of tall, good-looking boys, matched like footmen, done up in tails and white gloves like the entertainment at a hen party.

Yermolov accepted a numbered wooden paddle and saw me to my seat.

'So, maybe I'll see you tomorrow?' he asked quietly.

'Maybe.'

He kissed my cheek then continued down towards the stage. Flanking the platform, the telephone bidders waited by their polished, old-fashioned bank of landlines. Another innovation – they were done up in the House colours, the young men important and solemn in lounge suits and pale gold silk ties, the same shade as the matching strapless evening gowns worn by the young women. Each rested a hand lightly on the receiver, their pose adding to the tension in the room, like racehorses lined up before the gun. Pandora caught my eye and gave me a quick, conspiratorial smile. She looked proud and nervous. I spotted da Silva over my shoulder seconds before the lights went down. He was wearing a dark-blue shirt with a big white Polo logo, not one of the things I'd bought him. But he was there. I felt my muscles ease, loose and rangy with anticipation. *Game on.*

Speakers blasted the fourth movement of Beethoven's Ninth as the strobes went up, the screen behind the podium illuminated with the House logo. The chorus line of phone buyers lifted their sets as the 'sizzle' kicked off to whoops and cheers from the crowd, who applauded as each lot streamed up, the images morphing through the letters of the artists' names. Phones mushroomed everywhere, grabbing the action – any minute now they'd have their lighters out. The film segued through twenty of the major lots, from Manet to Pollock, to abrupt blackout. Silence. Then the first notes of the theme tune from *Rocky*. Jesus. The lights threw up a stream of electric pink and blue like fireworks as the de Kooning and the Gauguin – my Gauguin – flashed up side by side, while Charles Eagles jogged down the central aisle in a velvet dinner jacket, the crowd applauding and fist-pumping his entrance as he climbed the rostrum. What had *happened* to the House?

Poor Rupert. Eagles waited like an actor as the lights came up, absorbing the tension. The Dreamboys carried on the first work, a Basquiat, and set it reverently on the stand. And we were off.

Exuberance switched to concentration. Eagles made his way through the first few pieces with no surprises – the Basquiat, which went for eighty, followed by a Caillebotte and the Manet, each exceeding the reserve by a couple of hundred thousand. Number four was the Pollock, set at one fifty. Immediately, a girl in the bank next to Pandora raised her paddle, her opposite number bid, a sign from the floor, another phone bid, a quiet sign from a Japanese lady on the front row.

'One hundred and fifty,' called Eagles. 'Do I have your bids?'

The mounting price flashed on the screen behind his head in pounds, dollars, euros and roubles. A new bid from the bank, then another and a collective exhalation concentrated the room. One eighty. And then, as the invisible buyers seemed to become infected with the lust of the mob on the sales floor, Eagles could hardly keep up with the bids, each one winding the thrill of the figures ever higher. Two thirty. You could buy a hospital for that. Two fifty. Two sixty. The bids dwindled until there were just two figures moving in the bank, the original girl and a fiercely concentrated boy, eyeing each other as they spoke behind cupped hands, urging the buyers on. Two seventy. Two eighty. A long pause.

'Do I hear two hundred and ninety million?'

The boy was muttering rapidly, but his face had already conceded defeat.

'Going once . . .'

The boy signed a cut-off.

'Going twice and . . . sold! Ladies and gentlemen, for two hundred and eighty million pounds.' Roaring from the spectators.

I dug my nails into my palms as the next few lots dragged by, holding my back straight, trying to appear cool, unconcerned. Yermolov had not so far raised his paddle.

'And now, *Intersection*, by William de Kooning.'

At about four metres square, the canvas gave its handlers some trouble raising it into position. Even under the spotlights, it had a faded look, the usual vivid colours typical of the artist seemed bleached out, a rackety assemblage of bamboo and pale pewter spindles hunching round a single flash of deep manganese blue. It unnerved me. There was something cold and spidery in its density that I had to admit was powerful, the forms skittering across the picture, crisp and horribly predatory. It pulled at the eye in a way which was almost hypnotic – at least, not a picture you would feel quite safe turning your back on. You'd want to see what it was doing. Eagles was tensed forward on his toes, loving the anticipation.

'Ladies and gentlemen,' he said slowly, lowering his voice to a seductive murmur, 'opening the bids at sixty million.'

The reserve was twice that – it had been all over the newspapers and was printed in the catalogue, yet the room thrilled sensibly. Almost immediately, Pandora picked up her phone. *Fuck.* Zulfugarly was bidding.

'I have seventy million, ladies and gentlemen. Do I hear eighty?'

The bids climbed, the figures above Eagles's head barely spinning fast enough as his hands moved like a conductor, summoning mounting gambles from all over the saleroom.

It passed the reserve and climbed towards two hundred. Pandora was still speaking, raising her hand to counter as each new price was raised. *Had Zulfugarly changed his mind? Was he going for the de Kooning instead of the Gauguin?* Rupert would be on the verge of a coronary. No more than the fat bastard deserved, but the last thing I needed.

At two hundred and fifty million there were three bidders remaining. One on the floor, a silver-haired American I had seen in the drawing room, two in the bank. The American pulled out at two seventy.

'Do I hear two hundred and eighty? Two hundred and eighty million pounds?'

A nod from Pandora. A nod from her counterpart in the bank.

'Three hundred million pounds.' If they went any higher they would break the record. I forced my breath into my stomach, praying that Zulfugarly was being strategic, exhausting the ammunition of a potential rival for the Gauguin.

A squeak from the floor. In the front seats, where a tiny, elderly Asian woman in black had calmly raised her paddle.

'Three hundred and ten million pounds, ladies and gentlemen.'

The de Kooning was now officially the most expensive painting in the world. In the stands, the journalists were tapping their feeds, breaking the news even as Pandora motioned, casting an anxious glance in my direction. The other phone raised. The little old lady made another slight sign.

'I have three hundred and thirty million pounds. Now it's against you, miss.'

Eagles nodded to Pandora, who paused, spoke, paused. Was she raising? No, she was out. *Thank Christ*. If they'd carried on any longer I would have suffocated, along with half of the room – for the last few minutes I'd forgotten to breathe.

'Between the lady and the buyer at the telephone. Do I hear three hundred and forty million?'

She raised, even as the other handler on the phone shook his head.

'Three hundred and fifty million pounds for Willem de Kooning, *Intersection*! To you, madam.'

The sum had bludgeoned the exuberance from the crowd. Momentarily, the room shared a moment of silent awe. Then the blind rush, the swarming release. Most of the House employees managed to retain their professional composure, but Eagles was panting audibly into his microphone, offering out his hands to the love.

'And now, the last lot of the evening, Paul Gauguin, *Woman with a Fan II*.'

I could feel the eyes of the group from the reception seeking me from every corner of the room. As the picture came in, I couldn't resist a look at da Silva. He seemed calm, absorbed in the screen of his phone, barely glancing up as Li's work was positioned on the stand.

'Phew!' joked Eagles, echoing Rupert's gesture with the handkerchief. 'Quite an evening, ladies and gentlemen, quite an evening. But now, do I hear an opening bid of fifty million?'

For a horrible second, I half expected someone to stand up and denounce the painting. Knowing it as I did, I was suddenly unable to see it properly, each line and layer of colour screaming 'fake!' Now it was exposed, the thousand times my eyes had traversed the canvas seeking the slightest millimetre of a flaw seemed to count for nothing. I had a wild urge to call it myself, to stand up and throw everything away. What did I care if Raznatovic got his money, if da Silva was reprieved? I sat on my hands, stared fixedly at the stiff collar of the man in front of me. *It has to sell. If it doesn't sell, it's not over.*

The first bids were already climbing before I focused on Yermolov's back, searching for a hint of movement. The number above Eagles stood at eighty-five. Yermolov raised his paddle. One more look over my shoulder. Da Silva was sure as fuck paying attention now, his eyes like mine streamed on Pandora. She raised. Yermolov countered. More bids from the floor. One hundred, one hundred and twenty, one hundred and fifty. From across the seats, I could almost feel da Silva's relief. Raznatovic had his price. But I wanted more.

'Ladies and gentlemen, I have two hundred million pounds.'

Eagles was dropping his voice now, focusing the whole energy of the crowd on the duel between Yermolov and Pandora as one by one the other bidders cut. I fixed my eyes on my lap, willing Yermolov to continue. *It isn't about the money for these people. Boats, planes, girls, pictures. The money is just how you keep score. I had to hope that Zulfugarly's desire to win would conquer. He'd gone to three thirty for the de Kooning – was that the limit of his insane idea of a budget?*

Two thirty, two fifty. Yermolov continued raising his paddle, an impassive flick, as though he were playing ping pong. Two seventy. You could have heard a Tiffany coke straw drop. Two ninety, three hundred, on they went, urged by the silent, contained frenzy of the crowd.

'I have three hundred and twenty million pounds.'

A long pause. Then, slowly, Yermolov raised. *He couldn't buy it. I couldn't do that to him.* Pandora was speaking rapidly into the receiver. She waited. Eagles waited. Pandora was still whispering.

'To the gentleman in the front row at three hundred and thirty?'

Fuck, no. He had to bid, he had to. Pandora was looking out into the crowd, uncertain. The silence stretched while I caught her eye. *Say the name, Pandora, say the name.* Remind him it's Yermolov. I was prepared to believe in telepathy, anything to get those three syllables from her lips. She cupped her hand tighter around the receiver, turned away. *Good girl, good girl.*

Pandora nodded abruptly and signalled.

'Three hundred and forty million for Gauguin's *Woman with a Fan II*. Against you now, sir.'

But Yermolov was already shaking his head, laying down the paddle.

'At three hundred and forty million pounds, I'm going to close the bids.'

I tasted blood on the inside of my lip.

'Sold.'

I was off the blocks before the crowd were on their feet, pushing my way to the back of the saleroom, heading for Rupert's office. Angelica was across the room in full Instafrenzy, hopping about like a war reporter. There was just time to catch da Silva's eye as I barrelled through the doors. Rupert was standing at his desk, beneath the large screen which had live-streamed the sale, watching the mayhem, Eagles strutting down from the rostrum as though he'd just scored the winning penalty in the World Cup final.

'Rupert?'

He turned, slowly, half-transfixed by what he was watching. There was actually the glimmer of a tear in the crease of his jowl.

'Three forty,' he whispered. I scrunched my eyes tight as I stepped into his embrace.

The corks were already popping in the chairman's drawing room as I made my way towards the warehouse. I'd explained to Rupert that I was too overwhelmed to join the party, and after his brief efflorescence of emotion he had said that he quite understood. With me gone, there'd be no one except Eagles to steal his limelight. I was more than happy to let him have his moment. I hovered about in the passage as the works were returned, checked off by a House expert as they entered the warehouse where they would remain until the paperwork was completed before shipping. I tugged at Jim's sleeve as he passed with a trolley.

'Jim! Isn't it wonderful!'

He grinned at me. 'Best sale ever. We'll be done in a minute. Got a lock-in at the York if you're interested?'

I laughed. 'Thanks, I wish I could. But I have to get back up there.'

I rolled my eyes wearily to the noise emanating from the drawing room. 'Listen. I wouldn't mind having one last look at her, but my pass is in my coat upstairs. Would you mind?'

'No problem, miss.' I held my breath as he let me past the door.

'Thanks. I'll only be a minute. Oh . . . but Jim.' I made a little helpless gesture at my white dress. 'Could I possibly borrow?'

'Oh. Oh, of course.' He unpopped his brown overall.

'You're a star. I'll leave it by the rack for you. And here,' I handed him the two fifties I had ready in my hand. 'Get the lads a round on me.'

'That's very kind of you, miss. Congratulations!'

If I'd ever planned an art heist, this was the moment I would have chosen, immediately after a big sale, the time when everyone is distracted and the works are being moved back into the warehouse, the only tiny tear in the canvas of the House security. I hid in the sedan chair with the Minion until the last of the works were stored and the porters left for the pub.

28

The basement was dim and cool, the only sound the faint thrum of the temperature units. I checked my watch – 10.40, da Silva would be arriving in about fifteen minutes – then texted Elvis: *Get moving.* Time for a quick wander. Most of the works were stacked in cases, but in the space reserved for British Pictures towards the back several canvases were propped on the counter adjoining one of the large viewing benches. I felt for the switch under the rim of the table and flicked on the UV. William Etty. Creamy Victorian thighs and blushing Victorian bosoms, languishing in every coy posture of Victorian desire, the flesh rendered a surreal blue by the artificial glow. Perfect. Pulling the House overall from my bag, I slipped off my shoes and knotted my dress at the hip, trotted over to the door that led out into the area loading bay. A queue of low wooden trolleys was parked along the wall, waiting for the next day's deliveries. I wheeled one carefully back inside, the overall flapping over my bare legs, and laid down the iron handle behind the viewing bench, moving my bag up to the counter, within reach behind a pair of entwined naked girls. I just had time to whip off my dress and the overall and hop onto the table before I heard da Silva's voice.

'*Amore, sei qui?*'

'Over here,' I answered, lowering myself on one elbow and stretching my length along the wood, aware of the opalescent gleam of my own skin against the varnished sheen of the paintings. He gasped as he came into sight and I caught his gaze, travelling slowly along my body and then over the pictures, all those half-parted lips, rosy nipples, soft, heavy limbs.

'You said . . .'

I put a finger to my lips. 'Shhh. It doesn't matter what I said. Come.' I sat up as he approached the table, opened my legs wide, trailed a hand down my neck, over my breasts and along my thigh to the lips of my cunt, opening it for his mouth as he sank to his knees in front of me. His hand moved up to rub and squeeze at my breasts as his tongue pressed inside me. I let my head fall back as he lapped and sucked at my wetness, my body answering him even as I reached behind me for the bag. He stood and released his cock, swollen and straining and made to pull me onto him, but I twisted away and patted the table beside me.

'My turn. Quick, lie down.' He obeyed and I straddled him, my legs flexed at right angles, only the very tip of his aching cock touching the lips of my pussy. Slowly I lowered my weight to take the head inside me, then pulled back, brushing him again with the mouth of my cunt. He groaned and I pushed his hands behind his head, spiralling my body in short twists, down, round, down, round, taking him deeper each time until just as he was buried there I lifted myself off him, paused at the summit then rammed him so hard it knocked the breath out of me. I settled back with my hips pressed against his, gripping his cock tight along its length as I made slow figures of eight, pulsing my muscles tight at the apex of each stroke.

'*Sei una meravglia.*'

Leaning forward, I let his teeth catch at my nipple, still grinding him, pulling him closer, closer, watching his face.

'You like that? You like it when I fuck you like that?'

He nodded, dumb, frantic, left of the bang.

'How about like that?'

He came as I popped the little canister from my bag and let the gasp of his orgasm become the first gulp of the butane. It was the Dupont that had given me the idea. The first hit sent his head thumping back against the wood; before he recovered enough to struggle I had the carrier bag over his head, counting to twenty as I released the second dose inside. He spluttered and was limp, inside and out. I slid off him, turned him onto his stomach and got the cuffs on before pulling off the bag. I didn't want him dead. Replacing the House overall, I hung my bag off the trolley handle and winched the base up level with the bench, then rolled him onto it, securing him with the nylon bands attached across the tray. Then I wheeled him out into the yard. I had to lean back to counter his weight as I pushed him down the slatted ramp that gave its name, 'Hilling', to the moving of works. As soon as we were on the flat, I texted Elvis.

Here?

Outside.

The night air seemed to be reviving da Silva: he was moaning and retching. I gave him another little snort to put him back under, then used the pass to open the warehouse gate. This was going to be the most difficult moment. There were no cameras in the warehouse itself – the House was too protective of clients' privacy – but anyone viewing those in the yard would see a porter and a trolley. The security detail might just check out the warehouse. They wouldn't find anything amiss – porters sometimes did move works at night, to catch early morning shipments – but we only had the time it would take for them to walk down before they saw us. The security booth was beside the lobby, so a couple of minutes at most.

As planned, Elvis had backed into the mews and left the van doors open. When he got down to help me I saw with a smile that he was wearing an ordinary denim jacket and had even sacrificed his pompadour quiff. Silently, I gestured to him to help me position the trolley.

'This the package, then?' he whispered wryly.

'Cover him up and start the van. Hurry. I'll put this back.'

The security gates glided shut as we pulled out of the mews. No sound from inside the warehouse.

'Have you got my stuff?'

'There. Next to whatsit in the back.'

I reached over the seat, conscious of my bare arse under the overall, but Elvis had his eyes on the black cab that was passing in the street. For an agonising moment it slowed as though to let out a passenger, but it drove on. My briefcase and the small trolley lay next to the mattress on which da Silva was beginning to come to. Straining round the seatbelt, I shoved him onto his side. He'd puke, and I didn't want him choking. I wrestled jeans, sweatshirt and sneakers from the trolley and pulled them on.

'You brought the chair too?'

'Everything, just like you said. The kit's in the backpack under the seat. Kevin said to give you this,' added Elvis impassively. 'He said you were partial.'

He handed me a Crunchie. Lawrence used to serve Cadbury's Treatsize instead of canapés. How sweet of Kevin to remember. Elvis lit a fag and peered over the back seat.

'How's he looking?'

'Bit green. All right though.'

I extracted the cash-fat envelope with Elvis's fee from my handbag.

'There you go. Three grand, in twenties like I said. You've been just brilliant, thank you.' Christ knew why I was whispering.

'All right. Glad to do a favour for Kevin.'

'You're not a chatter, are you, Elvis?'

'What?'

'Doesn't matter. You'd best get going. I'll have it back here tomorrow at four.'

'Sure you can manage him?'

'No problem.'

It would have been much quicker and easier to have Elvis help me with da Silva and the kit, but I didn't want to implicate him any further than I had to. Besides, I needed to do this alone.

The van was bigger than anything I'd ever driven before. In fact, I'd never driven anything except the driving school Vauxhall I had taken my test in. Christ might also know where my licence was. I stalled embarrassingly on Piccadilly and somehow found myself in the bus lane near Chinatown, but finally got the hang of it as we crawled through Soho, up Dean Street towards Oxford Circus. Crowds of tourists and partygoers milled in and out of the bars, lingering in the warm summer air. Three girls, arms linked, swaying on the currents of the night, clacked in front of the van in their platform heels, lovely and arrogant and out on the lash. One of them blew me a kiss. I sucked sweet melting honeycomb from the roof of my mouth. The drive would take about four and a half hours, so we'd be there just before dawn. I made the chocolate last until we were crossing the Westway, heading for the M1 and the north, then I switched on the radio to keep myself awake as the van began to peel off the dark miles, climbing the spine of England, towards Liverpool.

A few times, when I was little, my mum took me to Crosby Beach. Except no one called it that: it was the Erosion, the wide basin of the Mersey Estuary where the ships heaved in, stately behind the puffing tugboats, to anchor in Liverpool Docks. Ships from America, from Greece and Norway and China. My mum and I would try to guess the flags as we sat with our picnic of apples and folded white bread and jam. I remembered the grit of the reddish sand, the way its scratchiness got everywhere, under my jumper, into the turn-ups of my jeans. You weren't really allowed to swim, the currents and the quicksand were too dangerous, but my mum would take me for a paddle, and once I think there was a fishing net. And 99 Flakes from the ice-cream van, Mr Whippy with bright raspberry sauce. Breaks your heart, doesn't it?

My journey was punctuated by da Silva's mutterings and the rasping presence of Darth Vader on Elvis's satnav, faint thumps and occasional expletives in Italian. Towards the end I almost dozed off, jolting awake as Anakin Skywalker growled at me to turn left on Marine Terrace, towards the boating lake. My watch said 4.35, fifteen minutes until dawn. Dulled with fatigue, I opened the back door and took out the chair. Up here, the air was dismally cold; a spiky wind off the Atlantic gusted seaweed and rot over the rails of the promenade. Aside from the street lamps along the front, the foreshore was black; I held the small torch between my teeth as I carried the chair and the ropes down to the sands. Tentatively, I began to pick my way towards the first of the motionless figures guarding the horizon.

Anthony Gormley's *Another Place* was installed in Crosby in 2005. One hundred cast-iron figures, each moulded from the body of the artist, each weighing 650 kilos. They watch for three kilometres along the coast, staring up to a kilometre into the waves. According to the artist, their objective is to challenge human life against planetary time, which was pretty much what I had in mind too, if not quite in the manner Mr Gormley intended.

About a hundred metres out the give of the sand shifted beneath my feet as it turned from dry to wet. The tides in the estuary turn on a five-day cycle: high tides in the morning range from just after midnight to about 6.30 a.m. Today's was due at 5.47. Encumbered by the chair I moved slowly. I wanted to hurry as I could sense, rather than see, the first stripes of dawn behind me, but I knew I had to place each step with care, testing the give and suck of the waterlogged sand. I passed several of the ghostly, sea-mangled figures until the ground collapsed, engulfing my leg up to the knee with a greedy slurp. Backing up a little way, I set down the chair, then jogged back the way I had come.

Back at the van, Selena Gomez warbled wistfully about neat whisky. I cocked the Caracal and slung the backpack onto one of the benches along the prom. Da Silva didn't smell too good – lighter fluid and half-digested canapés don't make for an alluring fragrance. The vomit had dried in long spools down his neck and soaked his collar and there were welling purple bruises beneath his bewildered eyes. I got the gag on, then tried to hoist him forward, but he resisted, loosening his body into a dead weight. It was impossible to look at his face, impossible to look at those eyes. So I just jammed the Caracal against his ribs, which got him moving. I held it there in an echo of our walk from my prison shed in Calabria as I marched him down the beach. What passed for the sun in these parts was up now, but from behind we'd look like a couple out for a romantic dawn stroll. He was still dazed, stumbling against me as we progressed towards the brown waves.

'OK, lover. Have a seat.'

I tied his legs together first, looping the rope around the legs of the chair before unbuttoning his horrible Ralph Lauren shirt, tearing it along the seams to get it over the handcuffs. He began protesting at that point, jerking from side to side, trying to kick at me.

'I wouldn't do that if I were you. You'll only knock yourself over. That'd spoil the view.'

I knotted him round the chest to the chair back and threaded the third length of rope round his neck and tightly through his cuffed wrists to keep his head in place, then stepped back to admire my handiwork. Immobilised by his bindings, motionless on the chair, da Silva from the back looked as stolidly immobile as the Gormley figures nearby.

'This will be *ciao*, then,' I called, as I gathered his soiled and shredded shirt and shoved the gun into my jeans. I didn't look behind me until I was back on the front, lighting a fag on the bench and watching the sea change from murky brown to a paler murky brown. Five a.m. I wondered how long it would take him to work out that he had forty-odd minutes before the sea closed over his head. He had tried to kill me on a beach, after all – I suppose it was even quite poetic. Already, the water was reaching straggly nicotine-scurfed digits towards the chair.

There's always something mesmeric about watching the sea. That knowledge that whatever happens, those waves will still break on the same shore for an infinity of tomorrows. I supposed that was what the artist was gesturing towards, the strange comfort of our own smallness. We waited together, and after a while, in the lulling susurration of the waves, I almost forgot that the seated figure was more human than its companions. It didn't seem to matter much. Certainly, it hadn't mattered to da Silva. I recalled him in the farmhouse in Calabria, casually explaining the way the boats sometimes dumped their human cargo. That indifference was the source of the only affinity we had ever truly had.

Because we were alike, he and I. I'd watched him. The ease with which he lived with doubleness, the ruthlessness, the calm embrace of necessary violence. And I had thought, just like every sad bitch who'd ever sat right here and wept her heart out to the indifferent waters, that it meant that he could love me. Just be yourself, and you'll find someone who wants you just the way you are. Da Silva had seen me, he knew what I was, what I had done. In Tangier, I'd told him that the best weapon a woman could use was surprise. But love is the best of all. In the end, I had convinced myself that love would deliver him to me, would deliver us both. Perhaps it could have done. I had made and remade myself so many times, but he was a chance to be new. And he took it away from me. Not even when I realised he would sacrifice me, but when I knew that he would do so and feel nothing at all. He wouldn't save me, so I couldn't save him.

The water was lapping the front of the prom now. Da Silva's head had long since disappeared beneath its glossy surface. The thing with love is, it makes you gullible. It makes you credulous. It makes you slow. So if a man thinks a woman is those things, it makes him weak. I had been gullible, credulous, slow. But in the end, da Silva's own image in my eyes had made him relax just long enough to underestimate me. He had thought me transparent, pellucid. We had both believed for a time that he could see me, which turned out to be his mistake. I bundled the shirt, cast a quick glance along the front for early-morning joggers and dropped it into the waves. It unfurled in the water, spreading helpless arms. Somewhere, above the tilt and whistle of a wind from across the Atlantic, someone was crying. Maybe it was me. Maybe because forever had turned out to be a bit short.

Time for the next thing. But maybe breakfast first. There was a caff open on the main road behind the prom, salty fat brimming out into the salty air.

'All right, queen?' asked the bloke at the counter.

I grinned. 'All right, ta.'

Bacon and double fried egg sandwich, rust-scalded tea, HP sauce. It was good to be home.

29

My mother was meeting me at eleven in the café of the Tate Gallery in the Albert Dock. I had the van parked in Hanover Street by eight and huddled down on the front seats for a couple of hours' sleep. I didn't fancy the mattress in the back much. When my phone woke me I brushed my teeth with a bottle of water, cleaned my face with a wet wipe, changed into a navy cashmere sweater for the summer weather and walked down to the Mersey.

She looked good. I felt so fucking old sometimes that it was hard to remember she was only forty-seven. Her face was drawn, but since she'd had that tooth fixed and her hair highlighted, her skin looked quite fresh with a bit of bronzer. And she'd dressed up – a white shirt and a bright scarf, brown ankle boots to match the Mulberry bag I'd sent her.

'All right, Judy.' No one else called me that, now that my old friend Leanne was dead. I'm taller than her, and when I stooped to kiss her cheek I tried to stop myself sniffing suspiciously, but she caught my hand and held it for a second against her face.

'I'm all right, love.'

'Yeah. You look lovely, like you've been taking care of yourself?'

'I've been going to the pool at the leisure centre. With Mandy. They've got a steam room now and everything.'

'That's great.'

'Do you want to order something?'

'Just a black coffee. I had breakfast.' I was itching for a fag.

'I'll have a cappuccino, then. Are you ... staying?' Such frailty in the hesitant question.

'I can't ... I've, I've got to get back to work.'

'To Italy?'

'Yeah. I just came up to deliver something. A piece.'

The coffees came and we stirred them. When we raised our cups simultaneously she caught my eye and set hers down without taking a sip.

'I seen the papers. It's amazing. I didn't say anything though,' she added hurriedly.

'Yes. It went really well. My clients are thrilled.'

'Yeah. Listen, I'm sorry, Judy.'

'What for?'

'All of it. The drinking. I know I can't make it up to you, but I'm sorry. I ... I understand, why you've stayed away.'

For twelve years, I'd stayed away.

'I'm dead proud of you though. All that – with the picture? On telly and everything. You've really made something of yourself.'

'Mum, we're not on *Jeremy Kyle*. Give it a rest. I understand about the drinking. Why wouldn't you fancy a drink when one of your daughters had killed the other?'

'Don't say that.'

'It's true though, isn't it?' I leaned forward over the table. My Americano had come in a jam jar. 'I killed Katherine.'

'It was an accident. We know that. A terrible accident.'

'Which you let me take the blame for.'

'What choice did I have, Judy? They would have taken you away.'

'No. It was because you know I did it.'

'Is that why you came? To torment me?'

'No. I wanted to see you. I wanted to—'

'To understand? I don't understand. I know myself, I know what a failure I am. I do my best to get along, that's all. But you? Why you're . . . as you are? You know better than I ever will.'

I have a lot in common with my mother. Our faces. The way we think. But she'd never made me feel stupid before. She was pressing her lips together, as though she was trying not to cry, but the strained white lines in her make-up didn't show sorrow. It was contempt.

My mother put a ten-pound note on the table and picked up her bag.

'Bye, Judy. Take care of yourself. It's been lovely to see you, give me a ring.'

I wondered how much cash she had in her purse. How far she'd get before she gave in and opened the door of the nearest pub. I imagined her, falling out pissed at three o'clock, crying on the bus home, and somewhere, the image gave me pleasure. She was like me in lots of ways, my mother, but she was weak. Which is what had made me strong.

My sister Katherine, who smelled of almonds. She was born when I was twelve. For a while it was good, the three of us. My mum stopped drinking. She'd come to meet me from school with Katherine bundled in the buggy in her little pink hat with fluffy ears. On Fridays we'd go to the café at Gregg's bakery and my mum would buy me a hot chocolate. We'd share a vanilla slice, with Katherine's puddingy weight in the dark-green lap of my school skirt, and her fat tiny fingers furling and closing around her bottle as I helped her drink her warm milk.

I loved Katherine. But then my mum started going down the pub again, crashing in late with some fella she'd picked up, screeching at me to wake up and see to the baby while they banged the sofa against the wall. I was tired all the time, my eyes felt peeled with it. I dropped things, forgot my textbooks, dozed off in class and got a D on a maths test. I couldn't do my homework because there was always Katherine to see to, Katherine to change and feed and her cot to make up and the bins to be put out, and the wash to run, getting her in the buggy to go to Tesco when there was some money in my mum's bag, trying to cook the tea with the baby on my hip while my mum slept it off in front of the telly. In the end, it seemed easier not to go to school at all. I didn't want to leave her alone with Mum. The head had me in for 'a little talk'. He told me I could be clever, that I could get into university, but his eyes were on the clock on the grey wall of his office, which stank of Bensons. It was round the school that he kept a bottle of vodka in the drawer of his desk. He was marking time, just like everyone else on our estate. I felt sorry for him, for his horrible breath, the pouches under his eyes. Stuck. But I started going to school again and when I got in Katherine would be screaming in her cot, soaked and filthy, and sometimes I just left her there and shut the door, because it wasn't fair.

So that day, when I opened the door, the flat smelled of sweet almonds. The light was on in the bathroom, but the flat was dim and airless. My mum had run Katherine's bath with the special baby oil, then she must have forgotten about it, because there were empty bottles next to her on the sofa. Katherine was slumped against the bars of the cot. She tried to cry again when she saw me, but she must already have sobbed herself hoarse because all her poor little voice could manage was a rasping croak. I picked her up and cuddled her.

And then I thought. 'You won't be able to leave.' I was twelve. Four years, five, I could get out. But Katherine would only be about four, and I knew I couldn't leave her. That's how it would be. And in a bit I'd end up just like my mum, nothing to look forward to but getting pissed the day I cashed my cheque from the social. We went and stood over my mum. She didn't wake. I bent down and Katherine reached for her face, but I drew back and carried her into the bathroom. I got out a clean towel and unpopped the wet buttons underneath her Babygro, ran some more hot into the cloudy water. When she was naked, pink and wriggling, I kissed the soft place at the corner of her eye.

'I'm sorry, baby,' I whispered.

It didn't take long. Afterwards, I wrapped her in another towel, her special towel, the yellow one with the hood. Her face was grey, her eyes all glassy. My legs were shaking when I carried her back to the sofa.

'Mum,' I said then, over and over. 'Mum?'

My coffee was cold. I wandered out through the brave smart shops lining the arcade and held on to the railings where the river flowed. There wasn't anything else I wanted to see in Liverpool, so after a bit I went to find the van, and the ring road and then the M1. The radio was playing 'Hot Love' by T. Rex, but I had a date with Elvis.

30

The Bunch of Grapes, in Duke Street, for old times' sake. I'd brought my old black Chanel suit from Italy, nipped-in jacket, flippy pleated skirt. Dave was waiting at a table with a pint and a glass of what I knew from experience would be nasty white wine.

'Got something for you.' He pushed a dark green Hatchard's bag over the glass-rimmed wood. 'Hardback of my book.'

'Oh, Dave.' I flipped to the back first, the author biography, Dave looking smart and serious in his regimentals. Then to the front – he'd signed it. *With love and thanks always, Dave.*

'What are the thanks for?'

'You know.' It had been my fault Dave had lost his beloved job at the House, but then the sale of a Richter painting, my first acquisition as a dealer, had enabled him to take his teaching qualification. Still, that was nothing to what I owed him.

'I am *so* proud of you. I'm so lucky to have you as a friend.'

We both took a long, British sip of our drinks.

'I hope it's a ticket to the Bahamas. Now you're famous and all. "The girl who found the Gauguin". Like the new name.'

'Yeah, well. Professional reasons. I won't be needing it again. But you' – I humped my briefcase onto the table – 'you really are going to be famous. The BBC are going to love this.'

I started to unpack the notes I had taken on the *Lady with a Fan II* provenances, the photos I had printed up of Li at work. I'd been careful to only shoot his hands. Dave stared at them, running his fingers back and forth across the glossy paper.

'You what?'

'It's a fake. Rupert sold a fake. For three hundred and forty million. And it's yours. The proof. You can destroy him, Dave.'

'Why would I want to do that?'

'He fired you! He fired me! He chucked us both away, like . . . like the butts of his fucking cigars. This could make you famous, Dave – you could be an expert, a newspaper columnist, all sorts! Don't you want that?'

Dave stacked the papers and photographs neatly, taking his time about it, then pushed them back across the table. His face had shut down, all the warmth and enthusiasm locked away.

'I don't know why you did this, and I don't want to know,' he began. 'But it wasn't for me, was it? It was for you, Judith, or Elisabeth or whatever you call yourself these days? Because you always have to be the superstar, don't you? That business back at the House, with the Stubbs? It was all about you. You used me then, and you've used me ever since.'

'I made it right,' I answered sulkily.

'You did, and I'll always be grateful. But that's not the point. Why would I want to drag all this down on me? They'd want to know how I got it, how I know you – I just want a quiet life. Always have.'

'So why did you help me all those times?'

'I felt a bit . . . sorry for you, I suppose. You're a good girl, deep down. I always felt there was something missing though. Like, when I first knew you, back at the House, people said you were . . . funny.'

'Because I wasn't born posh? I thought you of all people understood that.'

'Not that. Like I said, something missing. People said you looked at them as though they weren't real.'

Watching, all the time. Imitating, working out what was expected. That's what everyone does isn't it? I'm just . . . faster than most.

'Stop there, Dave,' I spat. 'Just stop there.'

'OK. I'm sorry. I always thought you were all right though. And when you got yourself in trouble, I wanted to help you out. But this – this isn't anything to do with me. I'm sorry.'

I got to my feet, placed the provenances back in my brief-case, imitating his care. Then I leaned forward, looked into his kind, honest face. There was pity there, which might have been unbearable if unbearable was something I actually under-stood. But there was nothing to say. I wasn't angry: Dave was absolutely right. I could make no further use of him. He was an irrelevance.

I straightened my back. His silence followed me out into St James's.

Maybe that's how it should have gone. Us against them, plucky crusaders for truth, taking them down fraud after snob, the crooks and the social climbers. The ones who believed that beauty is only ever business, that oil paint can temper bloodstains. That isn't ever how it goes though. Which was why I was going back to the House for the last time on my own.

I didn't even bother speaking to the girls on the desk, just made for the carved staircase in the central hall, the one it had always made me feel so proud to climb.

'Elisabeth!' Rupert was all smiles for his record-breaking seller. 'How are you? What can I do for you?'

'I need to speak to you urgently. In private. Would you mind locking the door so we're not disturbed?'

'Of course.' He bustled past me, locked his office, turned and found me seated on his desk, with the Caracal aimed at the congested flab of his heart. His first reaction was a shrill titter, an absurd queef from deep within his bulk.

'I'm not laughing, Rupert. Come and have a seat.' I pushed out the chair with the tip of my Saint Laurent stiletto. When he had inserted himself between the arms, I hopped down and circled him, bringing the pretty little 'O' of the barrel to rest on the bulge of flesh above his collar.

'Open the briefcase. Get the papers out. Take a look. Do anything else and what passes for your brain will be in White-hall before they get up the stairs. Go on.'

Watching him set out Li's work, I wondered how fake it really was. A perfect Gauguin, just not by Gauguin.

'Fuck.'

'Language, Rupert. Though yes. The fucking fucker's totally fucked. The fucker being you.'

'What do you want? Money?' He had grasped the situation with admirable speed – I had to admire the control in his voice, the fact that he wasn't wasting time on incredulity.

'No.'

'Then what?'

There were various answers to that question. Option one: I leave with the papers, take a cab straight to Kensington and hand them in at the Daily Mail. *Au revoir* Rupert's career. *Option two: I let him withdraw the picture – shame and embarrassment – Raznatovic kills da Silva. Oh wait, da Silva was already dead. Option three: I let Hay-Z hang it in whatever hideous monument to ego his architect had designed and just leave it there, only me and Rupert knowing the truth. Shits and giggles, forever and ever. I was quite tempted by option three.*

Rupert's attempt at sangfroid collapsed at that point. He began to cry, big ugly sobs.

'It's a picture. It's just a fucking picture,' he wheezed.

Option four: I smear Rupert's medulla all over his desk. At least he had a medulla. But I've always liked to play fair. What was it Raznatovic had offered? The collective option.

'Nah. I don't want money. I don't want to ruin you. I don't even want to kill you, all that much. What I want . . .' I walked slowly round his body, which was quite the workout, and resumed my seat on the desk. I twitched the tip of the Caracal between his head and his heart. 'What I want is to play a game. It's simple. All you have to do is tell me my name. If you get it right, I pack up the papers and you never see me again. The Gauguin hangs, you get a promotion and eventually a knighthood, for all I fucking care. If you can't, well – oh dear.'

At that moment, a car alarm went off in King Street below us. Suit your art to your circumstances was something I'd learned from Caravaggio, so I took the opportunity of the noise camouflage to slightly shoot Rupert in the left foot. The slug made a little firework underneath his Edward Green brogue as it lodged in the parquet. He reared out of the chair, attempting to clutch his injured limb, but he was too fat to reach it.

'No screaming.' The flanks of Rupert's cheeks were as pasty and damp as fresh mozzarella, he gulped and sucked desperately as the pain hit, but he didn't cry out.

'Sit back down. Good. Now, are you ready? I'll make it a bit easier for you.' I buttoned my silk blouse primly at the neck, the way I had worn it as a junior, and quickly knotted my hair into a ponytail.

'Ring any bells?'

I'd never seen anyone drool with agony before. It was running down his chin, mingling with the sweat on his collar. I could actually smell the high reek of his fear.

'Come on, have a go.'

'Er . . . er.' His desperate eyes remained uncomprehending.

'Well, you're getting warmer.'

'Please,' he burbled. 'I don't understand. What have I done? I haven't killed anyone!' *That makes one of us.* 'Do you want a clue?'

He nodded frantically.

'It'll cost you.' I leaned down and trailed the gun over his face, the wet front of his shirt. 'Which bit of you are you willing to trade for a clue? Another toe? How about an ear?'

'Please, please.' He was sobbing again now.

'Oh go on, I'm getting bored. Stubbs?'

'Er, er . . . Georgina?'

'Nope. Like the lateral thinking though. George Stubbs, *The Duke and Duchess of Richmond Watching the Gallops*? Remember that picture? You should.' I pointed to the photographs of Li's hands, laying in the ground for the Gauguin. 'The same guy altered it for you, back when you fancied going into business with Cameron Fitzpatrick.'

'I don't know, I promise, I really don't – oh. Oh.' The moment of his epiphany was really quite beautiful to see.

'Judith? *Judith?*'

'Bingo, Rupert. You got there.' I began to gather up the papers, keeping the Caracal trained with one hand.

'Judith. I don't understand, but I'm sorry. I'm sorry if—'

'Save it. What is it they say, "Never complain, never explain"? Though I'd prefer another cliché. Shall we go with "water under the bridge"?'

Rupert knew how his pal Cameron Fitzpatrick had died. Murdered on the riverside in Rome. The painting they had been faking, the one that got me fired, disappeared.

'Shall I tell you how Cameron died, Rupert? What I mean is, would you like to know the details?'

I got his torso over the quay in one heave. He arched back, and the back of his head cracked against the stone embankment. I put my knee on his chest to ease the stuffing from his mouth, then shoved against his thigh to work the body round until it rolled into the water.

'That was you.' He said it flatly.

'That was me. Right again. But I don't really have time for a chat about the good old days at British Pictures, Rupert. Now, in a minute, I'm going to leave. You can recall the Gauguin if you like, or you can sign the chit and wave it off to Baku. I imagine you'll do the latter, because your integrity is in inverse proportion to the size of your revolting arse. Speaking of which – undo your trousers.'

'What?'

'Do it. Now, stand up. Hands on the desk and bend over please. Now spit.' I held out the gun. 'Spit on the barrel.'

As da Silva had once explained to me, there's quite a vocabulary for snitches amongst the Mafia. *Vomitini* ('pukers'), *muffuti* ('moulderers') or, my favourite, *ammalati di sbirritudine* ('sufferers from coppitude'). It's rare that they live very long, but if they do find themselves in prison with 'men of honour', a particularly degrading punishment for their betrayal is buggery. I'd wondered if, like the blond hair and blue eyes which sometimes pop up in the gene pool of the Italian south, whether this was an atavistic custom retained from the Vikings, who were given to raping their male prisoners after a successful battle. Once the gun was good and slippery, I circled round Rupert's slumped body and gingerly approached the elastic of his Y-fronts, easing it down with the barrel.

'Now if you can just keep quiet a bit longer, I think we can keep this meeting to ourselves, yes?'

'Yes.'

'Oh, Christ. Yes what?'

'Yes, Judith.'

I had no wish to get any more intimately involved with Rupert's anatomy, but I took my finger off the trigger and nosed the barrel gently into place.

'You might want to put a fist in your mouth. Careful when you take it out, it's still cocked, if you'll pardon the pun.'

Heigh-ho, in we go. Tensing my right forearm, I hit it hard with my left fist, just under the elbow. Most of the Caracal disappeared into Rupert, who managed a stiff upper lip.

'As I said, gently does it. Don't whatever you do touch the trigger or your breakfast will be back at the Wolseley. Bye, Rupert.'

I picked up my briefcase and sashayed out of the door in my high heels.

On the staircase, I saw Angelica. She almost walked right past me as I descended in my black suit, until something made her turn.

'Oh hi – Elisabeth? Elisabeth?'

I gave her a little wave.

Most artists don't die artistically. Artemisia, exhausted and fevered with plague, Caravaggio, a helpless staggering pilgrim, on an empty Italian beach, Gauguin crazed and starving in his spoiled paradise. We prefer to make our ideas of their lives from the images of the work. The three of them linked by violence, by sacrifice, by blood. Caravaggio only ever signed one of his pictures, and he did so in a saint's blood. He had killed a man in Rome and the Pope had offered a reward for his head. Ending up in Malta, at the headquarters of the Knights of St John, Caravaggio offered his talent as a plea bargain. Membership of the order would commute a potential sentence. The books said that Caravaggio failed to comprehend the nature of the deal, that he was exchanging the scaffold for a prison of his own making, but I like to think that he was afire to paint again, and thought he'd chance it. He always preferred trouble to obedience. Caravaggio's Beheading of St John *was the largest altarpiece of his career, made for the cathedral in Valletta where he would be received as a knight. He placed the saint in the grim courtyard of a night-time prison, a version of the frigid stone enclosure where Gauguin watched Prado's execution. The party's over, the palace is sleeping, the hall where Salome danced is abandoned to the wraiths of wine fumes and incense. Somewhere within, she dreams her prize. The executioner bends over his bound victim, his sword on the ground at his side. He has done his work, but the job is not finished. The sword has sliced deep into John's neck, but the head is not yet severed, the wound gapes and gushes. Grasping John's hair for purchase, the executioner reaches impassively for the knife at his belt to wrestle the last bone and sinew from the still-living trunk. The victim neither lives nor dies; he is petrified in endless, remorseless agony. Blood spools in a crimson skein and when you look, its creeping tendrils embroider Caravaggio's name. It might be understood as a portrait of redemption, the painter re-baptised, washed clean of his murderous sin in the blood of the saint's ebbing mortality. Or, perhaps, Caravaggio is saying, this is where I am, forever, brutally frozen on the cusp of a pitiless mercy.*

* * *

It was about six in the evening, the time when the city churns again on its axis. I was waiting on the platform for the Piccadilly Line at Green Park, just another woman in a black suit amongst the resigned, sallow-faced commuters. *I do what is in me.* Inside my tatty leather briefcase, a card with a number, the provenances for a fake Gauguin, a small but genuine Rembrandt, a pair of one-hundred-carat diamond earrings, a passport. In a vault in France, a painting and a box full of headless remains. In Amsterdam, the man who held the current record for the world's bestselling art forgery was waiting in a hotel. In the South of France, another man would be expecting me. In New York City, a third. Behind me, a low, collective groan rippled through the crowd. Someone on the tracks, probably.

THE END

Acknowledgements

I should like to thank the following people for their passion, dedication and immense hard work:

Jane, Kate, Julian, James, Stephen, Angie, Georgia and Imogen at Bonnier Zaffre. Bill Massey, Emily Burns at Brandhive, Annabelle Robinson, Carol and Andrea at Roca, Camille, Glenn and Sandrine at Laffont, Giuseppe, Tommasi and Raffaella at Longanesi, Stefano, Cristina and Achille Mauri. Meenakshi at Bloomsbury India, Henrik at Norstedt, Tomas at House of Books, the irrepressible Jochem Bouwens. Frank McGrath for poisons, Erikkos, again, Rosie Apponyi for more than I can ever say. Dominique de Bastarrechea and Christopher Maclehose, who made it happen and Michael Platt who did the hard bits.

And Mark Smith. Publisher extraordinaire, visionary, Ernie. Mark, you changed my life. I will never be able to thank you enough. Also Kate Smith, whose patience and generosity made that possible.

L.S. HILTON
READERS' CLUB

If you enjoyed *Ultima*, why not join the L.S. HILTON
READERS' CLUB for exclusive writing, giveaways
and news from L.S. HILTON by visiting
www.bit.ly/LSHilton?

Dear Reader,

Ultima is the last in the *Maestra* trilogy, and I'd like to thank all the readers who have stayed with Judith to the end. Thank you for your letters, your lovely messages and your very helpful suggestions. One of the great privileges of working on this series has been the chance to meet so many of you – in France, Italy, the Netherlands, Australia, Belgium, Spain, Switzerland, India, Germany, Sweden and the US, and to hear from you in places as diverse as Bulgaria, Singapore, Norway and Ukraine. When we were bringing the books out, my publisher, Mark Smith, talked about the forty-two countries which have published the Maestra series as a 'family', and I'm honoured to have you as part of that family.

Ultima will, I hope, keep you turning the pages right up to the last (and first?) scene. The ending is one I'm keen to hear your opinions of – in a way Judith Rashleigh has come full circle, but where could she go next? I was pleased to bring back Yermolov, Dave, Rupert and Carlotta, and hope that the story will prove satisfying as part of a coherent narrative, as well as an independent read. One of the questions that came up in editing is why, after Artemesia Gentilleschi and Caravaggio, I chose Gauguin as 'the' artist for the last book. Party, I think, because the first two are Baroque artists, and I believe that as a symbolist Gauguin owes much to the baroque, and partly because these three painters are connected through a sensuality and a violence which adapts them to Judith's (very idiosyncratic) take on the world. And more distinctly, without giving too much away – well, severed heads . . .

Judith is a complex and disturbing character in many ways, but I have found writing her to be immensely pleasurable. Her world is one to escape into – violent, sexy, exotic, but also humorous. So, whilst *Ultima* is in some ways the darkest of the books, I think it's also the funniest. The series has provoked some pretty strong reactions, both positive and negative, but as a passionate reader myself, I think any book that makes people talk, makes them angry, makes them laugh, makes them engage, is doing its job. I can't wait to hear how it will make you feel.

If you would like to hear more, you can visit www.bit.ly/LSHilton where you can join My Readers' Club. It only takes a few moments to sign up, there are no catches or costs and new members will automatically receive an exclusive message from me. Bonnier Zaffre will keep your data private and confidential, and it will never be passed on to a third party. We won't spam you with loads of emails, just get in touch now and again with news about my books, and you can unsubscribe any time you want.

And if you would like to get involved in a wider conversation about my books, please do review *Ultima* on Amazon, on GoodReads, on any other e-store, on your own blog and social media accounts, or talk about it with friends, family or reader groups! Sharing your thoughts helps other readers, and I always enjoy hearing about what people experience from my writing.

Thanks again for your interest in this novel, and I look forward to hearing from you and sharing your reactions to *Ultima*.

With all best wishes,

Lisa

Find out where it all began . . .

MAESTRA

THE NUMBER ONE BESTSELLER

GLAMOUR'S **WRITER OF THE YEAR.**

**WHERE DO YOU GO WHEN YOU'VE
GONE TOO FAR?**

By day Judith Rashleigh is a put-upon assistant
at a London auction house.

By night she's a hostess in one of the capital's unsavoury bars.

Desperate to make something of herself, Judith knows she
has to play the game. She's learned to dress, speak and act in
the interests of men. She's learned to be a good girl. But after
uncovering a dark secret at the heart of the art world, Judith
is fired and her dreams of a better life are torn apart.

So she turns to a long-neglected friend.

A friend that kept her chin up and back straight
through every past slight.

A friend that a good girl like her shouldn't have: **Rage.**

Available in paperback, ebook and audiobook now

And don't miss . . .

DOMINA

THE GLOBAL THRILLER PHENOMENON

Judith Rashleigh has made it. Living in luxury amidst
the splendours of Venice, she's finally enjoying
the life she killed for.

But someone knows what Judith's done.

Judith can only save herself by finding a priceless
painting – unfortunately, one that she's
convinced doesn't even exist.

And she's not the only one seeking it.

This time, Judith isn't in control. Outflanked and out-thought,
outrun and outgunned, she faces an enemy more ruthless
and more powerful than she ever imagined.

And if she doesn't win, she dies.

Available in paperback, ebook and audiobook now